MW00928519

The Raider Christian Jack

D.G. Snipes

This book is a work of fiction

Copyright © 2012 D.G. Snipes
All rights reserved.

ISBN: 1-4681-4237-2
ISBN-13: 9781468142372

To my Father and Thomas Schultz

And all who—in Truth—encourage

PART ONE

~ 1 ~

The countless miles of unbroken prairie had begun gradually rolling in waves...

From the saddle and crest of the next swell, Christian Jack studied the small settlement huddled closely together below. Beyond the weathered-grey raft in its ocean of parched grass, the late afternoon sun glinted off a brief strike of river. He removed his worn and faded black hat, its headband darkened with perspiration collared by a white marbling of old sweated-salt. He brushed at the tickle of the scar above his left eyebrow—-reminding him it was still there.

The large bay stallion pumped its head and spoke. He could smell the water.

"Yeah, Hest, I see it," Christian Jack said.

He donned the flat-topped Appalachian hat, patted Heston's solid neck and, with shadow in tow, started down. He needed coffee, jerk, bread, tobacco, rolling papers and lucifers.

At twenty-six, lean and just under six-foot booted, he was not a physically imposing man. But survival over the forging years fighting and living on the move and ground under hoof had aged and tempered him considerably. Square, daily meals had not been privilege, and sustenance consisted of what happened to be available; that of late being prairie dog, rabbit and jerked beef.

On the porch in front of the trade post, two young fellows stood facing a posted placard. As he neared, they departed, eyeing him guardedly from over their shoulders as they side-gaited away. It was the provident way of folks if they didn't know someone, or, in his case—-did.

He dismounted and flipped the reins over the hitch post, then mounted the springy wood step and stoop. The strained warning of loose plank nails blended with the rusted squeak of the swinging door.

"Howday, pil...grim," an elderly man greeted, his voice trailing with concern.

Disregarding the greeting, Christian Jack swept the empty and sparsely stocked store. Outside of Heston, the shadow and himself, he hadn't spoken to anyone else for some time. He hawked his throat and told the clerk what he wanted.

The white-haired, careworn man, peering over the bridge of his spectacles, tensed as though he'd just seen two rattlers inside the open wings of the stranger's coat. As he bungled about filling the order, making nervous conversation he said, "Headed fer Cheyenne, are ya?"

Again Christian Jack said nothing and eyed the apron wearing man.

"Don't mean no 'fense," the clerk added. "It's just all folks have been chewin over late."

"What'd that be?"

"Big ta do they're throwin this week after season's roundups. There'll be fiddlin, saltatin, horse racin and shootin con...tests... too." Thinking he needn't have mentioned the *shooting* business, his eyes fell to the stranger's revolvers. They were worn high with handles forward and centered in a manner suggestive of their probable expedient, if not frequent, usage.

"Near every cowpoke and sod buster in the territory'll be there," he added.

"This week, ya say?"

"Yep, kicks off Sat'day. There's a postin tells of it out front, there."

"What's today?"

"Day's Tuesday," the merchant said setting forward the cloth sack of goods. "Eight bits'll cover that...sir."

Skidding a Union silver dollar across the counter, "How far's Cheyenne?" Christian Jack asked.

"Sixty or so miles due west. We're last trade 'twixt."

The young, yet seasoned and serious-eyed stranger with the intimidating Colts and blue scar over his eyebrow said, "'Bliged," and, taking up the poke, started for the door.

"Ya betcha pil…grim," the clerk said rhyming with the door's worrisome hinges as it swung open and shut.

Out front, Christian Jack stopped before the posting. He could read but as a rule didn't care for where ink trails left on paper by men tended to lead. They were usually misguiding or trying to sell something.

According to the placard, there would be both pistol and rifle contests with a three-dollar entry for each. Take would be awarded for first and second place. Turning and stepping from the porch, he scanned the short empty street where eyes watched unseen, but felt, from shadows, behind corners, cracks and shutters. He divvied the poke between his saddlebags, mounted and rode on.

The river he thought he'd seen from the rise earlier was only a wide, played-out and shallow autumn stream. Still, it and its thin stand of cottonwood and willow were welcome. Up wash from Heston, he filled his canteens, then cupped handfuls of the water over his head and face until his almost shoulder-length, straight, dark hair was thoroughly wet. He tasted the salt tinge of sweat mixed with the grit of trail dust as the cool water trickled over his sunbrowned face, through his moustache, to the cut of his mouth. He stood there beside the stream for a moment motionless, senses trained—-watching, listening, smelling and absorbing the surroundings. Overhead, the turning leaves shimmied and whispered in the warm zephyr that carried the gone-to-straw scent of summer's spent grasslands. Shadows had begun stretching long into nothing, running from another setting sun.

On the river cobble in the small campfire, he placed a two-fisted tin cup of water. The aroma of the fresh coffee grounds smelled inviting as he twisted and tied them into a ball within a brown, once yellow, Union neckerchief. When the water was steaming, he dipped the knot of grounds in to let it steep. As he sat pulling from a slab of jerked beef and fresh bun of bread, he listened to the evening. The crackle of the fading fire and constant chorus of crickets, along with the occasional, distant yip of coyote were normal. The only difference was the comforting whisper of the sliding stream and the breeze in the branches overhead, reminding him of the plentiful spring-fed brooks and sheltered woodlands he'd left far behind in Missouri.

~ 2 ~

Before the risen sun had fully burnt off the morning mist that cloaked the good camp amid the trees beside the stream, Christian Jack was on the move, sights set on Cheyenne and its contest money. Ambiguous, risky, or not, man needs objective, and in life—he reminded himself—it and money were ultimately flip sides of the same coin. Like the air you breathe in then out; if you're alive there's not the one without the other.

Up till now, destination had been trying to shake the past, all the while trailing the sun west. He'd heard a hundred stories of how a man could disappear and breathe easier there and, as he had countless times already, once more found himself entertaining the notion of going up to those Rocky Mountains where, hopefully, he'd be able to do just that. There, maybe find a cave or build a shelter; hunt, fish and trap. Maybe even pan for trading color. He'd been thinking along those hazy maybe lines all the way from the Mississippi across Missouri, through Nebraska and, any day now, Wyoming territory. Knowing too how tools and supplies would be beneficial, he thought how beyond the Cheyenne contest and what it might garner, he might be able to land some kind of inconspicuous work over the winter until he could stake enough to better outfit himself. *Maybe distance will afford chance*, he thought.

"Maybe you should knock it off with all the blasted maybes," he cursed. They were nauseating. Leaning forward, he spat emphatically over Heston at the mimicking shadow ahead. He pulled from the cigarette he was smoking and as he expelled the smoke grumbled, "Maybe's no real as grabbin smoke, Hest."

On the note of smoke, beyond his own, he saw a blurred cloud of dust being stirred against the skyline ahead. Sensing it trouble, he reined the bay. Standing erect in the stirrups, he saw as three riders emerged over the roll of the trail. They were approaching and riding hard. He thought there might be Indians after them, but with the morning sun at his back, he could see for miles and no sign of anyone in pursuit.

"People," he grudgingly muttered, annoyed by the development. He didn't want to leave the trail and ford fields of thigh-high dry prairie grass. He'd had enough of that and wasn't in the mood. *Leavin's one thing—-flat-out runnin's another.*

Settling back into the saddle, he took a final, hard draw from the cigarette, then, resigning himself, ground its cinder between his left trigger finger and thumb. Flicking the butt to the side of the trail, "So be it," he said.

Heston reared his head and snorted as though he were in agreement.

Pulling his arms free of the faded black duster, he felt the familiar quickening of blood in his veins. Then, for yet no justifiable reason, he could hear the old call to rally—-*Strike and send 'em to hell before the devil knows they're on their way.*

He bunched and draped the coat across Heston's withers at the saddle horn. From his saddlebags, he drew two revolvers and, thumbing each cylinder, checked the ease of their rotation. Then he removed from his holsters each of the two steel-blue Colts, replacing them with the larger pistols. The riders were nearing. With a Colt in each hand beneath the folds of his coat at the saddlebow, he gave the mount a light tap of his boot heels.

"What fool man would run a horse in the ground if he weren't bein hounded, Hest?"

The bay nickered and Christian Jack bowed his head as they started slowly on. With bearded chin brushing at his chest, he squinted past the sagged brim of his hat and watched as the three grew larger until they began to rein in. Their mounts were blowing like locomotives and were streaked with dirty lather from their being run hard and no doubt long. Through the dust cloud just beginning to gather about them, he saw that as they were tucking the right wings of their coats behind their holstered side arms, they appeared to be plotting amongst themselves. Then, at about forty yards out, they spread blocking the trail, halted and waited.

"How do?" the center man hailed.

Acting unaware of both greeting and presence, Christian Jack kept his face bowed and eyes squinted in the shadow of the brim of his hat. Heston plodded slowly forward.

"Where ya out from...fella?" the same one asked. This time he'd spoken in a lower voice, not wanting to awaken him should he be asleep. And, too, Christian Jack noted, besides his being nosy, there was a definite inflection of attitude in the way he'd expressed *fella,* suggesting both inquiry and intent were anything but friendly.

"He looks kinda sick," the left rider said.

Recognizing now that his holstered revolvers were safely away from the ready reach of his hands, the faces of the three coiled in opportune sneers. Suspicions confirmed Christian Jack remained unresponsive, head slumped and bobbing with Heston's casual gait.

"Might be he'd like ta do a little horse tradin," the same rider mused followed by a ridiculous sounding snicker.

You piece of—-Christian Jack thought to himself tempted to grin. Rather, he watched through slit eyelids as a wolfish darting of eyes now passed between the three and, too, as their right hands settled securely over their revolvers.

"Well..." the third rider in a deep, rough and resolute tone of voice began, "he ain't showin any sign of cedin the trail now——"

Before he'd completed his challenge, Christian Jack had folded completely forward putting his heels hard to the bay and brought up both hidden revolvers blazing. As Heston lunged and his Colts spit fire, there was the usual frantic confusion of startled, rearing and screaming horses and wild churning hooves. Blasting through and past, he was certain he'd hit the flank men twice and, too, that they hadn't loosed a round between them.

Clutching the free reins, he broke and sharply swung Heston, then stuffed the leather straps into his mouth and clamped. With barrels raised, he peered through the swirls of bluish-gray gun smoke and settling trail dust. Two men lay on their back not moving. The three riderless horses, too tired to gallop long, loped halfheartedly along the trail. Flopping as lifeless as a sack of coal from one was the third, his right foot caught-up in its stirrup. Then the body twisted free, rolled and was still.

One of the two lying side by side moaned.

Christian Jack nudged Heston and approached the downed men. The center rider, the first he'd shot, was hit below the left eye. His revolver was still holstered. The one who'd been concerned about his not conceding the trail and who was now moaning, he'd hit twice in the mid-section. His revolver lay free in the dirt and his bloodied hands clutched at the pooling as he blinked to clear the shock from his eyes. As though trying to make out something from afar, he searched the reposed face of the rider above.

"Who the...tarnations are ya?" he ground through clenched teeth.

Letting the reins drop from his mouth, Christian Jack thought how he'd yet to settle on a name and felt unprepared. Not that this fellow needed to know, but it was a strong reminder of unfinished business that needed tending. Then the man's graveled breathing ceased. He noted how his still wide-open eyes, like most he'd seen, were fixed in that glazed and confused trance of fear; as though they'd seen a ghost or the Devil himself.

After reloading the empty chambers of his Colts, he rounded up each of the three dead men's tuckered horses, stripped the saddles and bridles and set them free. He then went through each set of saddlebags and the men's pockets, but found nothing that would indicate they were bandits. They had only a few dollars between them. And except for a couple plugs of dirt and lint-embedded tobacco chaw, and some greasy slabs of what smelled like gamey buffalo jerk, there were no other provisions. All of their weapons were unimpressive and sorely in need of cleaning and oil. He slung them and their rifles off into the fields. What he might be able to glean from bartering them, their mounts and tack, wasn't worth the suspicion it could raise. Their hats were fresher than his, but he'd never wear another man's; that, or their long johns or foot stockings. Outside of the cartridges and the few dollars they had, he took nothing other than their lives and left them where they lay.

Into the freshest of their hats, he emptied one of the men's canteens and held it for Heston. While the mount drank, he half-wondered what it was they'd been running from. He thought how, like himself, everyone seemed to be running or skirting one thing or another, some just faster and harder.

After Heston finished drinking, Christian Jack twisted himself a smoke. Then he mounted, struck a lucifer with his thumbnail, lit the cigarette and continued on. Like the steamed breath of a winded horse in winter, he jetted streams of smoke from his nostrils and said, "Hest, they didn't have enough for tradin."

Riding on, he could hear the graveled echo of the one who'd asked who he was. Half-wondering what it really mattered considering, he was reminded of his need for a new name. He'd been trying to settle on one, as well as a past to go with it. Something in the event he tried to land work or wanted to dispel idle suspicion. A background where he'd never been to Missouri, knew what jay-hawkers, bushwhackers or raiders were.

Just then, it dawned on him how no one knew his middle name—-Lucas. It was so obvious, he hadn't considered it before. He thought how it would be easier to remember. Then, along that same note, he thought, *Why not stretch Jack into Jackson?* In a way similar to how he might work a new hat or revolver, trying to get used to the fit and feel, he voiced it aloud, "Lucas Jackson...Lucas Jackson."

Reflecting on both new name and partially fabricated past, he came to where the three riders had left the open fields from the south joining the trail eastward. He scanned the direction from which they'd come, but could detect nothing that might explain their riding full out as they were. Nevertheless, he'd keep watch just in case.

While satisfied over having at last concluded the name issue, he knew better what it was that usually gave him away; that being the two-inch scar above his left eyebrow that had since healed blue. Over the years it had ridden with him and was known by citizen and blue-belly alike. It was, unfortunately, easily recognized and it preceded him like a curse, even supplying the exaggerated far-fetched stuff of infamous raider exploits. As if by chance it might disappear, he occasionally brushed his fingers over it, just as the near fatal Minie ball had, leaving its mark and earning him the brand of *Cain* among fellow raiders. But unlike the Biblical Cain said to have killed his brother, he never had a brother and hadn't killed anyone he knew personally. And that religious premise that all men *were* brothers was absurd. While it was something his parents had mistakenly held to, he knew firsthand better. Life in this world was each man for himself.

A shadow darted across the trail before him and, looking up, he saw it was a lone eagle, no doubt on the prowl for prey. As he watched it soar, he wondered what it must be like not to be hunted; that and having wings and being as free. It suggested something he'd heard somewhere about having or, being on the wings of eagles and he tried recalling the impression, but could not dredge it further.

For some time, the eagle drifted in wide circles above. Then it banked and glided north. He thought how it had its place and knew where it was going. Beyond Cheyenne and somewhere west, he did not. He only knew that any certainty of any future was only as sure as each stride Heston took; that and as long as he remained vigilant. Other than that, he was as tired of trying to project tomorrow as he was ruminating the past, which was never done with him. It and its shadow that every time he thought he might have finally shaken it, would reappear, announcing who he was, or what he'd once been——a Missouri bushwhacker and one of Quantrill's raiders. Names that just the mention of caused folks to seize breath and tremble or seethe with hatred. Turning aside he spat, and his mind drifted back.

The war for him began when he set out to avenge the senseless murder of his father by Kansas jayhawkers. That was over seven years ago and before the War Between the States began. And now, the only good he could glean from Cause, was that the notorious jay hawk instigator known as *The Grim Chieftain*, had put a pistol in his mouth killing himself. The same blasphemous mouth from which he'd vomited his murder-inciting charge: *Missourians are wolves, snakes, devils, and damn their souls, I want them cast into a burning hell.* An ominous curse he'd seared to memory so that given the opportunity, he could repeat before killing the Kansas hatemonger and casting him along as well. But now, like everything else, the Grim Chieftain, too, was one with the unshakeable shadow of the past that refused to be buried and continually haunted him.

Therefore he was in essence, branded and unpardonable. And whether people actually knew who he was or not, just the notion that their suspicions had arisen and he'd find himself moving on again. And that not as much out of fear of dying—since everyone had it coming eventually in one way or another—but simply out of the natural instinct to survive. The only alternative, outside of giving himself up for a necktie party, was to shoot or kill them before they did him. For that reason alone there could be no quarter for fear. For to possess fear, was to be possessed by it. Fear was a disabling burden and preoccupation that only brought you that much closer to its dreaded outcome. Yes—-fear was better left for your adversary, be it a vengeful jayhawker or Yank looking down his gun sights with an itching trigger finger, or just men looking to gain some kind of distinction for having killed a known raider. Nevertheless, regardless of who or their reasons why, he wasn't going to simply lie down because of what jayhawkers and that damn war had made of him.

His thoughts turned to the Younger's, Jim and Cole, and the James', Frank and Jessie. He wondered how they were getting on. He'd heard rumors about some of the trouble they'd still been raising and how authorities were gunning after them. He thought how he could have continued riding with them, but how, by then, he'd wanted, or rather needed, to be alone. He was tired of people, their faces, opinions and arguments. He'd finally come to the reclusive opinion that being free meant complete disassociation not just from raiders, but *all* people.

Realizing the extent in which he was once again ruminating the past, he disconnected himself from it. Returning to present, he glanced skyward and saw that the eagle was now but the small black speck of a lone predator drifting across a vast blue and empty sky. He imagined its being similar to the way that he, mount, revolvers and shadow must appear as they too drifted over the sun-blanched, barren plain.

Finding his thoughts somewhat astray once more, "Good Lord," he grumbled. He thought how his having nothing to objectively focus on, presented the unavoidable tendency for his mind to randomly wander, thereby letting his normal vigilance lapse. In diligent response, he purposed himself to scan thoroughly, full circle from saddle to horizon.

Having done that and sighting nothing, he thought how while the abundance of nothingness afforded his excessive woolgathering, there was also the measure of comfort in his having seen so few people. Besides the three riders, the few people at the trade post, and an occasional homestead sitting far off alone in the distance, there'd only been the time just after he'd first struck out, when he'd seen the three Indians. He'd reckoned they were Sioux, but paid them little attention and continued on as if they weren't there at all. He remembered how they sat calmly on their paints watching as though they were part of the landscape itself. It was like they knew all they'd get from him was hell.

~ 3 ~

It was nearing noon Friday when he saw the dirty brown haze hovering snug on the horizon ahead. Because there was a light, yet steady breeze blowing into his face, and the dusted blur remained fixed and continuous, he discounted his initial notion that it might be buffalo and reckoned it was likely the frontier town of Cheyenne. When he'd gone another mile, confirming his hunch, the rooftops rose into view from the long, sweeping downs that surrounded it.

While the high plains town was small with few permanent structures, as he began passing outfits of men camped about its outskirts, he also knew with certainty there was no lack of people. A shiver, the likes vermin might raise, crawled slowly from behind his ears to the nape of his neck and down his spine. Then, just as he was about to enter the town itself, Heston sharply bucked his head and whickered a warning followed by the piercing scream of a train whistle. It was as though it were expressly announcing his arrival and it set him further on edge. The temptation to bypass the bustling town was great, but focusing on his ultimate purpose and needs, he consoled himself with the notion that it wasn't like he was riding into Kansas City or St. Joseph. Compelled by necessity and the town's remoteness, he tweaked the brim of his hat further shading his scarred brow and continued in.

Fording his way up the busy street, he saw there wasn't room to hitch Heston if he'd wanted. Then he picked up on the intensely tempting aroma of beef-steak being cooked. His stomach groaned audibly for it. Finally, at the far side of town, he came to a livery. The stableman told him the barn was out of sleeping space, but mentioned where he'd likely find the cheapest rooms if any were still available. He'd also remarked what a fine-looking mount Heston was and asked if he was planning to enter the horse races. Tempted to say that a good mount was too valuable for folly,

Christian Jack did not, replying only that he wasn't. He paid the stableman for Heston's keep adding two-bits for a nose bag of oats along with a solemn warning that there'd be hell to pay if anything happened to him. The stableman, glancing down at his holstered Colts, assured him nothing would.

Taking his rifle and saddlebags with him, he headed back along the busy street. He thoroughly disliked the idea of being away from Heston, but there were things needed done; not the least of which was his regaining of at least some measure of acclimation to people.

The two-dollar room he took was more like a closet. There was a thin, flat pillow and mattress spread over a rickety wood frame that wasn't much wider than the narrow foot space beside it. Serving as a night stand was a small produce crate on top of which sat a half-burnt tallow candle in a rusted jar lid that also doubled as an ashtray. There was no window, only a couple of large, square-headed nails half-hammered in the wall. He had twenty-two dollars and four bits, but still needed a bath and shave, his clothes cleaned and to get something to eat.

Behind the hotel was a laundry and bath house which was convenient. After having a bath and shave, he returned to his room followed by a complacent baldheaded Chinaman who wore a shiny silk frock and a long, single patch of hair down his back. After he'd disrobed, the Chinaman, holding up the breeches, peered through their thinly worn seat and suggested his having them patched, but shaking his head, Christian Jack declined. The Chinaman smiled, politely bowed and departed, taking the clothes to be laundered. In the meantime, he sat naked and hungry on the bed and cleaned and oiled his revolvers and rifle. All he could think about was a hot meal, tomorrow's contest and his getting out of the busy town.

Early evening, after his clothing was returned, he stood in a long line of men waiting to get into one of the eating tents at the edge of town. There, he overheard talk of a town deputy who'd recently been shot during an encounter with three men who were said to be horse thieves and rustlers. Evidently, the deputy, who happened also to be related by marriage to the town sheriff, had been attempting to arrest the men when he was shot by one of them and had his horse stolen. The men in the grub line said that the sheriff, along with his posse, had set out in pursuit of the suspects, leaving behind a couple of hastily deputized greenhorns to keep over the town. One said that he and his posse had followed the culprits south into Colorado. Another remarked how the sheriff wouldn't let any state lines stop him from running them down.

Christian Jack thought about the three men he'd encountered on the trail. Though they'd been headed east, he half-wondered if they weren't the same. That and if there'd been any reward posted on them. But that was only useless speculation, knowing that even if there had been he'd never be so foolhardy as to present himself to the law in order to try claiming it. He did however, consider it good news that the sheriff wasn't likely to be around for tomorrow's contest.

The sun had fully set and the smell of food had his empty stomach digesting itself by the time he sat down. The cheapest fare offered was watery potato soup with a bun of bread and coffee. When he'd finished two servings, there wasn't a drop of the soup or a crumb of bread left.

Returning to the hotel room, the celebration of revelers could be heard from one end of town to the other. Saloons were packed as tightly as a madam's corset and the bluster of voices strewn with the wafting cadence of piano notes, streamed with tobacco smoke from their batwing entrances. Boardwalks and alleys were already lining with men, many passed out drunk.

Back in his room, he cocked the produce crate against the door, lodging it securely beneath its doorknob. After disrobing and neatly folding his freshly laundered breeches and shirt, he placed a revolver beneath the rock-hard, flat pillow, and another beside him under the blanket. Through the second-storied, thin clapboard wall, he could hear the raucous whooping and howling in the street below. But it didn't bother him. He hadn't slept off the ground or under shingles for a long time and had no trouble at all falling off and sleeping soundly. That is until morning when he was awakened by an odd dream concerning his hat.

The wind was gusting like the river beside him was rushing, and it ripped his hat from his head. It raced off tumbling on its brim over the rocks like a runaway wagon-wheel. He flew from the saddle to give chase and almost had it in his grasp when it dodged and skipped off into the water where it was carried away with the current. Looking downstream, he saw a woman who'd waded out into the rapids apparently to retrieve it. Then, looking up, he saw that there were men standing along the cutbank taking potshots at his river-swept hat. Reaching for his own rifle, he glanced downstream again to see that the woman had gone down with the surge of the current and that her head was bobbing away like his hat.

Waking with a start, he blinked and checked the wall for his hat. It was hanging from the nail where he'd hung it. The odd thing about it was he rarely remembered dreams, but the notion of losing his hat had been most unsettling.

In the grainy light before sunrise, he left the room and went to eat. It was all or, naught now, so he figured he might as well put a good breakfast in his belly. After eggs, hash, skillet-fried potatoes and a stack of flapjacks, he went to register for the contest. It was set to start when the opening ceremonies at noon concluded. From there he went to check on Heston and his tack. Afterwards, at the far corner behind the stables, he sat atop a pole-fence and twisted a cigarette. As he smoked, he watched as riders and wagons streamed in for the coming out. When his shadow had drawn itself small beneath him, he hopped from the fence and started over.

~ 4 ~

Threading his way through the clustering mob of people, Christian Jack headed to where the shooting contest was to be held. After checking in, he wandered back alongside a small set of seating stands. It wasn't long before there must have been fifty men milling about the vicinity of the firing line. If they were all contenders it meant the contest would take a while; and too, that the prize money would be sizeable. He noticed how many of them fidgeted nervously with their revolvers, repeatedly removing them from their holsters every few minutes to inspect and recheck them. While most looked like working ranch hands, there were also a number of men who wore suits. Some looked like businessmen, others gamblers. He thought how more than likely the latter probably fancied themselves as gun slicks. Slicks or not, in light of its being almost a matter of survival for himself, the contest would be tantamount to riding into battle; only without the blood, and, he'd be standing, not riding. As for his dapperly attired opponents, he figured it was likely a matter largely of boasting rights for them.

Finally, a tall, older fellow stepped forward and upon gaining the crowd's attention, addressed the participants and audience:

"On behalf of our local ranchers, I welcome you to the Cheyenne pistol contest. As you can see, interest is large. We have thirty-one entrants. Therefore, on the first round at ten paces, contestants will be limited to three shots each."

A disappointed groan arose from the bulk of shooters. Christian Jack knew it was because it took some a shot or two to sight-in and adjust. He also knew that having the three shot limit would narrow the field much quicker.

"I know what some of you are thinking," the judge remarked, "but it can't be helped in the face of time. Now, if a shot breaks the line of an inner circle, it will be considered a score. In the event of ties, there will be a second round at twenty paces, then thirty and so on. Are there any questions?"

"Is it possible to take first and second place?" one of the better-dressed men quipped. His immediate group of cronies and some of the people sitting in the stands, which were now almost full, laughed.

"I'm afraid not, Mister Stenerson," the judge replied.

"Will we be limited to three shots on tiebreaker rounds?" another asked.

"That will be determined by myself and the other judges, depending on how many contestants are still in the hunt. Now, when your name's called, check the name on your target and make sure it's yours. There'll be three shooters on the line at a time. Names will be called in the order of registration. So good luck, gentlemen, and let's keep it safe."

As the judge was calling the names of the first round of shooters, from the corner of his eye, Christian Jack caught sight of two Union officers moving through the crowd. His hackles instantly rose. *I don't believe it,* he groaned. Maneuvering to get a better look, he saw that the blue-bellies were in full uniform and that they had two women with them. That was good, he reckoned, counting them a distraction. As he was better able to view, he noticed that besides being armed, they wore the same army boots he was, only theirs issued and polished and worn outside their yellow-striped leggings, while his own, he'd scavenged and were scuffed and covered by his pant legs. He wondered if they were participating in the contest. Chances were, they'd never seen or heard of him, but he'd been wrong thinking that way before. He spat at the shadow between his Union boots. *What's the odds of your runnin into Yanks all the way out here?* No sooner had the thought posed itself than he knew that with the rails spreading across the country, chances were much more likely. Then he thought how if the women were their wives, they might be stationed at some nearby frontier garrison. *At any rate, you've done placed the ante, now play the hand and deal with it,* he thought telling himself.

The contest started and instead of watching how the shooters at the line were faring, he kept himself back and his eyes on the blue-bellies. As the second round of shooters began firing, he saw that the two women with the soldiers were covering their ears from the cracking gunfire. Then the men began leading them away. He breathed easier watching as they departed. He set his bags and rifle down and started rolling a cigarette. Meanwhile, the official called for the next round of contestants:

"Gillam, Jackson and Wolfitz."

Two men stepped to the line and were checking their targets. Then the official called, "Where's Jackson…Lucas Jackson?"

"Blast it," he muttered stuffing the half-rolled cigarette into his shirt pocket. He'd already forgotten that *Jackson* was his name, or at least the one he was using. Grabbing his bags and rifle, he hustled through the group of shooters and spectators up to the line. Once there, he was met with laughter.

"Lucas Jackson?" the judge asked.

"That's me," he answered setting down the saddlebags and rifle. Stepping forward he confirmed the name on the target was his, or, the one he was using at least.

Once the targets were set, "Fire when ready, gentlemen," the judge signaled.

Christian Jack—alias Lucas Jackson—calmly drew his left revolver with his right hand, leveled and fired without a pause between pulls. When he dropped the smoking revolver into its holster, the other two contestants were still carefully aiming and firing. He saw there were no hits outside the center of his own target. Returning to where he'd been before, off to the side of the stands, he scanned the audience for the Union hats.

"Good shootin," a young fellow standing nearby said.

Turning his attention to him, Christian Jack straightaway detected the unassuming smile in the shade of the fellow's cowboy hat which was about as worn and battered as his own. And, too, that he was wearing an equally old and worn gun belt and revolver. He looked to be in his late-teens.

"Thanks," he said with a straight face.

Then, squinting his eyes and bunching his nose in obvious curiosity, "What kind'a pistols are *them*?" the kid asked.

Although he didn't welcome the interest at all, considering both source and situation, he reminded himself that it was part and parcel of it all.

"Colt Police five-shot," he replied.

"What ya gonna do if they go ta six shots?"

Looking the inquisitive young fellow dead in the eyes, he half-smirked and tapped the handle of his right side revolver. He'd been asked many times over the years why he used them. He liked their natural balance and line and they were less restrictive than the six. He preferred the immediate advantage of speed and accuracy over the extra round since it was usually the first shots that settled most business anyway. Besides, when he rode into battle, he had at least two more six-shot Colts shoved in his belt for back-up.

"My name's Charlie, what's yours?" the kid asked.

Pausing to get it right, "...Lucas," he answered.

"Good ta meet ya, Lucas," Charlie said offering his hand. Lucas met it and they shook.

"Are ya shootin, Charlie?"

"Yeah, but I ain't so good."

"Just relax and trust yourself."

"I'll try," Charlie said. "Are ya on at one of the ranches, Lucas?"

"Nope, I ain't."

The judge was calling the next group of contestants.

"Well, that's me," Charlie said. Setting snug his hat, he headed for the line.

Lucas fingered the loose rolling paper from his shirt pocket and drew the cotton pouch of tobacco and proceeded to roll another cigarette. As he did, he reminded himself that his name was now *Jackson—-Lucas Jackson*. When Charlie finished shooting, he saw that two of his shots had narrowly missed the inner circle.

"Fair shootin, Charlie," he said when he'd returned.

"I knew them first would get me. They always do. Maybe I'll do better with the rifle tomorrow. Are ya in it, Lucas?"

Striking the lucifer with his thumbnail, he lit the cigarette and scanned the crowd for the blue-bellies.

"Naw," he said. "Think I'll go mosey a spell, Charlie."

"Okay, Lucas. Good luck to ya."

"The same," Lucas said lifting his bags and rifle. The kid was okay, just young, nervous and kind of talky was all. Working his way further back alongside the stands, he noticed a couple of older fellows who seemed to be humorously appraising him between themselves. Knowing intimidation was the only skill some fellows possessed, he ignored them. He considered, too, how they might just be thinking him lucky.

It was over an hour before the judge stepped forward and announced that there were nineteen contestants who would be moving on to the second round at twenty paces which, he'd also added, would be a three shot round again.

When he was next called to the line, to his left was the fellow who'd asked earlier about taking first and second place. Wearing a cocky smirk the comedian said, "You sure they called you?" Some of the men standing nearby laughed.

Lucas confirmed the name on his target then set his saddlebags down and propped the Winchester over them. "I'm here," he said from the corner of his mouth eyeing the level of the target being set down range.

"Fire when ready, gentlemen," the judge called.

Lucas calmly pulled his left, leveled and let it go, one-two-three in the center of the target. When the mouthy fellow next to him finished firing, he saw that two of his shots had just edged the center line counting him in.

Through the growing mob of eyes, he worked his way back along the stands. There, he reloaded his revolver.

"Good shootin again, Lucas," Charlie said. Lucas acknowledged him, this time faintly revealing a smile.

Finally, the judge came out and announced that the contest was down to nine men. He read the names and said it would be six shots at thirty paces and called the first round to the line. The audience, which had grown steadily larger throughout the afternoon, now went silent and the air tense. Standing back, he noted how the remaining shooters had begun hard-eyeing one another as well as himself. Called in the second grouping this time, next to him was the same mouthy fellow as last.

"It's too bad you got those five-rounders," he remarked with a grin.

"That right?" Lucas said appraising the target as it was being set.

"Yeah, good luck," the fellow scoffed.

Lucas turned and looked him hard in the eyes thinking *Yeah, you too, you pestersome*—-

"All right, gentlemen, fire at will, six shots each," the line judge signaled.

Lucas drew and raised his left revolver pulling three rapid rounds during which time he'd drawn and leveled his right in his left hand, squeezing off three more just as fluidly. As the gun smoke lifted, he could see no shots outside center. Taking up his gear, he could feel the eyes of the entire audience upon him. He kept his face tilted and forehead shaded behind the brim of his hat. It worried him making a show of himself, but he needed the money and this was his opportunity; and that was how he shot, when he shot to count. *It counts anytime you shoot*, he thought.

"Dang, Lucas!" Charlie exclaimed. The kid was looking about as though he was proud to be in his company and Lucas couldn't help but openly smile at him.

After the remaining shooters had taken their turns, the officials studied the results for another hour. At last, the main judge stepped forward and hailed the audience's attention.

"Ladies and gentlemen we have an outright winner and ongoing three way tie for second. Our winner is Mister Lucas Jackson."

"Ya did it, Lucas, ya won!" Charlie exclaimed. The gallery lightly applauded and Lucas turned toward them and tipped the brim of his hat, purposely drawing it lower over his brow.

After the shoot-off for second place concluded, the judge called the two winners forward. The runner-up, who wasn't the one who'd had so much to say earlier, was awarded $31.00, one-third of the gate. Christian Jack or, rather Lucas Jackson, received the remaining two-thirds of the take in the amount of $62.00. Again the audience applauded as he shook the judge's hand. The attention was extremely disquieting and he could feel his body temperature rapidly climbing. He wanted to get out of there and felt very much like a cornered animal desperate to escape.

Taking his bags and rifle, he stepped from the line and began working his way through the crowd. He couldn't help noting the disappointment on most of the contestant's faces. As he was approaching the two who'd been humorously appraising him earlier, he caught the unmistakable, serious look they now had in their eyes. He felt as that tinge of warning was triggered from the nape of his neck down his spine. No, they weren't grinning and mocking him now, they were clearly calculating and sizing him up. *If you ever seen that hungry, schemin dog look before* he thought telling himself as he passed by them, *there it is bigger'n the Mississip.*

When he'd reached the less crowded area off to the side of the stands and was setting down his gear, Charlie came over.

"Ya oughta enter the rifle contest tomorrow, Lucas," he said.

"Naw, that one's yours, Charlie," Lucas replied looking beyond him to the two who still had his attention. Like a couple of hungry vultures they were still watching. Focusing now on Charlie he said, "Get ta bed early and put a good breakfast in ya. Remember, trust yourself and leave the frettin to the others."

"I'll try. Well, it was good meetin ya, Lucas."

"The same, Charlie."

The two of them shook hands again and as Charlie departed, Lucas glanced towards the two men to find they were still watching. He got the distinct impression that they were glad to see Charlie leaving and that he was indeed on his own. Feeling pressured enough as it was already just his being there, as he began reloading the empty chambers of his revolvers, his jaws set tight and he growled within. He thought how more than likely they would try tailing him until he was away from so many people before making their play. Then he began to wonder if perhaps they knew who he was, but then, thought how if they did, they wouldn't have been mocking him as boldly as they had earlier, or, acting the blatant conniving way they were now. Surrendering to his instinct of engaging potential threats head on and without delay he thought *So much for keeping a low profile.*

~ 5 ~

Christian Jack—hopefully known only as Lucas Jackson—slung the bags over his left shoulder and resting his right hand over the handle of his left-holstered revolver, set out cutting an unmistakable straight path towards the two suspected conspirators. As he thumbed back setting the hammer on the holstered Colt, he simultaneously ratcheted the Winchester in his left hand with a sharp, snapping jerk, leaving its muzzle leveled directly at them. As he approached, he acknowledged them with a careless, almost crazy-eager grin, which then shifted to a penetrating, dead-serious look that read—-*Let's say we deal with your problems right here and now.*

Recognizing his unexpected advantage of ready arms, as well as his intent and boldness to bring both weapons and themselves to bear right then and there in front of all who were present, the sinister, calculating looks drained instantly from their faces. Reflecting expressions of self-preservation now, they began shifting awkwardly on muddled feet, then, pivoting, hastily sloughed off into the safety of the exiting crowd.

The one thing he wanted even less than a scene now was to be stalked and ambushed later. He could have continued to ignore them but by bringing it to head on his own timing, figured it might diffuse any further unfavorable notions they might decide to entertain later. In gambling terms, he'd called their hands and they'd been wise in folding.

Just then, blocking his view of their retreat, a short, older and well-dressed man, wearing a high-crowned Western hat and absurd looking wide smile, stepped abruptly before him and stopped. His suit coat and tie made him look like a banker or businessman, but the hat said he probably had something to do with the cattle trade.

"Congratulations," he said. "One of the best displays of marksmanship I've had the pleasure to witness…and using both left and right firearms as well."

Looking beyond the peculiar man, Christian Jack flashed on the two and saw they were still exiting. Returning straight-faced to the man before him he said flatly, "Thanks."

"Name's Valentine...Augustus Valentine," the man said extending his hand.

Careful to get it right, "Lucas...Jack...son," he said slowly and clumsily. Then he met and shook the man's thick, doughy hand.

"Pleased, I'm sure," the man who might have been in his forties said. He was really beaming.

Lucas tried exerting something of a smile himself, but standing there alongside the current of people made it difficult so that what he was able to muster was hesitant at best. He still had that agitated feeling similar to the one you get when you realize the enemy is closing in around you.

"I'm a rancher, Lucas with a spread just a day's ride from town," the man said. Turning, he gestured towards the entrance behind him. "That's my wife, Geneva, and two daughters, Katie and Jodie."

The three brightly dressed women standing on the other side of the pole-fence flashed complimentary smiles that seemed to evaporate as quickly as they'd appeared. Lucas nodded in recognition.

"Excuse my curiosity, son, but are you presently employed at one of the area ranches?"

"No sir, I'm not," he answered bluntly. As if they were the center rings of two targets, he bored into the blacks of the provocative man's eyes. He was resistant about anyone questioning his business, and he wasn't particularly fond of being called *son*, either. He did, however, on further reflection, get the distinct impression that the man who'd just mentioned *employment* appreciated his having been addressed as *sir*. Since he held no man in high regard, his having said it wasn't so much a sign of respect as just old habit from his youth that would occasionally resurface.

"I see. Well, are you currently interested in attaining employment?"

Focusing on the aspect of potential employment, Lucas paused trying to rein in his apprehensive nature. He didn't want to come across too coarse, eager or desperate.

"That's possible, I suppose," he said.

"Father," one of the man's daughters called.

She had flame-orange hair and wore an emerald-green dress and beret. Overhead, in her also matching green-gloved hand, she held an open parasol. Besides being slightly taller, the way in which she held herself suggested she was older than her blonde-haired sister who wore no hat or gloves and carried no parasol. From behind the thin dust veil that hung from the front of the wife's hat, the strained expression on her face showed that she, too, like the redheaded daughter, was evidently tired of waiting. The rancher raised his arm and open hand to them.

"Well, Lucas, if you're interested, I'd like to discuss with you the position I'm looking to fill. I'm quite certain you'll find it lucrative in light of standard compensation and worthy of your time and consideration."

"Father!" the redheaded daughter exclaimed again.

Lucas figured she desperately needed to visit the privy.

"So, Lucas…in let's say a couple of hours if that's convenient for you. I have to get my family back to the hotel just now. I apologize."

"All right, Mister Valentine."

"Good, I look forward to seeing you then, just over at Dyer's Hotel."

"All right…sir," Lucas said, deciding just at the last to add the *sir* for good measure.

He watched as the man joined his wife and daughters. As they departed, the younger, blonde-haired daughter turned, smiled and waved. Again, he nodded in acknowledgement.

Well, you got the prize money and maybe a job, too he thought telling himself. But no sooner had he, when he was reminded of the two he'd been prepared to challenge earlier. He swept the area without seeing them and thought how he'd still have to keep watch over his shoulder for them. Other than that, things were certainly showing signs of shaping up. That shelter of his in his mind and somewhere in the mountains might be a cabin yet. But that was only a fleeting thought as he also considered the fact that the position this Valentine character was looking to fill more than likely had to do with his shooting ability, not ranching skills. While experience hadn't been mentioned, *lucrative* compensation and the fact that the ranch was away from town had, and those factors in themselves certainly were tempting. His stomach rumbled. The shooting contest had taken the whole afternoon. He set out heading straight for the steak house that did its advertising with its enticing aroma. The one he'd smelled as he passed by on his way into town yesterday.

After eating a large thick cut of beef steak, baked potato, stewed carrots, green snap beans and plenty of freshly baked bread spread thick with creamy butter, he headed to the stables to check on Heston. It wasn't until he was there that it dawned on him how he should get himself a room squared. He'd been so busy enjoying the meal and thinking about his upcoming meeting with the cattleman that he hadn't thought of securing one. From the stables he went to two hotels without any luck. Then he reckoned it was time he headed over to meet the rancher. He'd just have to get Heston afterwards and ride out of town and find a place to camp. Then, of course, depending on how the meeting turned out, there was always the chance he'd be moving on anyway.

At the hotel entrance, there was a doorman who wore a black monkey jacket buttoned to his chin. He asked if he could be of assistance.

"My name's...Lucas...Jackson. I'm here to see a Mister Valentine."

"Yes, Mister Valentine is expecting you, sir. This way, please."

He followed the doorman into the hotel lobby. On the right, just past the check-in counter, a wide, rose-red carpeted staircase led upstairs. To his left was an open room that was half-full of people seated at round tables covered with white tablecloths. At the center of each table, candles glowed, their light fractured by cut crystal chimneys. Stretched against the far-mirrored wall was a polished wood and brass bar with matching stools. Not that he would have known from personal experience, but it felt as though he'd just stepped into some fancy Eastern hotel, not one in Wyoming territory. Then he saw Valentine seated at a table with two other men.

"Lucas, I'm glad you made it," the rancher said standing and extending his hand.

Switching the rifle to his left, he met and shook hands with the spirited cattleman. Meanwhile, the two elderly, suited men stood also.

"Gentlemen, allow me to introduce Lucas Jackson. Lucas, this is Mister Oates and Mister Wainsworth." Valentine acted and sounded as though he were proud somehow to be conducting the introductions. Lucas shook hands with the two men and noticed that theirs, unlike Valentine's, were hands that still, or at least had once, known physical work.

"That was a fine performance in marksmanship today, Lucas," the man named Oates said.

"Yes, most impressive," the silver-haired and mustachioed Wainsworth added.

Noticing as both men's eyes drifted to his revolvers, "Thanks," he said. Their compliments were fine, but he wasn't used to it and felt extremely out of place. He reckoned it as awkward as his being someplace like a church.

"Have a seat, Lucas. The porter will see to your things. What would you like to drink?"

"Coffee'll be fine, and I'll hold on to these," he said referring to his rifle and saddlebags. As he and the men sat, the doorman departed.

"Only coffee? I would have thought you a bourbon man, Lucas," Valentine remarked. While he'd said it with a note of humor, it was obvious he was actually pleased. If he'd been a soaker, he wouldn't have passed up the offer for liquor; that or he'd have probably been half-sloshed already.

A waiter approached the table, and Valentine ordered the coffee and another cognac for himself. He asked the other two men if they were ready for fresh drinks. Their glasses were yet half-full and they declined.

"Where'd you learn to handle firearms, Lucas?" the man named Oates asked.

Although he'd somewhat tried to prepare himself, rehearsing his fabricated past over supper, he now found himself feeling unprepared before the three older men. He'd only expected to be meeting with Valentine. Thinking how to respond, he noticed their expressions seemed unimposing enough, as if they thought perhaps he was being humble.

He cleared his throat and answered, "The family farm back in West Virginia, sir."

"Should have known," Wainsworth remarked. "There must be something in the air or water in those Appalachia's, the way fellas from those parts are known sure shots."

"Probably has some viable truth to it," Valentine said smiling agreeably.

Then the waiter brought the coffee with a silver cream pitcher and the glass of cognac for Valentine. He asked if there would be anything else.

"Not just now," Valentine said dismissing the waiter with a flick of his hand.

"West Virginia——" the one named Oates said and paused, apparently giving it further thought. "That was an undecided state, was it not?"

As Lucas poured cream into his coffee, not wanting to raise suspicion by his appearing reluctant he readily replied, "Still is, sir."

He noticed how the men's faces hung blank, and he thought perhaps he shouldn't have said it. That was why he'd settled on West Virginia as being where he was supposedly from, so he could remain neutral on the war issue and not have to claim either affiliation—Union or Confederate. Then the three men laughed.

"And he's got Appalachian wit and manners to go with the sure eyes and hands as well, gentlemen," Valentine said.

"What about that Major Mosby and his Raiders...did their outfit ever operate around your parts, Lucas?" Wainsworth asked.

He didn't know whether or not Mosby ever operated in West Virginia, but gambling that these three didn't either, he once more readily answered, "Not so much around us, but we heard of 'em. And I believe he was a colonel, sir."

"That's right," Mister Oates said. "And if memory serves me right, a self-promoted colonel at that."

Again, the three men laughed, and he smiled along with them, all the while thinking to himself how Mosby had been the leader of another group of raiders whose outfit operated more closely to Confederate command than the Missouri raiders he'd ridden with. But, like themselves west of the Mississippi, Mosby's Raiders had been a curse to Union forces throughout the war in the east. Still, he thought, humor aside, the subject was hitting uncomfortably close to home. Closer than he cared and they hopefully knew. Fortunately, the two men finished their drinks without asking any more touchy questions. Valentine asked if they'd like another.

"No thanks, Augustus," Mister Oates said standing. "It's time I got back to the missus. I'll see you gentlemen at the dinner this evening. Lucas, it was a pleasure to meet you."

"Yes, I should do the same," Mister Wainsworth said also standing. "Lucas, if Valentine here doesn't take care of you, you come see *me*, okay?"

"I found him first, boys," Valentine remarked with a chuckle as Lucas stood and shook hands with the two men.

When they departed, Valentine placed his elbows on the table with his hands together before him and in a lower voice began, "Lucas, I appreciate your time and patience. They're a couple of good friends and cattlemen with ranches of their own. But I'll get down to the business I asked you here for. Like my two friends, I've been having problems with rustlers and free grazers." He paused, watching for any reaction Lucas might possibly suggest. Sensing none, he continued: "Most of my men are ranch hands, and I'll be blunt, inexperienced at aggressive enforcement. A couple weeks ago, two of them were shot at and chased off by rustlers, and I mean to put an end to it. Now, the law's on my side here, and I've got a right to protect what's mine, and that's why I've asked you here. I believe having someone who's capable of confronting those situations will make all the difference and give the men the confidence to step up." The rancher paused again and took a drink, his eyes intent on Lucas'.

"My hands earn thirty dollars a month, Lucas, and just between you and myself, I'm prepared to offer you forty. That of course includes board, meals, mounts and ammunition."

"So what do I do with these fellas when I encounter 'em?" Lucas asked.

"We warn free grazers they're trespassing. If that doesn't work, we're left with little option but to let it pass or scatter their herds after dark. Something we've yet to resort to thus far. Of course with rustlers you use whatever force necessary. They know what they're doing is illegal, and they're armed and expecting it. I won't underscore their intents or boldness, if you get my point."

Just then, Valentine's wife and daughters approached the table.

"I'm sorry to interrupt you, gentlemen," the wife said. "Augustus, your daughters would like a word with you."

"Yes. In just a moment, dear."

"Father," the older of the two girls blurted, "Jodie and I are tired of sitting and waiting. We need money for shopping."

Lucas was surprised at the way she'd spoken to her father, telling, not asking, and now, couldn't help but notice the disapproving way in which she seemed to be appraising himself, as though he were the one interrupting. It was obvious she was spoiled, and she reminded him of some of the snobbish women he'd seen who were from wealthy plantations in the South. He also noticed that she'd changed her wardrobe and now wore a bustled, black velvet dress with matching hat, gloves and handbag. The contrast of her milk-white complexion and red hair to the dark suit was as striking as her natural beauty was to her unbecoming demeanor.

"Yes, Katie sweetheart. In just a couple of minutes, please," her father said.

"Come, girls," the mother said.

Katie, further revealing her displeasure, groaned audibly, then spun and followed her mother and sister to a nearby table. There, she flopped herself down into a chair and glared back over at Lucas and her father.

"I'm sorry, Lucas," Augustus Valentine apologized. "The girls have been looking forward to this visit to Cheyenne for some time."

Lucas tried exerting a look of understanding.

"So what do you think?" the rancher asked.

"Well, as long as I'm not breaking the law like you said, it sounds okay. When would I be startin?"

"Splendid," Valentine said. He looked very satisfied as he stretched his hand across the table and the two of them shook hands for the third time that day.

"Where are you staying, Lucas, if you don't mind my asking?"

"I'm not sure just yet. I reckon the hotels are all full."

"Not to worry, I'll square a room here for you, by all means. You'll be my guest." Turning, he glanced over at his wife and daughters and smiled. Then he turned back to Lucas.

"Excuse my inquiring again, Lucas, but do you have any particular plans set for the evening?"

"I reckon not now."

"The reason for my asking is, Geneva and I will be attending a dinner with some of the other ranchers tonight, but the girls, I'm afraid, refuse to. It's much too boring for them. Frankly, I'm concerned about their being on their own. I'm sure you understand. I wonder if I might put you on the payroll now and ask if you'd mind seeing over them just until after the dinner? It shouldn't be but a few hours at most."

Assimilating what he thought he'd just heard, he looked blankly at Valentine, then over at the women. Katie, the impatient daughter was staring back at him with a coy look on her face as if she already knew what her father had just proposed. Uncertain what choice he had in the matter at that point, he replied, "I suppose."

"Splendid. Geneva and I will be able to enjoy ourselves without concern. It means a lot to us. Thank you." Leaning slightly forward over the table, in a hushed voice he said, "Katie's a bit spirited and headstrong at times, as I'm sure you may have noticed. When she was younger, I called her my *Fiery Little Mustang*, but now that she's grown to a sophisticated young woman, she no longer cares for the endearment. And Jodie, well, she's the opposite, quiet as a stable mouse. Anyway, I'll go inform the girls and see to your room. Excuse me."

As Valentine informed the women of the arrangement, Lucas cringed as they all looked his way. A mixed feeling of being somehow exposed and having been taken advantage of swept over him. The wife and Jodie appeared pleasant enough, but Katie maintained that disdainful look of hers. Valentine left the women's table and headed for the hotel desk.

"What've you done gotten yourself into?" Lucas muttered to himself through set teeth.

A few minutes later, the cattleman returned and handed him a room key and a ten-dollar bill.

"That's your room key, Lucas. It's right across the hall from both of ours. You'll be able to secure your things there. The room's square through Sunday night, as we'll be leaving for the ranch first thing early Monday morning. That ten's in case you or the girls should need anything on the town. Feel free to help yourself."

Trying to reveal some semblance of gratefulness and not his reluctance or reservations, "All right, sir," he said.

~ 6 ~

The girls were sitting on a red padded, backless bench in the lobby and they both smiled at Lucas as he descended the matching red carpeted staircase. He figured their parents must have instructed them to be pleasant. Nonetheless, he skeptically studied Katie as though she were wearing a mask. Immediately, her eyes betrayed her, revealing her amusement at his obvious discomfort over the arrangement. Then, as she further appraised him, scanning from his floppy-brimmed hat to his hard-ridden boots, her condescending disapproval of his appearance was unmistakable.

"Are you *sure* you're up to this, Lucas?" she asked.

Looking as dispirited as he might after having just been taken prisoner by Union forces, Lucas surrendered himself to the task before him.

"I reckon," he muttered glancing sidelong at Jodie. Her kindly smile suggested an almost sympathetic understanding for him.

The way people gawked as the three of them left the hotel and paraded up the street, made him feel as though he were a five-legged dog and carnival attraction. He knew it was because of how old and worn his own clothes were in contrast to the girls who were dressed as though they were attending a governor's ball. It wasn't that he gave a hoot about what people thought of him or what he wore, he simply didn't want their attention at all. *It'll be dark soon* he consoled himself.

"We've changed our minds about shopping, Lucas," Katie said. "We're going to the dance being held at the grandstand."

As he considered how that was probably better than their gallivanting through the town and its shops she asked, "Do you dance, Lucas?"

She might have asked him if he spoke French the way he cocked back his head and arched his eyebrows making Jodie snicker.

"Nope, but you two go on ahead. I'll be right here in the stands."

"You know, Lucas, we're *not* children and we don't need a chaperone. I'll be twenty-one soon and Jodie's eighteen. We're certainly *quite* capable of taking care of ourselves."

"Like I said, I'll be right over here."

As the sisters made their way onto the dance platform, he climbed a few rows into the stands and sat. From his elevated perch, he noticed how the smaller group of women stood off to one side of the stage and the larger group of men to the other. In the back and center, a piano, fiddle and banjo picker were playing. Behind them was another fellow who sat tapping time on drums. He watched as a number of young fellows, one after the other, approached Katie, apparently asking her for a dance. One by one and empty-handed they departed, their bids obviously rejected. He also noticed that Jodie had now worked her way back into the thick of the herd and was not standing out front and center like Katie.

Fiery Little Mustang nothing he thought, *that one's a sidewinder.* He'd heard stories of how fire-strung some redheaded women could be and reflected on how there might be some truth to it. He half-considered the notion of whether the flame-like color of their hair might possibly be nature's warning of their potential for trouble; the way the hiss or rattle of a snake is.

"Look at you," he mumbled, "what'd she call you, a *chaperone?*" He shook his head thinking *The things a man'll do for money, it and a place of his own. That's why you're here, Bucko, remember? Still, if the raiders could see you whorin yourself now.*

In spite of the present awkwardness, he inwardly grinned as he considered how it had been for the most part a very successful day. Still—-the way everything was happening so quickly, it was almost as though he'd been caught up in a Missouri twister. Only this morning he was down to just over ten dollars and not sure what was next outside of the trail. Now, of all things, here he was watching over the two daughters of his new employer. Valentine no doubt trusted him, and he wasn't about to take that trust lightly, however odd an assignment it was. The girls would just have to suffer his presence for the time being. Then, when the actual job began, he'd do all he could to make sure the rancher never lost another head of cattle. He just couldn't wait to be away from Cheyenne and all of its nosing eyes.

He decided to roll a cigarette and drew the sleeve of rolling papers and tobacco sack from his pocket. There was a mild but steady breeze from the west and as he twisted his back to it, he glanced at the stage to see that a couple of men whom he recognized from the shooting contest were approaching the women's side. They weren't the two he'd almost confronted after the competition, but one *was* the mouthy fellow who'd stood next to him at the firing line. The comedian who'd asked about taking first and second place and had so much to say throughout the event. By the time he'd separated and creased the rolling sheath between his fingers, he saw the same fellow leading Katie to the center of the dance floor. He scanned the group of women and sure enough, there was the other fellow standing before Jodie. She was shaking her head, obviously resisting his request to dance. Then the fellow took her by the forearm apparently trying to further persuade her. Lucas rose to his feet and was about to make his way down and over when he saw that Jodie had freed herself and was now headed for the exit steps alone.

"You okay?" he asked when she'd made her way up the stands to him.

"Yes," she said. She smiled revealing her appreciation for his concern and with her gentle blue eyes fixed on his own added, "I don't care for him or his friend."

He smiled in agreement and for the first time, truly looked her over as she sat down beside him. As the last rays of sunlight shone upon her gently sculpted face and long, honey colored hair, he realized what a true beauty she was. And while her blue eyes were soft and kind, they were proudly set, suggesting she was much more aware of things than her quiet demeanor reflected.

"Who are they?" he asked shaking tobacco onto the rolling paper.

"The one dancing with Katie is Trent Stenerson. His father's the local land bureau agent. The other is Miles Clancy. His folks own a couple businesses here in town. The two of them think highly of themselves and strut around like they're important and irresistible."

Lucas chuckled aloud at Jodie's direct description as he finished twisting the smoke. At least she was of the same opinion about them as he was—-the Stenerson fellow, anyway. His initial assessment of him hadn't been too far off from hers. Now, sure enough, like birds of a feather, there was Katie saltating with him.

"Lucas," Jodie said.

"Yeah?"

"May I have a cigarette, please?"

"Sure," he said half-grinning. He sealed the one just rolled and handed it to her.

"Thank you," she said and smiled.

As he began building another, the music stopped and he looked for Katie and Stenerson. He located them and Clancy, too, together at the far side of the stage. Katie was tilting back a silver flask. Lucas subtly shook his head and finished rolling the smoke. When he had, he struck a flare and held it for Jodie. In the evening breeze the flame danced and fluttered in his cupped hands and Jodie snickered as she chased after it. Once she'd caught it, he lit his own.

When the music started back up, Katie and her two friends stayed where they were, passing the flask back and forth between them. While he and Jodie sat and silently smoked, they watched as a fellow with a ladder went around the stage lighting the oil lanterns hanging from the rope that was strung along its sides. The first evening stars were showing by the time he lit the last lamp.

"I wish Katie wouldn't bring them over here," Jodie said.

Her sister and her two friends were headed over. They were laughing and carrying on grandly, no doubt already feeling the effects of the contents of the silver flask. Lucas and Jodie, now finished with their smokes, rose and climbed from the stands to meet them.

"Mister Lucas Jackson, meet Trent Stenerson and Miles Clancy," Katie said making the introductions.

Neither of the men bothered extending their hands in formal greeting.

"Lucas is our *babysitter* tonight," she added. As her two friends laughed, she cast a teasing wink at Jodie.

"I remember Lucky...I mean...Lucas," Stenerson said.

As the three of them further chuckled over Stenerson's witty remark, Lucas thought how he was still wearing the same self-confident and cocky grin he had during the contest. He figured it was probably his permanent disposition. And as for his *Lucky* remark, that was fine. The less they knew about him the better. He considered it something akin to having an ace in the hole.

"We're going to the saloon, are you two coming?" Katie asked.

Lucas checked Jodie's reaction. She passively rolled her eyes. Meanwhile, Katie wasn't waiting for a response, and she and her two friends had started on.

"Your folks know about this?" Lucas quietly asked Jodie.

Jodie hesitated, then nodded *yes* and, stretching herself to his ear, whispered, "She has the last couple times we've come to town. Only I'm usually left sitting in the hotel room alone."

~ 7 ~

As he and Jodie followed the other three past the eating and beer tents into the heart of the busy town, Lucas imagined Stenerson and Clancy to be about his age; only their years vastly different than his own. He thought how war and fighting tended to weather a man differently than normal time and life—-whatever normal time and life were.

The three happy revelers turned into the doorway of the first saloon. There was so much tobacco smoke one might have thought the place on fire. Fifty different boisterous conversations at once formed a solid wall of confused noise. Occasionally, the din was spiked by the excited urgings and victorious cheers of the gamblers. There was a continuous clinking of beer mugs and pitchers behind the bar as the proprietors bustled to keep the unquenchable thirsts of their patrons whetted.

Without reservation, Katie pushed her way straight through the crowd to the bar with Stenerson and Clancy in tow. Lucas didn't care for the situation at all, but knew that Katie—especially now that she was drinking—was likely going to do whatever she wanted, and no one was going to tell her otherwise. He'd gathered that much about her well enough already. And that not just by her attitude towards him, but her behavior before her parents as well. And now, having her two friends to encourage her certainly wasn't a help, either.

A couple of men who were seated at a table near the doorway got up to leave, and Lucas and Jodie promptly sat down. From there, he watched as Katie and her friends huddled at the bar throwing down rounds of whisky. Jodie was watching wide-eyed all the goings on in the saloon. In order to be heard, he had to speak directly into her ear. He asked her if she wanted him to get her sister so they could leave, but she bravely shook her head *no*. He could tell it was probably the first time she'd ever been in a saloon;

one in full stir, anyway. Except for the two women serving drinks on the main floor, and those presently unseen, no doubt busy in the rooms upstairs, she and her sister were the only other females there.

About an hour had passed when Katie and her pals left the bar and came over to where Lucas and Jodie were. She set two mugs of beer on the table before them.

"These are for you...two," she said with a wink and slight but noticeable slur. "We're going to play roulette. Come on boys...let's win all their money they got."

If she wasn't drunk already, she was certainly nearing it. Lucas looked at Jodie who, looking at him, wrinkled her nose, either at the notion of the beer, or, the state of her sister. He thought how he probably should have gotten Katie out then, but definitely didn't want her making a scene and drawing unwanted attention. He watched as she cavalierly pressed her way through the crowd of men surrounding the roulette table, pulling Stenerson and Clancy along like they were a couple of pets.

"We have a lady who wants to place a wager. Let's give her a little room, gentlemen," the man working the wheel announced.

Leaning closer to him Jodie asked, "Do you drink, Lucas?"

"Used to," he said. His mouth curled at one corner and Jodie smiled as though she were glad of it.

It wasn't long before Katie's voice rose above all others in the saloon as she shrieked or groaned over the results of the clacking roulette marble. Then, about a half-hour later, in an especially loud and animated voice, she erupted:

"Must you always place your bets over my wagers?" she angrily demanded.

Breaking the brief moment of silence following her outburst, one of the men standing across the gaming table from her remarked, "Well, you're 'bout as pushy as yer old man, ain't ya Darlin?"

"Excuse me?" Katie blurted.

"Yer ears as full of manure as yer mouth? You heard me," the deep voice behind the bushy black beard shot back.

Some of the men around the gaming table laughed.

"You can't ta-talk to *me* like that you…you disgursting ba-bo-vine aminal," she said with a stutter and slur. "I'll have you know Wyoming erritory is innerducing legis-legslation and *I* have as much rights as any other man!" She had the whole saloon's attention now, and she was absolutely livid.

"What's wrong, Stenerson…can't control yer gal?" the fellow remarked, spurring a chorus of taunting hoots and howls.

Katie's two friends weren't saying anything, which was especially unusual for the normally quick-witted and mouthy Stenerson. Lucas could tell they didn't want any trouble with the bearded man or his friends who, like their larger, bear-sized companion, weren't fancy dressed town boys.

He started to rise from his seat, but Jodie laid her hand on his forearm and shook her head not to. He figured she was apparently thinking the matter would resolve itself—-that or she was trying to keep him clear of it knowing it was what he'd have preferred were it not for his having to be there.

Katie's enflamed face, when she turned back to her two shying escorts, was as red as her hair. Returning to her antagonist, she barked, "I'm not *his* or anyone's gal!" Then she lunged forward across the roulette table to slap the man who'd been going round with her. But he caught her by the wrist and held fast. As she squirmed to wrench herself free from his grasp, the whole saloon erupted in riotous laughter. With her being drunk, loud and surly as she was, and there in the middle of the men's rowdy arena, any respect or courtesy they might normally have afforded a woman were off the table.

"Shouldn't ya be gettin on home, Lassie?" the man holding her by the wrist said with a hearty laugh.

"I do what and where and…I want. Now let you go of me!"

Lucas turned to Jodie and could tell she was embarrassed.

"Act like you don't know her," she said.

"Here we go," he muttered standing. "Stay here, Jodie."

"What's wrong princess … used to getting your own way?" the man holding Katie said.

"Let go…of me," Katie said. There was a pitiful trailing-off to it that reflected her rapidly fading ability to scrap further. She'd gotten herself so wound-up that the whisky had gone straight to her head. Everyone was laughing except Stenerson and Clancy, who'd now begun distancing themselves from the deteriorating situation.

"Let her go!" Lucas sharply demanded.

Turning his attention to him, "Who the hell are you?" the man growled.

"I'm takin her out, so let her go."

"Maybe I'm tired of people givin me orders," the man growled. A couple of his friends laughed heartily, mistakenly thinking Lucas just another hilarious part of the overall entertainment.

Lucas pushed back the wings of his coat and rested both hands crosswise over the handles of his revolvers. Now, except for the scuffling rush of boots across the wooden floor, the whole saloon went silent.

"You callin me out, boy?" the man said, still holding Katie by the wrist. She'd quit struggling now and was bent limp and whimpering over the waging field.

"I'm gonna tell you once more, let her go," Lucas warned, staring straight into the grizzly's dark eyes.

Then, one of the man's friends lowered a hand towards his side arm. Lucas instantly drew, cocked and simultaneously trained both revolvers on the two men. Both flinched, but wisely held fast.

"What ya gonna do…shoot us all?"

Without hesitation, "You two for certain," Lucas replied.

The large, bearded man looked incredulously at Lucas. Because of the wild law he lived by himself, he clearly recognized it also in Lucas' eyes and knew he wasn't to be challenged. Even though he was half-drunk, he was familiar enough with the volatile situation facing down the barrel of a trained revolver. He'd been having himself a grand time up till then and, without having an edge in his favor, wasn't ready for gunplay or being shot.

"Her ol man oughta keep her on a leash," he snarled releasing his hold of Katie.

With unblinking eyes and revolvers yet trained, Lucas called, "Jodie, come take her out. You——" he said to the second man motioning with his revolver, "step aside and make room."

The man stepped back, distancing himself from Katie.

The roulette attendant, thankful the situation was showing signs of subsiding, gladly gathered and handed over Katie's remaining money. Jodie thanked him and dropped the coins into her sister's handbag. Then she wrapped her arm around Katie's waist. She was sloppy and whimpering. With Katie slumped against her, Jodie started away from the table then paused and scornfully measured both Stenerson and Clancy. Katie's silent cohorts cowered. There was a tense hush over the room until she, with Katie staggering at her hip, had made it outside.

"I seen this fella at the pistol shoot, Marsh," a fellow across the room said breaking the tense silence. "I don't think ya want ta dust with 'em none. He's the one who won it."

The scowl on Marsh's face changed immediately upon hearing that. Word had already gotten around town about the unknown gunman who'd dominated the contest, using both left and right revolvers. Naturally, there were also the unfounded rumors that he was a killer.

Still, obviously bitter, "I wasn't askin for trouble," the man called Marsh grumped. "We were doin just fine till she——"

"I know," Lucas said, cutting him short. "Now, I'm takin her back to her folks, unless——"

In the ensuing silence, he backed himself towards the entrance. From the doorway he said, "Have a good evening, gentlemen," and stepped out.

There, he found Jodie grappling to hold Katie upright against the wall.

"Can she walk?" he asked.

"I don't think so. She's awful rummied."

Lucas holstered both revolvers, bent and draped Katie over his shoulder, stepped from the boardwalk, and started up the street. She was half-in and out, but gone in either case. As they neared the hotel, he asked Jodie if she had the key to their room. She told him it was in Katie's handbag and started searching it. At the hotel the doorman grinned, but the clerk at the registration desk looked skeptically at them in much the same way everyone else who'd seen him with her slung over his shoulder had. Lucas smiled awkwardly and, raising a finger to his mouth, gave a *shhhh!*

The clerk, easing a smile, nodded.

Upstairs at the room, Jodie quietly opened the door and pointed to the first bed. Lucas poured Katie's limp body onto it.

Turning to Jodie, he asked, "You okay?"

She looked at him with a bevy of mixed feelings. It was the second time that evening he'd asked her if she was okay. Tempted to say *no*, "Yes," she answered instead. She was embarrassed as well as angry with her sister for having cut their evening short. But it was typical of Katie to make herself the ruinous center of attention. She did it all the time. Although she was her older sister, Jodie disliked that about her immensely and, as she'd gotten older herself, had done her conscious best not to be like her. It wasn't that she was so overly modest, it just appeared that way in contrast to Katie. Nevertheless, she truly was different from her. She'd much rather be out riding than in the house trying on the latest clothing fashions; that or honing her dignified countenance in the mirror.

Her eyes meeting now with Lucas', she blushed and her heart caught. While she'd never expected the situation in the saloon to escalate to the point it had, she'd also never seen such a display of valor and bravery before; and she considered what he'd done as having been absolutely gallant. She wasn't ready to say good night and wanted to remain in his company longer. She was tempted to throw her arms around his neck and thank him, but modesty kept her from it.

"She's gonna have a hangover tomorrow," Lucas said. "Your folks'll likely be plenty sore."

"Don't worry I'll explain it to them. It's not your fault." Then she turned and looked pitifully down at Katie. "She did just what she wanted, like she always does. They'll understand." There was an almost unforgiving tone in the way she'd said it.

Lucas hadn't been in his own room long when he heard Valentine and his wife out in the hallway knocking at the girl's door across from his own. He listened and heard the door being opened.

"You girls okay in there?" Augustus asked.

"Yes, father," Jodie answered.

"We'll see you in the morning, then," Geneva said.

"Okay, mother. Good night."

After removing his gun belt and pulling off his boots, Lucas raised the window sash in his room, sat down at the small table beneath it, and began rolling a cigarette. He'd just finished when someone tapped lightly at the door. He reached for a revolver and moved quietly over and cracked it open. It was Jodie. She was wearing her nightclothes and robe.

"What's wrong?" he asked.

"I'm sorry to disturb you, Lucas, but could I possibly bother you for another cigarette?"

He spread the door open and checked both ends of the hallway. Looking down, he saw she was barefoot and that her feet were white as snow, small and delicate. He also noted how both of his own large toes were poking from holes in his foot stockings.

"Sure, come in," he said.

~ 8 ~

Cheyenne was quiet early Sunday morning, no doubt sleeping Saturday night off. Christian Jack, still hopefully known only as Lucas Jackson, sat at a table in an empty diner having coffee and waiting for his breakfast. He watched through the front window as dawn gradually painted the false-fronted buildings across the street from gray to gold, then, to their final, man- brushed and painted colors. Regardless of what was next, he knew he needed a suitable change of clothing for winter and, depending on the cost, possibly a new hat. He'd asked the waitress about dry goods stores and she'd suggested one of the two mercantile in town and assured him that, although it was Sunday, most merchants would be open in light of the weekend events.

"Not even God comes before makin money, Honey," she'd said as she was refilling his coffee. He'd grinned, considering it as sound a gospel as any.

As he poured cream into his coffee, he reflected on how less than two days ago, he'd ridden light-pocketed into town not know-ing what lay ahead other than the contest and the inevitable, ap-proaching winter. He'd briefly improved his financial state and with the appropriate attire, would be better prepared to face the latter. What came now hinged on how the Valentines were going to react over Katie's getting drunk while on his watch, and whether or not he still had the job. As much as he disliked being reliant on anyone or thing, he knew he would, at least until the verdict was rendered. Beyond that, the real question was how long could he keep up the act? He was treading a precarious line trying to keep a low profile while repeatedly resorting to and publicly display-ing past skills. He took a swallow of the coffee and it went down the wrong pipe, seizing him until he'd hawked it clear. He wiped the resulting moisture from his eyes with his coat sleeves, blinked them into focus and took another drink.

Saturday had been some day all right. It was all going good until Katie's scene at the saloon. Men could have been killed, including himself. He could have been wearing a pine box now, that or sitting in the hoosegow or beating a fast trail out of town. He warned himself again about keeping as much distance from her as possible. *Remember,* he admonished himself, *trust no one.*

"There you go, sweetheart," the waitress said setting the two plates of eggs, hash, grits and griddlecakes before him.

As he dug into the breakfast, he thought about the things Jodie told him last night about her family and their ranch. Not surprising, it sounded as though her father was actually a businessman first and cattleman second. He'd moved his family out from New York representing eastern investors looking to profit from the beef market. Jodie explained how over the past two years the ranch had fallen short of its projected goals. One reason being the lost government contracts supplying Union forces with beef during the war; another being the lack of water and good grazing pasture. She'd also mentioned that her father blamed it on cattle losses too. Valentine couldn't control the weather or the war being over, but he could do something about the rustling and free grazers, which, if he still had the job, was where he came in. He could only hope that the ranch's remoteness would enable him the opportunity to assist his new employer in his lawful causes without raising any further suspicion; and, ultimately of course, buy himself a chance to stow an adequate stake before moving on. Maybe come early summer. He was anxious in his bones for that and the open spaces that never asked who you were, where you were from, or what you'd once been.

He began reflecting on something else Jodie had mentioned which had given him added cause for concern. She said that her father had hired an experienced Kansas cattleman to assist in the running of the ranch. He was the foreman and along with him, he'd brought another Kansan who was a blacksmith. She said they were both from Topeka. Lucas knew it was the state capital and likely where Lane, the jayhawker and politician whom he'd wanted to kill, resided. He'd taken part in raids reaching as far as Lawrence which was near Topeka, but never into the capital itself. At any rate, he still didn't like Kansans and trusted them even less than he did Yanks.

He finished the cup of coffee and folded a hotcake and was using it to mop up the last of the runny eggs, grits and hash when the front door opened. An older fellow wearing a dusty and dented brown bowler peeked in. He looked at Lucas, then the rest of the empty diner, back at Lucas and stepped in. There was loose dirt clinging to his wrinkled coat and breeches and he looked like he'd just crawled out of an alley where he'd probably spent the night.

The waitress returned from the kitchen, and seeing him, asked, "You here to order?" She stood firmly planted, her fisted hands upon her ample hips and elbows jutted out making her appear even larger. By the sternness of her voice, Lucas could tell she'd probably dealt with the man before.

The old sot sank his shaky right hand into his coat pocket and Lucas instinctively dropped his left below the table to his right revolver. The man fumbled around in his pocket a moment, then produced some eating utensils: a couple of forks, spoons and knives.

"I think these might belong to ya," he said. "I found 'em around back. Think I could get somethin ta eat?"

"When did you take those?" the waitress accusingly demanded.

"No ma'am, like I sez, I found——"

While he was yet speaking, the heavy-bottomed waitress reached forward and snatched the silverware from his hand. The sudden motion caused him to wobble and stagger sideward. Then the waitress, threatening to call the cook, pointed to the door and sternly instructed him to leave.

"I'll stake him biscuits and gravy," Lucas said.

Turning to him now, "You sure?" she asked.

"Yeah."

Sounding as skeptical as she looked, shaking her head as she started back for the kitchen, she grumbled, "It's your money."

"Ya got more coffee?" Lucas asked.

"Sure," she said. "Him too?"

"If he wants."

Reaching for the back of a chair at Lucas' table, the man nodded yes and said, "Thank ya, son."

"I ain't up for company, mister," Lucas said.

The man acted like he wasn't sure he'd heard correctly and, as he offered more gratitude, continued dragging out the chair.

"You're welcome, but like I said, I ain't up for company."

Blinking his watery, bloodshot eyes, the man mumbled an apology and shuffled over to another table.

While Lucas didn't mind the couple bits for the fellow's breakfast, he did the company. He'd had more than enough people in the past twenty-four hours. For a moment the bum had been something of a person perhaps down on his luck, but given the chance, he'd only become a pest. It was like making the mistake of feeding a stray dog. *That's what doing someone a turn gets you,* he thought telling himself.

After he'd downed the last of his coffee, he paid for his and the older fellows breakfast and left the diner. He went straight to the mercantile and from there, returned to the hotel. At the registration desk he stopped to inquire about room rates. It was a different clerk than the one who'd seen him lugging Katie in last night. The clerk told him the rooms were fifteen-dollars a night.

Thinking he'd misheard, "How much?" he asked.

"Yes sir, fifteen dollars. They're in high demand this weekend."

Ascending the red staircase, he thought how the room was nice enough, but also how it was like being robbed by someone without a gun. He could eat three months on fifteen dollars.

In the room, standing before the tall mirror on the door of the armoire, he again tried on the heavy, oiled-canvass coat he'd just purchased. He thought how his wearing the new hat, shirt and Kentucky jeans he'd also purchased might possibly make him look like someone else. He didn't know which was worse though, old, tattered and thin worn clothes, or stiff, store bought. Most of the outer clothing he'd worn had once belonged to someone else; men who'd already broken them in and no longer had need of them. The notion of his possibly looking like someone else made him wonder if there would ever come a time when he didn't have to be suspicious or concerned. Knowing the answer already, he was tempted to spit at the suggestion, but, looking at the fifteen-dollar-a-night room carpet, checked himself first.

After taking off the new winter coat, he pulled the thin, easy sleeves of his old duster over his arms and buttoned it in front so that the wings covered his revolvers. He wanted to check on Heston, then, he'd return to the room where he'd sit and wait for the ruling concerning the status of his employment.

It was silent in the hallway outside his room and behind the Valentine's doors. Locking his own behind him, he conjured the faces of the men at the saloon as well as the two from the shooting contest should he happened to meet them. Trouble has a tendency of doubling back in an eddy that way; and usually sooner than not.

As he was rounding the top of the stairs, he met Augustus, Geneva and Jodie on their way up. It was like he was being searched the way they were appraising him in the new clothes.

"We missed you for breakfast, Lucas," Augustus said.

"I wanted to pick up a few things in town, so I ate earlier."

"I see that," the cattleman said. His expression over his new attire clearly showed his approval. "Have you any plans set for the day?" he then asked.

While it didn't sound like the rancher was upset, which was good, he was immediately concerned that he was about to ask him to do something like watch over his daughters again. Trying to mask his reservation, he answered, "I was goin to check on my horse...unless—-"

"Aren't you participating in the rifle contest?"

"No sir."

"Well, if we don't see you there, I'd like you to join us for dinner here at the hotel afterwards. You'll get a chance to meet some of the other hands."

"Yes sir, that'll be fine. Oh—-" he reached into his shirt pocket and pulled out some folded bills and pushed them into the rancher's hand. "There's that ten and my room bill."

Augustus Valentine smiled. "I didn't expect you to—-"

"No, I appreciate it," Lucas said before the rancher could proffer refusal. It felt strange trying to make a good impression. A day ago he likely wouldn't have given it a blink of consideration. And, too, of course, if he'd been dismissed from his position, he definitely wouldn't have.

"May I go along with you to the stables, Lucas?" Jodie asked.

Geneva, surprised by Jodie's boldness and looking embarrassed said, "Don't trouble the poor man, Jodie. Besides, when your sister gets up, we're going shopping, remember?"

"Yes, but she won't be up and ready for hours. May I, father?"

"That's up to your mother and Lucas, dear."

"I don't mind," Lucas said.

Reaching forward, Augustus shoved two of the tens into Lucas' hand.

"Sounds like you earned that last night. Geneva and I thank you. That fella who was giving Kate trouble is one of our...how should I say with respect to the ladies present...one of our more troublesome neighbors."

"Do I have time to change, Lucas?" Jodie asked.

"Sure. I'll be downstairs."

"May I, mother?"

"Two hours, then I expect you back, young lady," Geneva said.

~ 9 ~

Sitting on the plush, backless bench in the lobby waiting for Jodie, Lucas thought how he'd consented to her going along. He hadn't wanted to say *no* before her or her parents. On the upside, he figured how she wasn't nearly as likely to scare up scenes as Katie was. It was awkward though, the way the Valentines, with the exception of Katie, were treating him. It was like he was family or someone they'd always known. Surely, after the scene at the saloon last night which Jodie had obviously told them about, the rancher must be more than just a little curious, regardless of whether he was pleased by its outcome or not.

He began thinking about Katie who was probably still in bed and paying the second-half charges for her whisky drinking. He shook his head as he recalled how many times he'd had to mount and ride, still half-plowed from the night before. Half the men he'd ridden with were drunk it seemed half the time. He'd finally gotten himself so skunk-drunk once after drinking some snake-bite concoction, that it made him green-sick for three days and his head pounded and spun afterwards for a week. He remembered painfully recovering and how as the last poisonous vapors lifted, he'd finally come to the conclusion that it wasn't worth it physically or financially. That was when he first actually realized that between the fighting and the drinking, it was something of a miracle he was alive at all. Now, he couldn't get the smell of spirits past his nose and to his lips without his stomach pitching.

"Are you ready, Lucas?"

Jodie was wearing a plain, buckskin leather skirt that fell just below the tops of her worn riding boots and a green and white calico shirt. Her long, golden hair was brushed out and sprang with a bounce over her shoulders and down her back. She was pretty and he liked the natural, easy way she looked.

As they were leaving the hotel, there was a man and two women walking up the street, and one of the women was ringing a hand bell.

"Free coffee. Come join us for Sunday worship services. Free coffee," the man was announcing.

"Have you ever been to church, Lucas?" Jodie asked. He looked at her hoping he hadn't made a mistake in letting her come along. That, and that she wouldn't be asking a lot of questions like that.

"Some when I was young," he said.

Noting his reservation, she looked aside. "Me, too," she said quietly.

"What'd your folks say about last night?" he asked.

"They're a little sore at Katie's all, and glad nothing worse happened. Thanks to you. Mother's embarrassed over how it might reflect poorly on the family, and Father just wondered who it was that had hold of her."

"A neighbor huh?"

"I guess so. I described the man and he said it sounded like a man named Marsh who, along with a group of his friends, has a ranch north of ours."

Lucas remembered how one of the men in the saloon had called the man *Marsh,* warning him about his having been the winner of the shooting contest.

"He said that Farliss, our foreman, had reported seeing him in town earlier," Jodie said. "I'm sure they're not happy how you handled them last night."

Their eyes met.

"That right?"

"Yes. According to father, he and his partners have a reputation for not being friendly; especially to folks from the larger ranches. He also says they're rustlers. Anyway, the established ranches don't like it that men like Marsh and his friends are filing homestead claims next to each other and joining forces." Jodie paused then added, "You know...competition. Anyhow, watch yourself, Lucas."

He liked the way Jodie spoke, straight to the point and without the all too typical, one-sided slant on things. He'd picked up on that last night as the two of them visited in his room. He also sensed in her warning just now that she actually cared about his well-being. The last persons he could remember actually giving a hoot about him were his parents, back before jayhawkers killed his father for no other reason than their family happened to be living on the Missouri side of the state line. Even though he still nurtured a healthy dislike for Kansans because of it, he knew that taking sides was never clear-cut. There were always drawbacks to every side of everything, and it sounded as though Jodie knew it as well.

As they approached the corral at the stables where Heston and a number of other horses milled, the large bay stallion stretched his head above the others and neighed. He strode over to meet them and leaned across the railing. His long, black mane draped like a wing along his dark-brown neck.

"Jodie, this is Heston."

"He's beautiful," she said stroking the bridge of his nose. "How long have you had him?"

"About four years."

"Where'd you get him?"

Lucas said nothing and only looked at her, and she, looking at him, sensed it and let it go. He had enough lies to keep track of already, as well as truths to keep concealed, and though she wasn't aware of that, he didn't need adding to them. He could make up another story, but it was simpler saying nothing. It would be just one less snare for him to stumble over later. He'd told her the evening before as they visited in his room, that he wasn't comfortable talking about the past just yet. She'd said then that she could appreciate and respect that, and when he'd looked into her eyes, he'd felt she meant it. That was how he'd looked now at her, and once more, her expression had showed the same unspoken understanding.

As Jodie cooed over Heston, he reflected on how he'd come to have him. It was during a night raid on a Union outfit asleep in their wooded camp. When his own horse had been shot out from beneath him, and he was thrown into a roll across the ground, there was a Union officer attempting to mount and flee. He shot the man taking his revolver and horse for himself. The mount, he learned the following day, hadn't been branded as Union property and, he'd assumed, had been privately owned by the man he'd shot. It was also obvious that he was a fine steed of good breeding, which he'd also come to suspect, might be a cross of Arabian and Morgan. He'd had a number of mounts in his time, but none ever as responsive and fine. Not long after that, he'd replaced the Union saddle and begun calling him Heston after his best friend growing up whom—at the time he'd recently learned—died fighting across the river in Tennessee.

After squaring with the stableman for another night's keep and oats, Lucas led Jodie to the far backside of the corrals where he'd sat the day before, waiting for the contest to begin. There, sitting once again atop the same pole fence, he rolled a couple of cigarettes. In the distance, could be heard the cracking report of the rifle contest that was underway. As they smoked, he listened as Jodie talked, telling him more about the ranch. About an hour and a couple more cigarettes later, they started back for the hotel and ran into Charlie, the young fellow Lucas had met the day before.

"Howdy, Lucas," Charlie said. Acknowledging Jodie, he tipped his hat and said, "Ma'am."

Jodie snickered.

"Charlie, this is Jodie Valentine. Her pa's just hired me on."

"That's good, Lucas."

"So, how'd the shootin go?"

"I reckon okay," Charlie said. "I made it past half-way 'fore I was 'liminated."

"That's alright then, Charlie."

"Yes," Jodie added.

"Well, maybe next year," Charlie said.

Just then, it struck Lucas how much Charlie reminded him of his old best friend, Heston Tyler whom he'd just been thinking about earlier. He hadn't connected it the day before, but could see the resemblance clearly now.

"Well, I better get goin, folks. I told the boss I would soon as I was done, on account we're headin back to the ranch. It was nice meetin ya, Miss Jodie, I mean...Valentine."

"You, too, Charlie," she said smiling.

"Charlie," Lucas said extending his hand.

After seeing Jodie to her room, Lucas retired to his own where he remained for the rest of the afternoon, sitting by the open window smoking and watching the busy comings and goings in the street below. When the sun had neared the horizon, he left the room and headed down.

At the entrance to the dining room, he saw Augustus Valentine standing and talking with two men who looked like working hands. One was tall and lanky, and the other short and overweight. They each carried rifles and had their saddlebags over their shoulders.

Smiling at Lucas as he approached, Augustus Valentine said, "Lucas, this is Herron and Jahns, our team's two newest additions. They come as a pair."

As Lucas shook hands with the men, he had two initial thoughts: the first being how the cattleman was arming himself up; and secondly, that he didn't like them.

"You'll be glad to know they're both proven shots with rifles," Augustus said. Addressing the two riflemen, he added, "I just hired Lucas after the pistol contest yesterday."

"We seen 'em shoot," Herron, the taller, redheaded one said. "And it looks like he's already wearin his winnins, too."

Lucas focused hard on him. He had an unusually long, narrow, almost pinched looking freckled face, nervous eyes and his mouth apparently naturally gaped, as though he were scoffing or in disbelief over something. Jahns, the obese one, apparently laughing, snorted over Herron's remark. Like his mouthy, opinionated partner, he, too, had nervous, fidgety eyes.

"Let's go in and I'll introduce you fellows to a few of the others," Augustus said.

There were only four men and Jodie seated at the long table in the dining room. She smiled at Lucas when he entered and slyly pointed at the empty seat across from her suggesting he sit there. He acknowledged her with a nod.

As Valentine introduced Lucas, Herron and Jahns to the others, he also cited each of their individual shooting performances respectfully. Apparently, the men from the ranch had been occupied with other interests and hadn't attended the contests. As for Herron, Augustus touted his having taken second-place in the rifle shoot while Jahns had made it to the final round.

At the expense of his overweight friend following Jahns' introduction, Herron remarked, "But you can call 'em anything if you're servin chuck."

Jahns chuckled, sounding as though he were snorting back nasal drainage as he did. Lucas got the impression that not only had the fat man heard the remark before, but that Herron was the obvious dominant of the two.

John Farliss, the Kansan foreman, was the first of the hands Augustus introduced. He said they called him *Far.* By Jodie's description, Lucas knew beforehand who he was. Outside of the Kansan's seemingly normal interest, he could detect no sign of his having been recognized by him. Like Jodie had described, he was tall, standing about six-four, and solidly built. His face was leathered and showed the years he'd spent in the elements. He looked to be in his mid-forties. At their meeting each other, the foreman's pale blue eyes were barely visible behind his squinted eyelids. He had a firm handshake and a deep authoritative voice that, along with his size, struck Lucas as being appropriate for being in charge of men. Both ends of his full, bushy moustache curled beyond the sides of his wide, squared jaw. It was light brown and salted with some gray, the same as his oiled and groomed, thin head of hair.

The second hand they met was also a sandy-headed fellow. His name was Todd Weller. He was the same height with a similar build to Lucas' and appeared to be about the same age. He actually seemed disinterested in meeting the new men as he kept craning his neck back towards the entrance of the dining room.

Then there were two older fellows who looked to be in their fifties. The first, Augustus Valentine proudly introduced as Mister Case, sparking an immediate round of approval from the others. Valentine said that Case was the personal family chef, butler, physician and barber, and, too, since he also manned the family carriage, their private teamster. He was a smallish, clean, white-haired man with an easy smile. Jodie had previously told Lucas that Mister Case, whom she considered to be her good friend and confidant, was from England.

Joseph Wooten, more weatherworn than Mister Case, was a serious, gray-eyed fellow who, like Farliss, looked as though he'd ranched most of his life. He was introduced as the ranch hand cook and bunkhouse boss. After Augustus introduced him, Farliss, the Kansan, added, "Woot's the most important fella you'll need to get along with or else the meanest, grumpiest ol lady you ever knowed." While everyone laughed, Wooten turned his head and without expression, squirted chew juice into a fancy hotel spittoon, making its thinly hammered brass ring like a bell. He wore a scruffy gray, goat-like beard that had orange stains from tobacco leach running through it.

"Where's Rocha?" Valentine asked, looking around.

"Ain't seen him," Farliss said.

"Well, if anyone does, remind our Mexican we're leaving *early* tomorrow morning. The rest of the crew you fellows will meet at the ranch."

After sitting, a waiter arrived, pushing a cart full of plates of steaks and bowls of other foods. As they began eating, Augustus explained that Geneva was looking after Katie, whom, he added, was not feeling well. But the truth was his wife was taking her meal in their hotel room because she disliked eating with the hired help considering it improper and undignified.

Jodie was seated next to her father directly across the table from Lucas. Each time he looked at her, she'd smile at him and he found it somewhat reassuring. Midway through the meal, Katie entered the dining room and Todd Welles stood as though he were a soldier coming to attention at the presence of an officer.

Although he was the only one who'd risen, Katie told everyone to remain seated. Without looking directly at him, she sat at the end of the table where Herron and Jahns were. It wasn't long before she was drinking wine and laughing as she visited with the two rifle-men. He noticed that her father seemed unconcerned about it. The thing he was most satisfied with, though, was that the Kansan didn't appear suspicious of him; that, and that they'd be leaving Cheyenne early morning.

~ 10 ~

It was midday well after noon before the Valentine production finally exited the Cheyenne stage and its growing gallery of on-lookers. Augustus Valentine's repeated plan that they would be leaving early in the morning had been little more than farting. The entire process preparing to leave, once it actually began, was a clumsy, confused undertaking in which Lucas found himself seriously questioning the resolve of his commitment. Along with miscommunications, there were headaches, hangovers and no shortage of pouty dispositions. Then, too, there was the haphazard assembling of carriage and wagon teams and missing persons, as well as the jumbled procurement and lading of supplies, packages and baggage. Finally, in order to console Geneva and Katie's distress over their having to leave Cheyenne, there was the necessity for the two of them to do some last minute, two hour shopping. Jodie remained with the assembled company of men inconspicuously keeping her eyes on Lucas.

That was when, following a small cavalry outfit that passed through, the town sheriff and his posse, looking trail-worn and bushed, rode into town and stopping, visited briefly with Augustus and Farliss. Keeping from open sight as best he could, Lucas busied himself re-securing the ropes along the far side of the loaded supply wagon. After the sheriff's visit, Farliss came over and reported to the rest of the Valentine crew how the sheriff said they'd trailed the three men they'd been after into Colorado to where they'd doubled back northeast to Nebraska. He said that it was there, right on the main trail, where they'd found all three men shot dead, still wearing their hair and boots and feeding the buzzards. Lucas arched his eyebrows and cocked his head exhibiting what he thought might be a normal interest and expected reaction.

The whole affair leaving Cheyenne had been most discouraging and it reminded him of the aimless and meandering year following the war still riding with some of the raiders. He couldn't help wondering if it wasn't an omen of things to come working for Valentine. As the cavalcade finally set out, he thought to himself how an entire army battalion with cannons in tow could have broken camp and begun moving with greater ease and efficiency.

There were twelve of them in all, with the Valentine women riding in the family coach piloted by Case, who followed Augustus and Farliss on mounts riding point. The overburdened supply wagon, with Wooten at the helm, swayed and creaked along behind the family coach. It was loaded full of ranch supplies and packages shipped from the East, along with the other things the Valentine women had purchased in Cheyenne. Alongside the family coach rode Todd Welles and Rocha, the spirited sombrero and bandolier of cartridges-wearing Mexican, whom Lucas had only just met not long before their departure. Apparently, he and Farliss had each overslept and had difficulty extricating themselves from one of Cheyenne's brothels, thereby leaving most of the work preparing to leave up to himself, Wooten and Case. Finally, bringing up the trail alongside himself, were the two still partially drunk yet talkative riflemen, Herron and Jahns.

From the moment they broke town, the two men jabbered non-stop, boasting about the amount of drinking and carousing they'd done in Cheyenne, as well as every other saloon and brothel from Pueblo to Denver and points between. Lucas wondered if they weren't somehow trying to impress him with their explicit sharing of the unpleasant details of their personal forays. Herron, in particular, struck him as the kind who'd do a snake if he could hold it still long enough. And as for the snorting Jahns, he couldn't look at him without feeling sorry for the women he'd been with as well as his overburdened, sway-backed mount. He found himself repeatedly reminding himself of his ultimate goal and reason for being there and tried ignoring them. He'd always figured there was only so much talking a fellow needed to hear or do in a day, and on the latter count, these two had more than exhausted their shares. On the upside, he didn't have to say much himself; at least not until Herron asked him where he'd learned to handle side arms.

He was reasonably sure by then that the two hadn't heard about the incident at the saloon with Katie. And since he wasn't beholding to them for their acceptance, he was tempted at first to reveal his outright dislike of them by simply ignoring Herron's inquiry. But then, he thought how instead of revealing his hand, it might behoove him to play them along. After all, his whole presence there was for the most part one of deception; and that, so far, without having to divulge any actual specifics of himself or his past. Acting as though he was opening up and attempting to gain their acceptance by confiding with them, he confessed how he'd actually been surprised himself by his good fortune at the pistol shoot. The two riflemen went strangely silent as they each considered his surprising declaration.

"It was the darndest fluke fellas…I'll tell you what. Bes I ever shot and some lucky day alright. Yes sir."

Jahns snorted and, implying he was lying said, "Hell, you didn't waste any time squeezin off them rounds."

"That's right," Herron said backing the charge.

"No sir, the longer I take aimin, the worse I shoot, fellas. I was nervous and just wanted ta get over with it. And doggone if every darn shot didn't wind up dead-square."

Still unconvinced, "Where'd ya get those Colts and that mount?" Herron asked.

"I got 'em give to me from my Uncle Leroy after he done come home from the war shot and unable ta ride or shoot no more hisself."

The initial skepticism on the faces of the two riflemen as they each studied him and the hokey-looking guffaw plastered across his face, gradually shifted to expressions of awed marvel as they'd gullibly swallowed his ruse. He thought how more than likely their opinions of him now, was that he was nothing more than a dumb-lucky hayseed fresh off the farm.

"Ain't that somethin, Jahns?" Herron said.

"Damn sure is."

"I knew I should'a entered that pistol shoot," Herron lamented.

Outside of the immediate company, the trail was easy and a steady wind out of the west pushed the caravan smoothly along. Lucas noticed how Todd Welles never got far from the coach window where Katie was. Like the two talkative riflemen, he also appeared to be holding quite a conversation with the Valentine women inside. Occasionally, Jodie would poke her head out from the other side of the coach and smile and wave. Herron and Jahns were sure she was flirting with them. It provided the two with further fodder as they considered the availability of the girls; that and how lonely they must get living in the country. They'd already fully speculated over Augustus Valentine's business and financial status, and were now sizing up and sighting in on his daughters.

"Ol Augustus has about the two prettiest split-tails around, wouldn't ya say, Lucas?" Herron remarked.

Lucas measured him sidelong and deciding to continue with his ruse grinned and said, "You're dead on far as that fiery, older filly goes. That's sure 'nough."

"Yeah, and I'd like to harness and break her fillyness sure 'nough," Herron said slapping at his leg as he broke into laughter.

Jahns snorted like a hog, belly bouncing as he laughed.

Later in the day, Herron and Jahns rode forward and asked Valentine and his foreman if they wanted rabbit for supper since there were so many popping up in the fields alongside the trail. They were easy targets the way the afternoon sunlight shone red through their long, thin, upraised ears. After demonstrating their rifle skills, much to the boss and his lead man's approval, and picking off about eight of the hares, the party stopped for camp. They were in a hollow partially protected from the wind next to a rare stand of scrub oaks and cottonwoods. Alongside the trees was a creek with but a trickle flowing through it. Lucas and the bandolier-wearing Rocha secured a hitch line between the trees for the horses and then set about gathering firewood. Farliss had the other men help pitch the large tent that the Valentine family would use. Rocha told Lucas that there would be two fires: one for the boss's family, and another set apart for themselves. Meanwhile, Case and Wooten busily dressed and prepared the rabbits and a first-class trail supper.

After they'd finished eating and it was dark, Katie wandered over from the Valentine camp and joined Lucas, Welles, Rocha, Jahns and Herron at theirs. The two elder cooks and Farliss had gone over and were visiting with Augustus and Geneva. It didn't take long for Lucas to see that Welles really had a thing for Katie, and, too, that he seemed troubled by her friendly consorting with Herron and Jahns. When Welles was finally able to get a word in, changing the meandering topic of their banter, he asked Herron and Jahns how much experience they'd had working cattle.

"*Really*, Todd," Katie exclaimed. "And just how much *skill* does it take to handle a mindless steer? You should certainly know." Her curt response and emoted facial expression gave the unmistakable impression that she was actually comparing Todd himself to a *mindless steer*. Having picked up on it, Herron, Jahns and Rocha howled with laughter.

Lucas shook his head and watched as the crestfallen Welles self-consciously gnawed at his lower lip, his face going as red as Katie's hair. Meanwhile, Katie poised in obvious satisfaction with herself, stretched her neck proudly and cocking back her shoulders so that her breasts were lifted prominently, appeared to loom larger as the downcast Welles seemed to shrink. Lucas thought how while she was easy enough on the eyes, her arrogance overshadowed any possible feminine grace she might possess. At any rate, he appreciated it that she still seemed to be ignoring him.

Having seen and heard enough of the Katie theatre and the group's mind-numbing discourse, he strolled over to where the mounts were corralled, then along the creek till he could no longer hear them. The wind had settled some with the evening, but still stirred, rustling the remnants of summer's leaves still clinging to the thinning branches of the trees overhead. Beyond the lower branches and just above the western horizon, a crescent moon was slipping. Overhead, the clustered Milky Way glowed brightly with the dusty haze of its starlight. Then, catching the trail of a shooting star from the corner of his eye, he wondered as he often had about things like how many he'd seen streaking across night skies, and whether or not they did during the day; and, if there might ever come a time when there wouldn't be so many left for falling; finally, why he even wondered about such things at all—-as if any of it mattered. He leaned back against the gnarled trunk of a scrub oak and, hunching his shoulders against the wind, drew and creased a rolling paper, then carefully shook tobacco onto it. As he began twisting it he heard someone approaching. It was Jodie.

"Am I interrupting?" she asked.

"Nope," he said then licked the cigarette sealing it and offered it to her.

"Thank you. You probably think that's all I'm after, don't you?" Though she snickered, she thought how she wished she hadn't said it.

"I don't mind," he said as he prepared to roll another.

"Do you know Jahns and Herron, Lucas?"

"No. Why?"

"Nothing really, I only wondered. I don't think I trust them… I think."

Lucas said nothing. He didn't trust or care for them, either. But then he didn't trust or care for anyone, really. Maybe Jodie some, was all.

"I don't see why Katie encourages them the way she does. And especially the way it affects Todd. She knows how he feels about her. He has ever since he came to the ranch. It's kind of…I don't know…sad."

"Dangerous," Lucas said. He'd just finished sealing the second smoke. He struck a flame and, cupping it from the wind with his hands, held it before her, then himself.

She liked the way he did that; liked the way he did everything. And she watched everything she could that he did. She even liked the way that he was quiet and reserved and hadn't easily opened himself up.

"Do you have any dreams, Lucas?" she asked looking past the fleeting smoke above.

"What you mean?"

"Anything…you know…something you think about away from all this."

Lucas saw again in her eyes, as well as sensed in her voice, that unobtrusive, easy feeling that she usually had about her.

"Yeah, I suppose," he said looking skyward himself.

Still sounding as though she were a child at play in a game of pretend, she asked, "Like what?"

"Oh, I guess I think about having my own cabin up in the mountains sometimes with just the silence, trees and seasons." No sooner had he spoken, when he wondered if that was actually him talking out like that. It caused him to feel awkward and out of sorts.

"That sounds nice," Jodie said.

In an effort to shake the trail off himself, he asked, "What about you?"

Jodie dreamily sighed then said, "Something like that, now you've said it."

They both smiled and for a moment, looked into each other's eyes. They'd done that a few times now, and Lucas thought how it was easy to do. Like looking through the clear, undisturbed waters of a calm lake and the way the moment just then feels almost special and rare. He could sense in her eyes a gracefulness that made her seem older than she was. Older like the way one gets not just from the passing of time, but from actually knowing. And speaking of knowing, registering the feelings just now beginning to stir and rise within him, he reined both them and himself in. *She's the boss's daughter* he reminded himself.

"Ya finished with that smoke?" he asked.

"Yes. Thank you, again," she said.

When they stepped into the glow of the campfire, Lucas saw Herron hastily stashing a whisky bottle beside him.

"And *where*…have *you two* been?" Katie asked.

"We're *certainly not telling you*," Jodie replied mimicking Katie's exaggerated tone. Turning she smiled at Lucas.

The other men, all but Welles, laughed. Jodie was only teasing with her sister, but Katie had a serious look on her face and in her eyes as she seemed to be sizing up the both of them. It made Lucas uneasy and he turned and looked towards the Valentine camp. He saw that Augustus and Geneva had already retired to their tent, and that Farliss, Case, and Wooten were also preparing to turn in.

"I think I'll call it, folks," he said.

"Me too," Jodie added.

She had other more pleasant thoughts to consider and wasn't interested in the drunken slipslop of the group gathered around the fire. She had her own private fire that flickered warmly in her heart to attend, as well as every new word of the brief conversation just shared between her and Lucas to consider and safely tuck away. They were hers alone to know and they, like his unspoken past, were to be equally kept and guarded. Beyond his rugged, handsome looks, the mystery she saw in his hazel-gray eyes was not threatening to her. And the feelings that swept through her whenever she was in his presence were real and unlike any she'd ever known before. If what she was experiencing was only an infatuation, it seemed to be just the one that she'd been waiting for.

"Good night, everyone," she said smiling at him.

~ 11 ~

It was not surprising the next morning that while everyone else had breakfast, Herron, Jahns and Rocha slept. Katie, too, was still asleep in the Valentine family tent. Throughout the night, Lucas had been awakened as they carried on. Todd Welles, who hadn't drank as much as the others, was up, but it was obvious he'd stayed awake well into the night not wanting to depart Katie's company and leave her alone with the other three men.

Farliss had everyone close up camp as quietly as they could. Case set aside some scrambled eggs and bacon for Katie, but Farliss instructed him not to save any for the men still asleep. Once Geneva and Jodie had finally managed to lead Katie staggering to the coach, the men, purposely silent, took down the Valentine tent and stowed it in the wagon. As the caravan quietly set out, leaving the three sleepers behind, Lucas and Farliss both grinned at one another. Augustus Valentine did not, but was going along with the lesson his foreman was giving. As Case and Wooten eased coach and wagon along the trail, they, too, were grinning from ear to ear. From atop the first rise, Lucas and Farliss could detect no movement at the camp behind and below.

"I'd give eight bits ta see their faces when they wake," Farliss said leaning sidesaddle to spit tobacco leach. "If they ain't dead," he added with a grin.

They hadn't gone much more than a few miles when Katie hung her head from the coach window and vomited. She was pea soup-green as she looked over at Lucas who raised his hand before his mouth to mask his amusement. After another mile, and with the coach still creeping along, the door swung open and Jodie hopped out shutting it briskly behind her.

Augustus and Farliss both twisted in their saddles to see what was going on.

"I'll walk before I ride in there," she said telling her mother through the coach window. She sounded adamant and shaking her head in disgust, looked up at Wooten piloting the supply wagon, then over at Lucas.

Extending his hand, he said, "Hop up."

She smiled and took hold of his forearm and, with his hand clasped firmly about hers, he pulled and she sprang gracefully up onto the saddle behind him. Then she wrapped her arms around his waist and laid her face lightly against the back of his left shoulder. Heston showed no protest over the added weight and Lucas felt strangely light as well.

"Katie got sick in the coach," she whispered in his ear.

Augustus dropped back alongside the coach to see what was going on inside. Lucas figured he might have a problem with his daughter riding with him and that he might have her join himself or even Case on the coach bench. But after talking with Geneva, he only turned and lightly smiled at the two of them as if to say he understood. Then he rejoined Farliss at point.

Lucas placed his free hand over Jodie's, which were clasped snugly about his midsection. She noticed that his stomach was firm and did not bounce or jiggle with Heston's gait. Lucas breathed deeply, drinking in her fresh, pleasant scent. It reminded him of spring meadows and of lying in their cool green and supple grass. Jodie closed her eyes and smiled. She was pleased now how things happened just as they had.

After riding silently for a couple more miles, Katie's head was again hanging from the coach window. When she looked over at Lucas and saw that Jodie was riding with him, her face contorted, making her look even worse than she already did. Lucas glanced back over his shoulder and saw Jodie was sticking her tongue out at her sister. Again, he couldn't help but reveal his amusement.

Once Rocha, Herron and Jahns had caught up with the rest of the party, they fell in quietly behind the supply wagon. Farliss turned and grinned at them. It wasn't long before Herron rode up alongside Todd Welles whose mount was a half-stride back beside Heston. Lucas overheard as he asked him why he hadn't wakened them, and glancing over, could plainly see that Welles was uncomfortable about it. Welles told Herron he hadn't because Farliss had told him not to. Herron shook his head and gave him a hard, disapproving look and snort, which Lucas could tell was further troubling to Welles. Seeing that his intimidation had succeeded, Herron sneered and worked his mount up alongside Heston. He then pointedly asked Lucas why he hadn't awakened them also.

"Don't ya know ta leave sleepin dogs be?" Lucas said.

Herron's facial expression over Lucas' insinuating remark reflected his obvious dislike for it as well as him for having said it; and particularly since he'd done so in front of Jodie who'd snickered when he did. Lucas let his unflinching eyes bore into Herron's. Like a poker player realizing he'd been hornswoggled, Herron blinked, swallowed dryly, glanced at Jodie, then quietly faded back, rejoining Rocha and Jahns.

It was out in the open now. Though the timing with Jodie being there was poor, Lucas was nevertheless glad of it. He hadn't liked Herron or his sidekick from the moment he'd first met them and didn't care to continue pretending otherwise. His impression of them was that they were the shady kind always on the prowl and looking for the easy mark; the unsuspecting and weak to take advantage of. And he was certain they did so without any reservation. It was perfect animal instinct and now unmistakably understood between them.

"I don't like the way he smells," Jodie said making Lucas laugh.

She was right, though, and he'd noticed it too. Herron and Jahns both really did have an unpleasant odor about them. Something other than the smell of sweated alcohol. It was sour and pungent, almost like curdled milk, and you could almost taste it.

"The ranch is just over that last rise," Jodie said. Her voice was soft in his ear, making it tickle. He searched for her fresh scent again and finding it, let it clear away the traces of Herron.

Save an occasional cluster of exposed rock, the long, slow rolling Wyoming grasslands spread boundless as far as one could see. In the wind, the yellow grasses swayed and flowed hypnotically back and forth, moving as if being feathered by an invisible hand from above. Lucas could feel Jodie's soft, long hair being blown and brushed similarly against the back and sides of his neck. It tickled like her breath and voice in his ears, making him feel fuzzy-headed.

When they'd crested the long, gradual rise that Jodie had pointed out, the ranch came into view. There was a sizeable, sturdy looking stone and wood home that stood not too far from a large barn and a number of other out structures. Most homesteads and ranches had an almost fort-like appearance having been intentionally laid out like that in case of Indian attacks. He'd asked Jodie that night back in his hotel room if they'd experienced any trouble with Indians, and she'd said, *Thank God, no, we haven't.* She'd further explained how it was probably because of the cavalry at Fort Laramie who routinely patrolled the Oregon Trail.

Surrounding the ranch house and outbuildings was a grid of many fences and corrals. In some were horses and mules, and others, cattle. Inside another large fenced area, there was a garden. Alongside the rows of old yellowed cornstalks were healthy clumps of green, leafy vegetables. Posted at both ends of the garden were two large, colorful scarecrow sentries. Then Lucas noticed there was a rider approaching from the ranch.

"Something must be wrong," Jodie whispered in his ear.

As the lone horseman reined up to Valentine and Farliss, Lucas could see he seemed to be going on with some urgency. Then Farliss twisted in his saddle and called, "Bring it in boys, we got work." With that, he and Valentine, along with the other young rider, quickened their pace down the hill to the ranch.

"Hold on, Jodie," Lucas cautioned before nudging Heston's flanks.

"Be careful, Lucas," Jodie said, her voice wavering with Heston's gallop.

When they'd reached the barn where Valentine and Farliss were dismounting, Lucas held Jodie's arm and eased her down.

"You'll be wantin fresh mounts, fellas," Farliss said as the others rode up.

"Fetch and ready mine, too, Hard," Valentine said. He was handing his reins over to a stocky fellow wearing a cowhide apron and holding a short-handled jack in one hand. Lucas figured he was the Kansan blacksmith who'd come to the ranch with Farliss. Looking back at Valentine he saw the deliberate side of the rancher and could feel the gravity in the air.

"You comin too?" Farliss asked Augustus. "We can handle this, ya know."

"You bet I'm coming, Far. I'll be right along." With that, Augustus Valentine turned and marched off towards the house where the family coach was just arriving.

"Be careful, Lucas," Jodie said. She had a concerned, yet warm smile that seemed to say more. Then she twirled and with a light skip in her step, traipsed after her father. Although he'd only known her for little more than a day, it seemed as though it had been much longer. He thought about her repeated warnings for him to be careful. It sounded funny, but he liked it.

~ 12 ~

While the others were dismounting and preparing to change out their mounts, Lucas led Heston to a water trough just beyond the front corner of the large barn. As Heston drank and he was loosening the saddle straps, he saw there were two young hands behind the barn splitting firewood. Seeing that he and Heston were there, they left their work and started over. As they neared, one called, "You want we should bring some hay for your horse, Mister?"

"Yeah, I'd appreciate that," Lucas said.

There was an open-sided hay shed attached to the side of the barn and they each stopped to gather some. When they'd reached the gate, "They're back in," one told the other referring to the crew gathered out front. They brought the hay over and spreading it on the ground, admired Heston. They were young and Lucas figured maybe seventeen or eighteen.

"Sure's a fine lookin horse, Mister," one remarked.

"Sure is," the other said.

"Carl, you and Johnny come help with gettin these mounts changed out," Farliss called.

"Yes sir," the two responded together and started off.

As Heston grazed on the hay, Lucas first inspected his hooves then, began massaging his forelegs. Aware that Farliss had come over, he glanced up and said, "We're fine."

"That right?" the Kansan said leaning to his side to spit. He'd drawn a thin grin revealing his skepticism over his declining to take a fresh mount.

"You got spurs?" he then asked.

Furthering the lead man's uncertainty, "Don't need 'em," Lucas replied. It didn't take spurs to urge Heston to a charge. A boot heel clip was all. He searched Farliss' eyes watching for his reaction, but they were barely perceptible behind the narrowed slits of his eyelids.

Turning now to Wooten, just pulling the dust tarp from the supply wagon, Farliss said, "Woot, we'll need you to stow enough fare for about ten and a couple days. Whatever's easy and available. Teller—-" he called aloud.

"Yeah, Far," another young hand a little older than the first two answered.

"You ready to ride?"

"You betcha," he eagerly replied placing his right hand over his holstered revolver.

"Good, then you and Gore help them others switchin out mounts. Johnny—-" he called to one of the two whom he'd only just sent to help with the change out. "Go fetch and help Woot ready a pack mule. Afterwards, you and Carl see ta gettin that supply wagon unloaded." Turning to the others, he said, "When you fellas are done ya can fill your canteens there at the well. If you're hungry, there's jerk. We'll sup later."

Although Farliss appeared uncertain about himself, Lucas, still trying to overlook the fact that he was from Kansas, actually appreciated the way in which he now seemed to be taking charge; especially after the lack of leadership he'd shown leaving Cheyenne yesterday. Even the raiders as sometimes scattered and wild as they were, understood the need for unity under the command of a single voice when riding into even the smallest of skirmishes. As he headed for the well to fill his one empty canteen, he watched as the large Kansas ramrod stood with his hands on his hips appraising the group assembling before him.

"How you sleepers feelin?" he asked.

"Fresh as peacheez, amigo," Rocha, the Mexican answered with a grin. "What we waiteeng all day long for, Far?"

"The boss is comin and anyone plannin on doin any more drinkin might as well light back for Cheyenne now." Although he seemed to smile as he further focused on Herron and Jahns, it was apparent he wasn't making light and was watching for any trace of attitude they might suggest. But the two riflemen, still light-headed and shadowed with hangovers, were silent, which was a welcomed change from the day before when they'd jabbered nonstop.

When Augustus emerged from the house, he bore the same determined expression he had earlier. Still, Lucas couldn't help thinking he belonged behind a desk pushing numbers on a ledger, not riding into a fight. He figured the reason he was going was probably to see what talents his newly hired trio had to offer.

"Men, the rustlers have stolen the last head of our cattle they're going to," he announced. With that, the short-legged, stocky boss turned and awkwardly tugged himself onto his freshly readied mount. It was a brief address, but had said enough.

It was about three o'clock when the ten of them set out heading north at an easy lope. As they rode, Farliss introduced Lucas, Herron and Jahns to Harding the Kansan, and the two younger hands, Gore and Teller.

"Hard's our blacksmith and second foreman when I ain't around, fellas," he said.

Lucas had been watching the other Kansan from the corner of his eye, but had detected nothing in his demeanor suggesting he might have any notion about who he was or what he'd been. He did, however, notice that when Farliss mentioned his *second foreman* status, Harding, apparently less than enthused with the designation, blatantly rolled his eyes. After the introductions, he said nothing and faintly acknowledged the three of them with a disinterested glance and nod. It reminded him of Todd Welles and the way he'd acted when they'd first met at the hotel. He got the distinct impression that the Kansas blacksmith was mopish; that or maybe resentful for not having been along on the trip to Cheyenne.

Then, in the course of being introduced to the two younger hands, Teller and Gore, Lucas couldn't help noting the hard-case way in which they each projected themselves. Whether it was meant to show they were toughs or to convey some sign of their seniority in the ranch hierarchy, he wasn't sure, but in either case it struck him as being almost as comical as it was pitiful.

They hadn't gone far before Teller, who was leading the pack mule and trying to keep pace with the rest of the group, started cursing it as it began lagging behind. Further appraising Gore, Lucas saw that he now wore that same eager expression that Teller had shown back at the ranch when Farliss asked if he was ready to ride to which he'd noticeably responded by reaching for his revolver. Gore looked more like he was going to a barnyard dance than a scrap.

He thought how it was always good to know something of the fighting caliber of the men you were riding into battle with, and, in light of his less than inspiring impressions of the group as a whole thus far, couldn't help being a little disappointed. While he hadn't expected to find himself in the position of confronting trouble this quickly, it *was* what Valentine hired him for. And as for the fighting abilities of the others, he remembered Valentine's saying at the hotel how they just needed someone capable of confronting those situations, and how then, the others wouldn't be as reserved about stepping up and using force. Nevertheless, he thought how perhaps it was good after all that Valentine had brought on the two riflemen, Herron and Jahns; like them or not. Then he remembered Rocha and the bandolier of cartridges he wore. Turning in the saddle, he glanced back at him. He saw that besides the belt of bullets, the Mexican was also wearing a grin that immediately projected the image of a jackass baring his teeth. Turning forward, no more encouraged than he'd been before, in an effort yet to glean some positive element, he reminded himself how you could never really tell how well a man would perform until he was in the actual heat of the fracas and death was on the wing.

When they'd covered maybe ten miles, the group slowed to a walk.

"Listen up, fellas," Farliss announced. "This is likely to get touchy. Just yesterday some of the Marsh boys were seen cuttin more yearling out of our stock, and knowin they was seen doin it, fired a couple rounds toward Johnny and Carl. Like the boss said, they know sure enough the score and could very well be laid up expectin our response. So keep yer eyes sharp and heads low.

There could be as many as fifteen of 'em hunkered in down there. Once we get a good look on things, we'll roust some grub and work our next move." Turning to Valentine, he said, "Maybe Marsh and some'll still be in Cheyenne."

Lucas had a gut feeling all along that he hadn't seen the end of the Marsh character. He remembered well the man's attitude in the saloon, knowing no one would dare try stopping him from doing whatever he wanted. And when he'd demanded he let go of Katie, he'd seen the defiant fire flare in his eyes. The big man wasn't accustomed to being told what to do, but facing down the trained barrel of a revolver was a language he understood well enough, brazen or not. And now, as Jodie had suggested, he's probably still none too happy about it.

After ground-staking their mounts and leaving Gore unhappily below to watch over them, the eight men climbed to the top of a long, gradual hillock, crouching and doffing their hats as they neared the crest. From there, with a steady wind at their faces, a few men could be seen moving around the barn below. Lucas figured it maybe three-hundred yards and, into the wind, well out of accurate rifle range. He studied again the two small ridges of rock outcroppings that were about a hundred yards down the long, tapered slope before them thinking how from the rustlers' side they might be ideal for the posting of rifles. Turning to his right, he saw that Valentine and Farliss were no longer using their field glass.

"Can I use the glass?" he asked.

"Why not," Farliss said, handing it over.

Lucas expanded the spyglass and raised it to his right eye. Closing his left, he shaded the open end with his free hand so it wouldn't reflect the setting sun and slowly twisted its eyepiece bringing it into focus. He scanned from the two nearby ridges of rock just below across the open spread. From the farthest hill beyond the ranch, he traced slowly down to the corridor that led between the cabin and barn, then over the yard and the other structures till he'd brought it back up to the two rock croppings below. The few men he'd seen moving about wore gun belts. One packed a rifle. But there'd been no sign of the unmistakable, bearded

Marsh. As he glassed over the closest rock break to his right, something dark caught his eye. He backed the glass and saw the short, dark tip of something jutting from the edge of the rock. Unless it was charred, it was too dark to be a tree limb or branch. Thinking it possibly the muzzle of a rifle, he lowered the glass and turning to Farliss said, "There's a chance there could be——-"

But before he'd finished, bullets were spitting at the ground and cutting past in the air, followed immediately by the cracking report of rifle fire. Going flat and edging away from the crest, someone to the left cried out. It was Harding, the Kansan. He'd been hit. Lucas saw he was still wearing his high crowned hat.

"Harding's been shot!" Welles frantically yelled.

"Where?" Farliss called.

"Arrghh...dammit!" Harding groaned. He'd rolled onto his back now and was clutching at his left shoulder.

"I think the shoulder," Welles reported.

"Hard, think ya can make it down and back to the ranch okay?" Farliss asked.

"I reckon," Harding said with a grimace.

"Gore," Farliss called down the hill. "Ride back to the ranch with Hard and bring Johnny and Carl back up with ya."

"Now...tonight?" he exclaimed.

"Yes, now! Try pluggin that wound from bleedin first then scat."

The rustlers had stopped firing and as Gore and Harding were mounting to leave, Teller, leading the pack-mule, arrived. Meanwhile, Farliss and Valentine lay on their backs against the hillside wide-eyed, breathing hard and perspiring heavily.

"What you think, Far?" Valentine asked at length.

"I don't know, Augustus," the foreman said swiping the sweat from his brow. His hand shook noticeably and his face was gray as granite. "It'd be suicide ridin in now. They've been waitin and I guess we'll have to, too."

"Before its dark," Lucas interjected, "we oughta post a couple men wide and get as good a read we can on how many they got and where they're fixed. And watch they don't try swingin on us."

Farliss was flustered and he studied Lucas blankly.

"I think he's right, Far," Valentine said.

The foreman leaned aside to spit, but all that came out was a cottony fluff. "Jahns," he called brushing it from his chin, "Move wide left and try and get a fix on their lay. Watch they don't mount and swing on us. Herron, you cover right. I'll switch you fellas out shortly."

"Might roust some coffee in the meantime," Lucas suggested. "It could be a wait."

"Sounds good too," Valentine said.

When Jahns and Herron had taken their new positions, the remaining five descended the hill. Lucas looked at Rocha who was beside him. The spur rowels jingled on his boot heels with each step he took. All the Valentine hands wore them, and though they were safely out of earshot of the rustlers, he thought how noisy they were and how they might as well be wearing tambourines. Rocha, from beneath the medium brim of his sombrero, grinned at Lucas, showing his mouthful of horse teeth. Thinking he looked funny, Lucas half-smiled.

At the base of the hill, Farliss instructed Welles to start a fire using some of the wood they'd packed in with them, and had the others scour the area for dried cattle chips and anything else that would burn.

"Let's just burn 'em out," Welles suggested.

"Can't with this wind, Todd, it'll burn every acre clear back to the ranch," Valentine said.

"There's nothin but dirt down there anyway," Farliss added.

It was true. What grass there was, was dry as tinder, and with the wind blowing out of the northwest, it would only drive the flames back the same direction from which they'd ridden.

In the dusk, now rapidly settling about them, they ate off the pre-cooked ham and biscuits that Wooten had sent with them. After emptying the first pot of coffee, they started a second. When it was brewed, they let the fire burn itself out, saving what little fuel they had. Then Farliss sent Rocha and Welles up to relieve Herron and Jahns. Lucas had expected the Kansan would send him, but now suspected the ramrod was in his own way, still punishing the men who'd stayed up late the night before.

As Herron and Jahns were helping themselves to the grub and coffee, they reported having seen about four men fixed in positions not counting those behind the rock outcropping, and each gave an approximation where. As the two riflemen ate, they fumed over their no longer having their Sharps rifles so they could better shoot from the distance. When Farliss asked what happened to them, Herron said they'd sold them to a pawnbroker in Denver because they were done with the buffalo hide trade. Lucas thought how it explained not only their rifle skills, but probably the odor they had about them. It was likely from the bison blood and guts that had permanently saturated their clothing, leathers and tack.

With each darkening minute that passed over the group as they sat silent about the flameless fire pit, Lucas was aware of the shroud of uncertainty that had grown until it hung over them as thick as a swamp fog that sight could not possibly penetrate in the hope of seeing its way through. The way the rustler's ranch was situated and having their riflemen posted as they were, there wasn't much the Valentine crew could do short of charging in. But like Farliss said earlier, even now in the dark, losses would likely be substantial, both for man and mount. If the Marsh crew hadn't known they were there, it might have been feasible.

Breaking the silence, he asked, "Do we got a couple of time-pieces?"

"What ya need the time for?" Herron garbled his mouth full of biscuit and ham.

Lucas peered through the darkness at him.

"Got somewhere else ta be?" Jahns added his mouth full also.

"I've got one, Lucas," Valentine said.

Further revealing his frustration over their predicament Farliss grumped, "Yeah, I got one. What for?"

"I'm thinkin I'll swing wide around the southwest side of their spread and make a quick pass through. I need you fellas to keep their attention this direction so I might catch some of 'em by surprise."

"You loco?" Herron remarked.

Again, Lucas looked at him, but said nothing.

"All right, Lucas," Valentine said. Standing, he dug a watch from his trouser fob and handing it to him asked, "What time?" Lucas opened the gold watch lid. It was just past eight.

"At midnight, start pourin steady fire at the bottom of those rock shelves and nothin else. Keep watch for me and when ya see me comin, hold your fire." Turning toward Herron and the still busy eating Jahns, he added, "Just don't shoot me."

Looking back at Farliss he asked, "What's yours read?"

"Five of," the Kansan reported. He snapped shut the watch lid staring curiously at Lucas through the dark.

"Close enough," Lucas said.

~ 13 ~

Except the constant brush of the wind cutting over the crest of the hill, it was silent as Lucas began twisting himself a smoke. He could feel the weight of the men's eyes on him in the dark, each wondering if he was really going to do what he'd proposed. Other than their calling it quits, he found himself with little recourse but to openly resort to his old skills. Again he couldn't help but wonder how much Farliss the Kansan knew about the raiders and bushwhackers, and if what he'd suggested doing might further cause him to piece it together.

Striking a flare, he lit the cigarette and was reminded of something peculiar that Rocha told him yesterday concerning Farliss. It was when they were preparing to make camp, and he and the Mexican were gathering firewood. Rocha said that Sunday afternoon, before Farliss had gotten himself spruced up to go to some private engagement, the two of them were both at a saloon, and that the men there were all talking about the unknown gunman who'd won the pistol contest. Rocha related how they'd all been speculating over who the gunman was and where he was from, and if he was a wanted outlaw and killer. At the time, what Rocha said gave him concern, but he'd only responded by smiling and shrugging dismissively. Then Rocha went on to say that when Farliss returned from his special engagement, he'd told him that the boss had in fact just hired on that very same gunman along with two riflemen. Besides confirming his own earlier concerns of having drawn too much attention to himself, it also struck him odd how at the dinner in Cheyenne, when Valentine had asked if anyone had seen Rocha, Farliss reported he hadn't. According to Rocha, he hadn't known about the dinner. Obviously, Farliss had purposely not invited him. Lucas wasn't sure what significance any of it had to do with anything, but he knew that Farliss was certainly capable of deception.

With the moon now below the horizon there was only the glow of starlight. That was one reason for his choosing midnight to make his charge, the other being that perhaps the rustlers would be tired and their guards down. Wearing his new black hat and old duster, he and Heston were but a large and dark shadow in the night. He kept the two of them far enough back that from the saddle, he could just see over the top of the hill to the backside of the rustlers' cabin below. The dim flicker of lantern light through the cabin's window was the only movement he could detect. He pulled Valentine's watch from his coat pocket and raised it before his eyes. It was almost twelve. He placed the watch back in his pocket and cinched snug the hat cord beneath his jowls. Then, bending forward, he stroked Heston's warm neck. Working his boots firmly into the stirrups, he started the mount moving slowly keeping behind the rise.

Heston was a good, sure-footed night mount, and he was thankful he'd opted to stay with him instead of taking a fresh, yet unfamiliar mount. He thought of the countless times the two had bull rushed unsuspecting soldiers. But then, there'd always been other raiders riding alongside. He thought how while these ranchers weren't soldiers, they more than likely weren't asleep, either. He put it from his mind as he lined Heston up, facing the alley between the house and barn.

From there, standing at the front corner of the barn below, he could just make out the form of a fellow apparently on guard. It looked like he had a rifle cradled in the fold of his left arm. Then, he saw the orange glow of cinder and that he was smoking. "Enjoy that butt, Bucko," he mumbled. "It'll likely be your last cause you'll prob'ly be first." He pulled the Colt from his left holster, placed the reins in his mouth and bit down firmly on them. Then he drew his right. From across the vale, the sound of gunfire erupted. It was time.

He put his heels sharply to Heston who sprang forward down the hill, charging toward the corridor between the buildings. Facing the commotion east, the fellow at the barn never knew what hit him as Lucas fired a single round with his left, catching him squarely rib-side. Just as he'd suspected might be the case, the one standing across the alley at the front corner of the cabin turned only in time to catch the single fire chest center from his right. Shifting his weight in the stirrups, Heston responded, banking right along the front of the cabin. He clipped his heels again to his flanks and as the powerful mount surged, leaning forward, he shot the fellow who'd just turned towards him in the open doorway, slamming him back inside. Raising his left, he pulled twice on the rifleman who'd been seen there earlier crouched in the open yard behind the pile of firewood. He heard the man yell. So far, just as he'd hoped, they'd all been facing the flashes of fire that illuminated the crest of the hill ahead.

Now they were out in the full open, racing straight ahead for the closest shelf of rocks. Standing behind the privy to the right, not far beyond the house, and rapidly firing at the hilltop, was the gunman who'd also been seen posted there earlier. Hearing Heston's pounding hooves on the hard-packed ground, the man reeled just as Lucas fired then folded to the ground. Putting his heels to Heston again, Lucas saw more muzzle flashes splitting the darkness to the right and sensed the drill of air as bullets whizzed closely past. He leveled and fired twice, emptying his right at the spitting bolts of muzzle flame. He wasn't sure if he'd hit the shooter, but Heston was charging and it was too late now. He shoved the empty Colt into its holster and yanked one of the fresh revolvers from his waist.

Behind the rock shelf dead ahead were two riflemen with their backs to him. They were unloading rounds at the top of the hill as fast as they could ratchet and fire. As he and Heston neared, one of the men crouched to reload and saw they were approaching. Firing the fresh revolver, Lucas hit him and saw as he toppled. This time with his left, he squeezed off two more rounds, catching the second rifleman and slamming him against the rock. The force sent his rifle whirligigging overhead. Leaning hard now to his left, he drew Heston towards the second ridge of rocks where two more riflemen were busy sending fire up the hill. That was where he'd seen the rifle barrel with the glass earlier. He shoved his empty left into its right holster and pulled the second backup from his belt. The Valentine crew had ceased firing, but he hadn't noticed.

He jabbed Heston's flanks again and charged straight for the last rock cover. The closest gunman spun, but before he could level his rifle, Lucas, with both revolvers blazing, cut him and the other gunman down, sending both into body rolls. Folded completely forward with Heston's mane whipping sharply at his face, he snatched the reins from his mouth, realizing only then that all the gunfire had ceased. There was only the rapid pounding drum of Heston's hooves and his hard blowing in the dark. As they flew over the crest of the hill, he also drew deep breaths. He never remembered breathing in the midst of making charges.

Slowing Heston gradually to a wide circling canter on the other side of the hill, then to a walk, he stroked the mounts hot and damp neck. After he dismounted, he led him over towards the other mounts and there, loosed the saddle straps and checked to make sure he hadn't been hit or grazed. Taking the pot for watering the horses, he filled it from the supply bag and after first gulping some himself, held it for Heston to drink.

"We made it through another, Hest," he said quietly to the horse.

Heston flicked his ears in response as he drank.

When Heston had finished two pots of the water, Lucas secured him to the picket-line and went over and sat down beside the cold fire pit where Valentine, Farliss and the others all stood silently watching. They were all amazed at what he'd done. And albeit dark, they had for the most part, peeking over the crest of the hill as they were firing, seen it with their own eyes. The whole thing had only taken a couple of minutes—-if that. He glanced briefly at them then dug into his inner coat pocket for his tobacco and rolling papers.

"Here, son, have one of mine." Valentine said extending a long, thin cigar to him.

"Thanks," Lucas said accepting the stogie.

"You're certainly welcome, Lucas."

He put the fold of papers and the tobacco sack back into his coat pocket. Then, after running the cigar under his nose, he drew it over his curled tongue. It smelled and tasted sweet. As he dug in his other pocket for a lucifer, he came across Valentine's watch. He took it out and handed it up to him.

After taking the watch, Augustus struck and offered up a cupped flame. As he held it over he asked, "How many you think you might have…gotten down there, son?"

Lucas breathed the fire in and out through the cigar a few times, giving it some thought.

"Maybe ten," he said, the wind whisking the smoke as he spoke.

Valentine straightened himself and looked at Farliss with a confident and satisfied expression that read: *I knew it, and that's why I hired him.*

~ 14 ~

An hour after Lucas' midnight strike and when he'd finished his smoke, the Valentine outfit mounted, fanned out along the crest of the hill and began moving in. Preferring the security of his revolvers close at hand, Augustus had Lucas hold back with him and Farliss before following the others. In the darkness below there were no visible signs of movement, only the painful moaning of an injured man. Jahns, who found him lying near the outhouse, shoved the muzzle of his rifle into the man's mouth and, without thinking, shot him, thereby warning any other potential survivors of their advance.

Later, Teller discovered another who was still alive and lying just inside the entrance of the barn. He'd been shot in the hip and had drug himself from the woodpile no doubt trying to reach the horses to escape. Lucas and Farliss had just finished making sure the cabin was clear when Herron, after first badgering the injured man in the barn, shot him between the eyes.

While Lucas had struck with sudden and deadly force, it was with sadistic relish the way in which Jahns and Herron finished off the two injured men. He'd seen men who'd gone mad with war and become twisted that way; some even so far as scalping and mutilating the bodies of the injured and deceased. But they were typically men who'd suffered the personal losses of their wives and, in some cases, even their children, and therefore, had become obsessed with inflicting as much vengeance upon the enemy—be they dead or alive—as they possibly could. He'd also figured that in their tortured minds, it was their way of sending the enemy as gruesome a message of fear as they could. But killing was the business of war, not game or sport, and the two disabled rustlers no longer posed a threat. Herron and Jahns didn't have to kill them, especially not in the manner they had, by heightening the level of terror in their victims first. His previous assessment of the two stood confirmed and, for a flashing moment, found himself seriously tempted to draw down on the both of them. If he hadn't been in the company of the others, he likely would have.

Coyote-eyed Herron had clearly detected the way in which Lucas at that moment was eyeing both himself and Jahns, and there was no mistaking what was on his mind. But after having seen the lethal results of his solo raid, he was in no way prepared to challenge him or the deadly accuracy of his revolvers face to face without an edge in his favor.

Marsh was not among the dead. More than likely, he and some of his men were either still in Cheyenne or on the trail back. If the two injured rustlers hadn't been so hastily executed, they might have learned when he was expected to return, but it was too late for that now. Nevertheless, emboldened by success, Valentine and Farliss decided they would wait out the remainder of the night and coming day in the event they should show.

After posing some of the rustler's bodies so that it looked like they were still on guard, they posted the Valentine men in concealed positions in and around the barn. Valentine, still preferring to have the security of Lucas and his revolvers nearby, insisted he wait in the cabin with himself and Farliss. Lucas said he would, but preferring not to be in the clear light of their scrutiny, insisted they extinguish the lantern. Lying, he told them how it had revealed one of the rustlers inside before he began his raid. Without hesitation, the two agreed and Farliss doused it.

There was a potbellied stove and after stoking it and closing its door to maintain the stealth of darkness, Farliss prepared a pot of strong coffee to help keep everyone awake. As he did, Lucas kept a sensitive eye on both him and Augustus, all the while hoping they wouldn't start asking uncomfortable questions about what he'd done. They were, however, obviously pleased with the results of his raid, and knew that had it not been for it, they'd still be sitting in a quandary on the other side of the hill; that or decided it was futile and withdrawn altogether. Though neither had seen the incident at the saloon in Cheyenne, Jodie's story of how impressively he'd dealt with the situation, they no longer considered exaggeration on her part.

When the coffee was brewed and Lucas and Farliss were delivering it to the men on watch, Gore, along with Johnny and Carl, the two youngest Valentine hands, arrived. They too, were posted on guard.

Sitting quietly in the dark and warm cabin had proven too much for both Valentine and Farliss, and it wasn't long before they were each bent over the rustler's rickety supper table with their heads on their folded arms asleep. Lucas was glad they were and, knowing the men outside were also tired and growing restless, busied himself making and delivering plenty of coffee. The initial excitement of victory had waned with their waiting throughout the remainder of the long night. They were not warriors. Still, he insisted they maintain silence and stay vigilant.

Since Marsh couldn't possibly know they were working for Valentine, Herron proposed that he and Jahns ride out to take him by surprise on the trail; if he was on the trail at all. But Lucas told them to hold their positions and remain alert. Now, having the boss or Farliss giving them orders was one thing, but they were resistant about answering to him or his. In their minds he was only a new hand just as they were. The two riflemen had both come to the same opinion that his solo raid had actually been an easy gamble and little more than luck. And now, he was sitting comfortably in the cabin with the owner and his foreman as a result. They sarcastically determined between themselves that his name was indeed—-*Lucky*.

"Easy for him to say, I ain't eaten and I'm cold and tired," Gore grumbled after one of Lucas' visits.

"Who's he think *he* is...our new boss?" Welles remarked.

Sounding as though he were joking, "I should'a winged him," Herron said. "He wouldn't be so almighty then."

"In all that gunfire, who'd'a known?" Jahns added.

A couple hours after sunrise, three riders paused at the top of the hill behind the cabin near the same spot where Lucas had begun his earlier midnight charge. Lucas saw them from the cabin's rear window, and that the large, dark-bearded Marsh was one. All the Valentine men had been instructed that should anyone appear, to hold their fire and let them commit to riding in close enough to insure they didn't escape.

As the three riders started down the hill, Herron and Jahns anxiously opened up on them, hitting two of the men, dropping them from their horses. Escaping the haphazard volley of unprepared shots that followed, the third man rode over the crest and out of sight. Marsh and the other lay dead, each shot in the head. Farliss glared at Herron and Jahns, furious at them. Lucas shook his head unsurprised. They were impetuous and not to be trusted.

Augustus told Farliss he was heading back to the home ranch and that he was having Lucas go with him. The foreman and the others would stay behind to bury the rustlers and round up their horses and livestock. They would also load all of the weapons and anything else of value into the rustlers' wagon and bring it with them when they returned.

As Lucas and Valentine set off together, the rancher expressed his concern over the man who'd escaped and his possibly reporting it.

"You wouldn't think a rustler would be reportin anything," Lucas said.

"Not if he was reporting the whole truth," Augustus said.

Turning to face the rancher Lucas said, "Yeah, I see your point. Still, I don't like the way Herron and Jahns opened up on 'em. Them or those other two, either. I don't like 'em."

Augustus grinned as though to say he understood.

"Well, that's one big problem out of our way at any rate," he said.

"There more?" Lucas asked beginning a yawn.

Hesitating to respond, the rancher looked curiously at him. "Yes," he said. "There's another outfit...the JK, farther north. Not as brash, though. Not like Marsh and his bunch. Then, of course, there's the free grazers along our east side who'll round up and drive anything on four legs, theirs or not. The biggest problem with them, though, is the critical water and grass they consume." He paused and saw Lucas was yawning again.

"It's the driest I've seen it, Lucas. There's not a drop of water in the ground. We got no choice but to graze next year's herd farther north." Once more he checked for any reaction from Lucas who was yawning yet again. The cattleman smiled.

Wiping his tired, watery eyes, Lucas half-considered Valentine and his investment partners and how perhaps they were trying to be too big. Obviously, the larger the spread, the greater the potential was for problems. And now the cattleman was talking about stretching out farther yet. *How much does a man really need* he wondered. A small cabin on a quiet mountainside with a couple head suited his imagination just fine. But then, he thought, Valentine was probably following some financial directives and trying to meet marketing quotas. Something like the way orders that needed to be carried out were handed down from generals through the ranks to sergeants and then, privates. Orders that usually made little sense to the men on the actual battlefield, but that, nevertheless, had to be executed, or, at least attempted. He yawned again, this time audibly. He couldn't stop from it.

Smiling at his new gunman who could barely keep his eyes open, Augustus said, "When we get in, I'll have Woot square you a bunk."

"Sounds fine," Lucas said.

"After you get yourself some rest, I'd like you to join me and the family for supper."

Lucas looked at the rancher and saw he appeared very satisfied; much the same way he had back in Cheyenne when he'd first hired him on.

"Sounds good, too," he said.

While he could certainly stand to eat, he'd been thinking more about the prospect of getting some sleep. His mind wandered and, considering the boss's invitation, found himself thinking about his seeing Jodie again. It seemed like days ago now, but it was really only yesterday that she'd ridden with him to the ranch. He remembered her spring-fresh scent and her soft, pleasant voice tickling in his ear, as well as the tickling sensation of her hair being blown in the wind like eiderdown against the sides of his neck. He'd liked it and how it made him feel, and just thinking about it now made him feel much the same way again. The two of them had grown easily close in a couple of days. It pleased him, as well as stirred a tinge of concern. She was, after all, the younger daughter of his new employer. *And you,* he reminded himself, *you're someone pretending not to be who you really are. Still, I've done nothing so far but take the hand I was dealt and played it just as I was hired to. And outside of not disclosing your past, your motives so far have been honorable—haven't they? Yes, I think so—I believe. And you, more than you know yourself, like the way it feels. That, like Jodie, was different too. What are you thinking?* he wondered. *Here you are, riding with the owner's daughter...I mean the owner who's just invited you to sup with his family...and while you're considering things like honor, you're also thinking about his daughter?* Once more, mindful of keeping his senses about him, he thought telling himself, *Jodie's not part of the job. Still, she is nice though.*

He was batty tired and it was like one part of him was telling him one thing, and another, another. Peculiar, almost hypnotic feelings had begun stirring within him. Like the surreal way that the wind had brushed and swayed the heads of the field grasses when the two of them were riding together.

You're crazy-tired he thought. *Dream-riding...like when you used to drunk-ride...remember? Ride while you were drunk, I mean. You're not used to thinking feelings like that...like her.*

Letting go his usual cautious nature, he surrendered himself to the intoxicating lure of sleep and, dreamily *yes,* to seeing Jodie again.

~ 15 ~

Lucas was aching to be out of the saddle and to stretch out and lie down long before he and Augustus arrived at the ranch. When they had at last, he unsaddled Heston and turned him out in the corral next to the barn where some of the other horses were grazing on freshly spread hay. Wooten, the bunkhouse boss and cook, briefly showed him around and led him to the bunkhouse. It was long and narrow and smelled musky of men. There was a cold potbellied stove and a couple of slat board tables with wood crates for seats near its only entrance which was at the backside of the building opposite the Valentine home. It had two rows of bunks on either side of a narrow aisle between them and high on the walls, just below the ceiling, were some open windows without panes for letting in light and fresh air. He thought how the bunkhouse resembled a large chicken coop. In one of the bunks, Harding was on his back asleep and snoring. His left shoulder was bandaged. Wooten said that he and Case had removed the bullet and that it hadn't been deep. Then he pointed out which beds were taken and told Lucas to pick the one he wanted from those available. He chose one at the far end and dropped his saddlebags at its head for a pillow. He sat on the bunk and yawned as he pulled off his boots. Stretching out over the bed, he fell immediately asleep.

It was about four hours later, when he awoke to find he was being sniffed by a large white dog with inquisitive brown eyes, large erect ears and a cold, wet, black nose. Startled at first, then, smiling, he said, "Hey there." The dog wagged its tail and put his two front paws up onto the side of the bunk.

Rising to his elbows, Lucas yawned and said, "You tellin me it's time to get up?"

The dog answered with an anxious whine and similar yawn.

"All right, I'm gettin up."

The dog hurried to the foot of the bunk and looked back at him as if to say—-*this way*. Sure enough, he led straight for the privy like he knew that would be the necessary first order of business. Afterward, as Lucas bathed and shaved, the dog lay patiently nearby, as though waiting for him to finish. It was quiet around the ranch since all of the hands, with the exception of Wooten and Harding, were still up at the Marsh place.

"That's Jodie's dog. He owns the whole cotton-pickin place," Wooten said and chuckled. "Don't ya, boy?"

Tonka tilted his head and looked at Wooten as if he were contemplating what he'd said. He had an intelligent look about him.

"His name's Tonka. It's Injun for big," Wooten said.

At the sound of his name, Tonka rose, shook and wagged his tail.

After getting dressed, Lucas strolled outside, leaned forward against the corral boards where Heston was, twisted and lit a cigarette. He was still tired, but the few hours of sleep combined with the bath had been somewhat reinvigorating. Squinting, he watched as the last of the sun neared the horizon, which had set afire in a spectacular red-orange blaze. Tonka dropped a stick at his feet and backed up, waiting for him to respond. Picking up the slavered stick he asked, "Ya want me to huck this?"

Tonka gave a single affirmative bark then tensed, ready to spring.

"Okay," he said launching the slobbery stick across the yard with Tonka ripping after it.

"Oh boy...you've got a friend forever now."

Lucas reeled, it was Jodie. She was wearing a white blouse trimmed with lace down its front and a sky-blue summer skirt the color of her eyes. Her long honey and strawberry-blond hair fanned in the breeze glowing bright as gold. Her blue eyes sparkled like jewels, the way the sun glimmers on calm waters. She was smiling and pretty, more so than he remembered, and he felt taken and unable to summon what to say.

"Father says you're joining us for supper."

"Yes."

"He can't stop talking about how you handled yourself. He's excited you're coming."

Lucas smiled, aware just then of how truly different he felt being in Jodie's presence than any of the other women he'd been around. As for her mentioning how he'd handled himself, he'd never said anything to her about why her father hired him, but figured now she knew.

"After we eat, if you're not too tired and the wind stays down, I was thinking perhaps, if you'd like, we might go for a ride and I can show you around some."

"That sounds good," he said.

"But you have to bring your tobacco," she said and snickered.

"It's a deal."

"Come on, let's go in. Supper's probably ready."

From the sitting room window, Katie watched as Jodie and Lucas walked together across the yard towards the house. She didn't like the way the two of them had in such short time become such good friends. It bothered her that she'd not curried his attention, as she'd always been able to do with most other men who were anywhere near her age. Then, too, there'd been the questionable incident in town at the saloon, where, according to Jodie, he'd *gallantly* rescued her. Being unable to fully recall the details clearly in her own mind, she seriously doubted the gravity of the situation and was sure Jodie had embellished upon it. The non-approving look on her face gradually gave way to a pleasant smile as she met the two of them at the door.

"I was just on my way out to find you," she said. "I hope you're hungry, Lucas. Case has been cooking all afternoon."

"It sure smells fine," he said. He could feel his stomach convulsing as it reacted to the inviting aroma that permeated the house.

After taking his coat and hat and hanging them beside the door, Jodie led him into the dining room. There, a large, fancy oak table was fully set. Around a pink, delicious looking baked ham sitting at its center were matching bowls of mashed potatoes, gravy, carrots, snap beans, yellow squash, sliced pickled beets and golden rolls of bread. Also matching were the crystal glasses of milk and wine. Empty and waiting to be heaped full, were gold-trimmed china plates with like coffee cups and saucers. At each place setting, there was ample, brightly polished silverware and neatly folded linen napkins.

Once the women were seated, Augustus said, "Have a seat and help yourself, Lucas."

As they ate, the Valentines watched as he eagerly enjoyed everything before him. He was aware they were watching, but it tasted so good he couldn't help but immerse himself and devour two heaping plates of the delicious food never touching the glass of wine. While Augustus, Geneva and Jodie all smiled at their ravenous guest, Katie studied him coolly. When he'd finished eating, Jodie poured him a cup of coffee.

"So, where are you from, Lucas?" Katie asked.

"Back east," he said bringing the cup of coffee to his mouth.

"Well, aren't we *all*," she replied.

Lucas smiled saying nothing.

"I mean...who are you, *really*? We know so little about you."

Jodie didn't like Katie's questioning him and she squirmed uneasily in her chair trying to refrain herself. But unable to hold back and coming straight to his aid, blurted, "He's the one who rescued you from that saloon while your brave friends, Stenerson and Clancy, stood by wetting themselves. That's who he is."

"Now, girls," Geneva politely cautioned.

Unfazed, and with dignity fully intact, "I assure you, Jodie," Katie calmly replied, "I didn't need *anyone's* help."

Suppressing the urge to laugh, "Of all the ungrateful—-" Jodie said adding, "And yes, Katie...then he carried you back to the hotel room, since you couldn't carry yourself."

"And *who's* room were *you* carried to, little sister?"

As though she'd been gut-punched, Jodie's jaw dropped as she looked in disbelief at Katie. What she was suggesting right there before Lucas and their parents had struck sudden and deep, leaving her completely stunned and speechless. She was no match for Katie, who now sat smiling smugly at both her and Lucas.

With tears beginning to well in her eyes, Jodie rose from her seat and without looking directly at anyone, excused herself and left the dining room. Augustus, Geneva and Lucas, also stunned, sat quietly. The atmosphere had gone thick and extremely uncomfortable as if someone had brought in a coffin and placed it right on the dining table before them.

Katie, although now acting surprised by Jodie's reaction, inwardly grinned. She'd successfully driven her first stake between Lucas, her sister and their parents.

Lucas, now noting the curious way that Geneva seemed to be eyeing him, felt extremely self-conscious. He thanked them for the fine supper and stood.

"Oh, won't you stay for dessert?" Katie said. "Jodie baked an apple pie."

Disregarding her, he turned to Augustus and Geneva and, patting his full belly said, "I guess I'm all out of room. Thank you again." With that he left the room, took his hat and coat and exited the house.

"Kate, I invited him and—-"

"So who is he really, Father?" she said, cutting him short. "He's a gunman. That's all anyone really knows about him. He does all his talking with a gun. I heard you say yourself that he dealt with those men like he was one of the riders of the apocalypse. Now, here he sits at our dining room table? What else does he want... besides Jodie?"

"Katie, that's enough!" Geneva exclaimed.

"Don't you see, Mother, the way she acts when he's around?"

Augustus, slamming both open hands down onto the table as he stood said, "Now you listen to—-"

"Augustus!" Geneva exclaimed.

"No, Geneva, you listen as well...both of you. Right now, I don't give a damn who or what Lucas Jackson is. Presently, he's possibly the most valuable employee this ranch has. And in fact, for your information, the very future of this ranch quite possibly rests with him and…his particular ability. We all need him for the time being until certain things have been accomplished. Once we no longer need his services, I don't care where he goes. But until then, I expect you to apologize and keep a civil tongue in your head, young lady."

Katie wasn't accustomed to being reprimanded or corrected, not even by her father. But when it came to the security and future of the ranch, reality hit home. She often entertained the idea that if anything ever happened to her father, she, being the oldest daughter, would naturally step in and assume his role. Beside her natural beauty, the ranch was the single and greatest source of her self-esteem and pride. She was no fool and shrewd enough to know that without it, her station in life—outside of having to sacrifice herself to matrimony and childbearing—would leave her to little more than that of a commoner. And she could not accept the abysmal thought of either occurring. Both were fates she feared as much as death itself.

Farliss and the others had returned and were busy stripping saddles and unloading the wagonload of spoils from the Marsh place when Lucas exited the Valentine home. Always aware of the boss's house, they all saw as he emerged.

Approaching the front gate, he muttered under his breath, "What were you thinking, being there in the first place? You weren't, that's what." He shook his head over Katie's implying there'd been some impropriety between him and Jodie that night in his room at the hotel. Other than their smoking and talking, that had been it. And now, all that, after the way she'd gotten drunk and the scene she'd made at the saloon? Muddled, he headed straight for the corral, aware of, but paying no attention to the inquisitive eyes of the men watching. He needed to be alone. As he prepared Heston to ride, he wondered if he shouldn't just roll up and leave altogether. Cinching snug the saddle, he remembered the ride he and Jodie were to take after supper. "Not a good idea, either," he mumbled. After closing and latching the corral gate behind Heston, he turned and was startled to find Katie standing there.

"Lucas, you're not leaving, are you?" she asked.

He said nothing save what she might have read in the sharp flash of his eyes.

"I'm sorry, Lucas. I didn't mean anything by anything. It just sounded that way."

He said nothing and, before he could take another step, she threw herself upon him, wrapping her arms about his neck. He didn't know what to do or make of it, only that he didn't like it at all. His jaws were immediately forged and he was tempted to sling her off as though she were a snake coiled about him.

"Please don't leave because of me," she whimpered.

He could see the other men watching and it made him feel even more uneasy. Trying to remain civil and ease free of her embrace he said, "I'm just going for a ride's all." Letting go Heston's reins, he put his hands upon her waist and as gently as possible, pried her free.

"I meant to thank you for helping me in Cheyenne, Lucas. I was just...embarrassed."

In the hopes it might be an end to it, "Okay, Kate. Take it easy," he said.

"That's what father calls me—-Kate," she exclaimed.

It was embarrassing and trying to think how best to respond, he thought how she sounded more like a child than someone who, according to her, as she'd so clearly pointed out in Cheyenne, was *quite capable of taking care of herself.* He just wanted to be away from her and without thinking said, "Look, there's just some things I ain't comfortable talkin about."

"I can respect that," she said. "I'm sorry, Lucas. Can you forgive me?"

Preferring to bite his tongue off, "Yes," he said. Turning back to Heston, he gathered the reins and began leading him away.

"May I join you for a ride?"

Lucas grimaced and without turning said, "Not this time, all right?"

Clenching tight her fists while her insides boiled, she forced herself to say, "Okay, Lucas. Thank you." She was almost never told *no,* and now had heard it twice in the short span of only a few minutes. And no one but no one had *ever* pushed her away before. She'd put herself out going completely against her preferred will, and his rejecting her like he had, and in front of the other men as well, had her seething. Growling as she spun and started away, Welles, who'd worked his way over, asked, "You okay, Katie?"

She cocked back her head and glared at him. "Yes," she spat. "And *do* mind your own business!"

Lucas raised his eyebrows as he passed Welles, who paid him an unfriendly look. Shaking his head in disbelief, he stepped into the stirrup and swung himself up. With a flick of his heels, he and Heston were off. *She's some kind of poison and you oughta leave now,* his inner voice warned.

"Where ya off to, Lucky?" Herron teasingly called.

Lucas heard him and although tempted to stop, ignored it and kept riding.

"Looks like ol Lucky's a lover boy, too," Jahns added with a snorting chuckle.

Jodie drew her window curtains closed and threw herself onto her bed. She'd seen Katie with her arms around Lucas and, once again, felt thoroughly betrayed by her.

Augustus turned away from the window in his den, satisfied that Katie had apologized and smoothed things with Lucas. Farliss, he'd also seen, was headed up the walk to the house.

"Come in, Far. Close the door. How'd it go?"

"Fine, Augustus. We rounded up near seventy scrawny head's all, most yearling; maybe twenty ours. It's hard to tell, though, some's been re-branded and runnin ironed so many times. I had Johnny and Carl run them that weren't over to the north pasture. The rest are in the back hold till we can get 'em branded. The Marsh spread's got no water, neither. A couple mud holes is all. Still, that cabin should make for a suitable line station come winter, don't ya think?"

"Possibly. Were you able to get—-?"

"Yup, after you left, Todd and I rode up maybe ten miles I'd say, 'afore we found 'em. The JK stock looks good and watered, too. Anyhow, I jotted this out for Hard." He pulled a quarter-folded piece of paper from his shirt pocket and handing it over said, "I told Todd we needed it for sortin the brands on the cattle."

"Good," Augustus said. He unfolded and looked briefly at the sketch of the JK brand, then handed it back to his foreman.

"Let's get Harding started on it as soon as he's able."

Farliss folded and returned the paper to his shirt pocket and nodded.

"Far, I want you to put together a line-stocking crew with Welles, Rocha, Johnny and Carl and send them up the east side tomorrow. Have Lucas go with them so he can get familiar with the layout."

Being practically Valentine family now himself, Farliss asked, "Everything okay? I seen Katie out there with him and——"

"Yes, fine. Just her and Jodie hashing out female business is all...I reckon."

"I see," Farliss said steady working one side of his moustache.

Returning to the earlier business, Augustus said, "Still, let's get him up there and put him to use. Leave Jahns and Herron back to help with the branding, and deal with the sheepherder. I think they'll be able to handle that. Besides, Lucas says he doesn't like them."

"I don't necessarily, neither. Speaking of Lucas, though, I've been givin some thought to what he done with the Marsh crew, and can't help thinkin he's got some kind of soldierin behind him."

"I had the same hunch, Far. Nevertheless, it was something, wasn't it?"

"It certainly was. Those Marsh boys never knew what hit 'em. Well, Augustus, I'll square and send 'em out tomorrow. Right now, I'm gonna clean up, eat and hit the bunk, I'm bushed."

"Alright, Far. Good night."

~ 16 ~

In the morning, Lucas dressed and straightened his bunk. Removing his old flattened hat which he'd kept in his saddlebags, he punched it somewhat back into form and placed it at the head of the bed as a sign it was taken.

It was timely he was being sent out before Katie could stir up any more of her scenes. And as much as he liked Jodie, he'd made up his mind that from now on, he'd avoid both girls as well as the Valentine household for good; and that not just for Jodie's benefit, but his own. All he wanted to think about was that place of his somewhere in the mountains away from everyone. If he could hold out, maybe come mid-spring he'd cash and go.

After breakfast, Farliss issued Lucas an old pair of leather wing chaps, then reimbursed the men for their spent ammunition used in the Marsh siege. When Farliss asked him how many rounds he'd expended, he answered twenty.

"Ten kills in twenty rounds. Now that's gettin yer bits worth, boys."

"Two weren't dead," Herron said.

"May as well been," the foreman quipped. "He had to leave somethin for you two."

Herron, shaking his head, sourly rolled his eyes towards Jahns.

Lucas was also thankful that the two of them weren't part of the detail being dispatched. He knew well enough, not that he cared, that he was capable of being more than unlikeable himself, but it didn't change the fact he didn't like them, their attitudes, mouths or smell. If they were to come, more than likely he'd eventually be tempted to do what he'd almost done at the Marsh ranch and shoot both of them; if they didn't bushwhack him first.

Welles, Rocha, Carl, Johnny and Lucas set out, with Johnny and Carl taking turns behind the reins of the wagon. It carried a full load of hay and firewood for stocking the line shacks, along with grub, some tools, two barrels of water and their bedrolls. Lucas hadn't seen a single head of cattle all day and later that afternoon questioned Welles about it. Openly revealing his contempt, Welles looked at Lucas and snorted sounding something like a horse.

"What eez wrong weeth you, Welles?" Rocha remarked grinning. "Are you seek?" He knew already what was bothering Welles, he was just bringing it to light.

"Nothin *you'd* understand."

"Cause I am a Mexeecan, gringo? Mexeecans geet cooter fever, too, you know. Stupeed Mexeecans, that eez."

Johnny and Carl snickered.

"I didn't sleep good's all," Welles retorted. Turning to Lucas he added, "I don't like seein womenfolk upset. It bothers me."

"Believe me, it ain't what yer thinkin, Welles," Lucas said.

Welles nudged his mount a few strides ahead of the others. While his having seen Katie with her arms around Lucas had been most troubling, he was also jealous over the new man's sudden rise in status and favor with the boss and Farliss. Finally, there was his having been invited to sup with the boss's family; a privilege after four years he'd yet to experience himself.

"That red pepper has a hook een heem bad, amigo," Rocha said in a low voice. Baring his usual wide grin, he added, "And heez pleenty sour as peez seeing her weeth her loveeng arms around *you*, amigo."

Johnny and Carl both chuckled into the folds of their arms.

"Well, I had nothin to do with that, and he oughta shake it."

"Love eez funny beezness, amigo."

Lucas nodded, turned and spat.

"The cattle's prob'ly all milled at the north creek for water," Johnny said.

"Sure needs ta rain. I hope this winter's better'n last." Carl said.

Lucas was about to mention how he hadn't seen many acorns on the ground leaving Missouri, suggesting a possible light winter, but thinking better of it, checked himself.

"Weenter weel be here soon, then you weel be wanteeng summer, amigos," Rocha said. Nodding north, he added, "See those beeg clouds?"

Lucas had seen them. They were large, grey and white clouds bunched up like mountains in the sky miles away to the north towards Montana. They looked like the kind of clouds back in Missouri that could spawn twisters that would touch down and cut a swath, flattening everything in their path. As he studied them now, he saw that beneath one large cluster, there hung a blurred curtain of rain.

"Eet does not matter eenyway, Valentine eez claimeeng everytheeng between heem and the north reever."

Welles twisted in his saddle and glared disapprovingly back at Rocha. No one said a word. Lucas partially recalled the boss mentioning something similar himself concerning the cattle and lack of water as the two of them were riding back in to the ranch yesterday. As he further pondered what Rocha said, he began thinking how Welles, like most of the others at the ranch he'd noticed, apparently didn't like the Mexican and seemed to keep a noticeable distance from him. Rocha, however, appeared immune to it and able to laugh it, and them, off. And judging by what he'd just said concerning both the boss's plans and Welles' infatuation over Katie, he obviously didn't let their coolness towards him stop him from voicing his opinions. It was kind of funny and he thought how the Mexican was probably half-full of it. And too, that he probably intentionally kept the others stirred so that they were easier to read. He seemed to be one of those fellows who took everything in stride, never letting much get under his bronze colored skin. On the other hand, he'd also gotten a distinct impression of apathy about him; like bottom line, he really didn't give a hoot about anything. He knew the attitude well, having been there himself; especially during those last couple years with the raiders. The trouble with apathy, though, was that when you had it, it was hard not only motivating yourself, but for anyone else to count you serious as well.

"So what do we do if we see Indians or any of these other cattle outfits?" he asked.

"*Indios* do not have meeny of theez, amigo," Rocha said patting the stock of his rifle.

"If ya see there's more'n a handful of 'em, fire a warnin shot," Johnny said. "Then leave the wagon and skedaddle."

"And cattle outfits," Carl explained, "we tell 'em they're trespassin and to move off east around."

"How far east?"

"Far enough we can't see 'em," Johnny said.

"Eet eez loco. There eez no cattle or water heer now. So who cares?"

Again, Welles twisted in the saddle and frowned sternly back at Rocha.

As though he were strumming the strings on a guitar, Rocha slowly drug his right trigger finger over the belt of cartridges he wore diagonally across his chest. Looking now at Lucas and sounding as though he were being earnest, he said, "I am a Mexeecan... so I am stupeed, amigo." With that he laughed hardily.

Lucas smiled. Rocha wore that belt full of cartridges like it was a shield. It was obviously meant for all eyes to see and it spoke in a language that all men, regardless of where they were from, clearly understood. He considered it likely the reason that none of the other hands had challenged him thus far.

"Guess the boss just wants 'em ta get used to the notion of not trailin through no more," Carl said concerning the free grazers.

Shifting uneasily in his saddle, Johnny grumbled, "I just hope we don't see none. Most don't cotton ta bein told ta shove off."

"*Ay*, do not worry about thees, amigos. That eez why *el pistolero* eez heer."

Over the following week they sauntered north along the east side restocking the line shacks, rounding a few strays and watching for free graze outfits. On the third day, they'd seen a sizeable herd moving north, but were far enough away that they were deemed fine. As they watched them from the distance, Johnny and Carl told Lucas that because it was getting on in the season, it wasn't likely there would be any more ranging through. They also mentioned their being surprised but nonetheless glad, that Farliss had sent the five of them just in case, since normally there were only two or three hands detailed at most.

The four line shacks were spaced about seven to ten miles apart and used in the winter when the hands had to go out to make sure the cattle weren't stranded in snow banks freezing to death and starving. They were nothing but small, shed-sized half-cabin, half-caves whose backs and sides were dug into hillsides for support. Because of the relentless punishment of the wind, only two had slatted-wood doors left at their entrances, and they, having been partially torn from their leather hinges, were almost beyond salvage. At the other two, they re-nailed cowhides over their entrances for doors. Inside the shacks were half-steel drums for stoves with a smokestack and just enough room for two or three men to sleep. But the men said they wouldn't stay in them unless it was raining or snowing because of the spiders, ticks and other vermin. Lucas had noticed the skeletal remains of smaller animals and shed snake's skins in a couple. Alongside each of the shacks, also partially anchored into the earthen slopes, were crude lean-tos which served as wind blocks for the mounts. Because of their rotting lumber and the battering of the wind, most of them needed bracing. Alongside each lean-to, they covered and staked with canvass a stock of hay and firewood for use during the snow months.

One evening, after eating, as they all sat around the campfire, Carl and Johnny got to swapping stories about scraps they'd gotten into when they were younger. Welles, who hadn't said much at all, especially to Lucas, spoke up and said, "Tell 'em why they call you *The Butcher*, Rocha."

"That eez right, amigos, you see these teeth?" Rocha grinned, showing his pearls the way a horse or mule might. "Do not mess weeth these teeth, amigos," he cautioned.

Lucas grinned as Carl and Johnny chuckled.

"One time me and two of my *compadres* were geeteeng drunk een a cantina down by the border and these beeg, fat drunk peeg who was eveen fatter than that Jahns comes een all loud and sees me and my amigos dreenkeeng tequila. And then these beeg peeg, he sneefs een the air and says that greasers steenk."

Rocha paused and slowly shook his head wearing a regretful looking expression as if to convey both the audacity and shame of such a thing. Then, smiling, he continued:

"Eveen that fat drunk's eyes looked like peeg eyes, I mean eet. So eveen though me and my amigos were drunk and deed not want to be een eeny trouble, I say to heem—*So do you, you steenking, fat peeg.* And then that peeg was queek, and he comes rusheeng at me like a crazy hog weeth rabies and I was drunk and before I could know eet, that beeg peeg grabs me and eez squeezeeng the guts out from me. I mean reelly squeezing my guts and I could not do notheeng but bite heem. So I bite heem hard in heez fat neck until he was screameeng and dropped me."

Rocha paused and grinned, proudly flashing his teeth the way a braggart might flex his muscles. Johnny and Carl were laughing hysterically.

"So then he sees the blood on heez hands from heez neck and he grabs me before I could geet away 'cause I fell over a chair or some damn theeng. Only heez got me upside down now and heez tryeeng to squeeze the guts out from me again and I could not do notheeng but bite heem again. So I bite heem again as hard as I can with theez teeth deep in heez fat reebs."

Again, he paused. Johnny and Carl were on their sides howling.

"So then theez peeg, he geets squealeeng again and he drops me on my head, but I was too drunk then to feel eet teel later. Then I seez that peeg's on heez kneez holdeeng heez neck and heez roobs and steel squealeeng like a beeg baby. So me and my amigos are geeteeng out of there away from that crazy peeg, and when we are leaveeng, he eez cryeeng how I beet heem and I told heem, *Peegs are for eateeng,* and you should have seen the look een heez eyes amigos, like he was goeeng to the butcher and goeeng to geet eaten. So do not mess weeth these teeth, amigos."

Lucas couldn't remember laughing so hard before. Meanwhile, Johnny and Carl were doubled-up on the ground in obvious pain. Even Welles couldn't help snickering, and he'd heard the story before. He figured that what made it so funny was watching Rocha and the way he'd told the story, all the while grinning and flashing those big white dangerous chompers of his.

The following day, as they were headed south, about a half-mile east, Lucas and Carl spotted a large herd of cattle being driven north. There must have been two thousand head of longhorns strung out with cowboys riding point, followed by a chuck wagon and swing men along the flanks. He saw that Welles, Rocha and Johnny were converging from their different points towards the herd, then, too, that some of the cowboys from the drive were headed over to meet them. Pulling his spare revolvers from his saddlebags, he shoved them into the front of his gun belt and told Carl, who was in the wagon, "Wait here," and clipping Heston's flanks, charged off to backup the other three.

By the time he'd ridden to where the two parties were assembled, there were six men from the cattle drive present and a couple more who were beating their way over. The oldest of the group, probably the trail boss, was obviously upset about being told to turn and was going on vigorously.

"Sonsabitches, we're already a month behind schedule and there's talk of Sioux trouble east'a here. We've run into one snarl after another all the way from Texas. Hell, it'll be snowin 'afore we reach Montana at this rate." Turning, he spat with conviction, apparently determined to keep his course.

Then, one of the cowboys who'd been curiously eyeing Lucas, spoke up and asked, "Ain't we met somewhere 'afore, mister?"

Lucas squinted blankly at the fellow without responding.

"Sure...was a few winters back, jus north'a Waco," the cowboy said. "That's it, I never forget a face." He appeared quite pleased with himself now and giving it more thought said, "Cain ain't it? Its yer blue scar there 'minded—-"

Before he could say anymore, the fellow beside him leaned over and whispered something to him. Then that same fellow, now wearing a concerned expression and looking at the others, quickly darted a finger over his left eyebrow as though relaying something unspoken to them. Their faces all drew tense and, with a different intent now, seemed to be studying Lucas and his four revolvers, one of which he had his hand set over.

As though he were speaking exclusively to him now, "Well, we're sorry 'bout that," the trail boss said. "We'll get 'em turned, then. Pay no mind to Duke there; he rattles off like that now and again." Swinging his mount he said, "You heard 'em, boys, let's get 'em turned."

Up till then, that trail boss hadn't shown any signs of conceding. After all, if bluff came to show, he had plenty more men and guns than the Valentine crew. But then, all of a sudden, he went real polite and changed his tune without any further protest. Welles and Rocha both looked quizzically at Lucas, then each other. As the group of cowboys beat it back to their herd, they kept checking over their shoulders as if to make sure they weren't being tailed.

"*Ay*, amigo! Soon as they seed you, they sure were happy to turn they cows. I never deed see notheeng like eet."

Welles, who still hadn't warmed up to Lucas, stared curiously at him and said, "Sounded like they knew you, Lucas. What'd that fella call you—-*Cain?*"

"That fella's got loco-mouth. Ya heard what his boss said."

As they watched the outfit turning the herd, Rocha laughed and slapped at his thigh. Johnny, greatly relieved, exhaled deeply and smiled. But Welles didn't. Neither did Lucas. He couldn't believe it. He'd only been to Texas a few times where the raiders had wintered through bad weather, staying in one town or another, and mostly drunk the whole time they had. There was one particular incident though, he could faintly recall. It was the time he'd shot a couple of gamblers who were fixing to draw down on a fellow raider who'd just accused them of cheating. Standing at the bar, he'd just caught a sniff of it from the corner of his eye.

Seeing that one of the sharps was drawing his revolver beneath the table, he'd reacted without hesitation. As he reeled and shot the first, the second came up armed and he shot him, too. That was all he remembered about it. He couldn't remember the names of the towns, nor the saloon girls he'd been with. When the raiders would first ride into a town, they were treated something like heroes, but it wouldn't take long before they were unwelcome. They were a wild and rough bunch who took orders from no one, including the Confederate command. No rules were their rules. Not even the Texas Rangers wanted anything to do with them. Those cowboys must have remembered him from one of those winter visits and, judging by the way they were eyeing him, it was probably where he'd shot those two sharps. Here he was out in the middle of nowhere, yet once again the shadow of his past had found him.

~ 17 ~

Teller and Gore had on previous occasions exhibited roguish tendencies and behavior akin to the likes of Herron and Jahns. Farliss, assured of their eager commitments to the task, as well as its secrecy, dispatched them along the north side of the Frenchman's homestead to keep watch. Once the two younger hands had reached their assigned points, Herron shot the Frenchman as he emerged from his cabin. Then, after Jahns picked-off the Frenchman's wife as she knelt shrieking over her fallen husband, Herron shot the sheepherder's dog and the five cattlemen opened up with their rifles, slaughtering the chaotic flock of frightened and confused sheep. With the sheep all down, Herron and Jahns drug the lifeless bodies of the Frenchman, his wife and dog into the small cabin and proceeded to set it and the small barn on fire. Sitting atop their horses, the five now watched as the tinderbox cabin and barn blazed.

"That wood's as dry as kindlin. It won't be long 'afore there's nothin left," Teller observed.

Admiring the flames that would finish their handiwork, Herron added, "Nothin but ash and scab-herder bone."

It was a perfect day for a bonfire with a cool, relatively mild wind out of the north. It didn't take long for each of the two wooden structures to collapse, succumbing to the ferocious appetite of the fire. In less than half an hour, the roaring flames had settled to a calm burn.

"Let's go, fellas," Farliss said wheeling his mount. "We don't gotta worry none 'bout its gettin outta hand the way the sheep have cropped the grass down to dirt around here."

"It's practically burnt to nothin, anyway," Gore said.

"Hooee!" Jahns hooted. "That was fun. 'Minds me of buff huntin." He admired the small vale, dotted with the carcasses of dead and disabled sheep. "Stupid varmints ain't smart enough 'cept to run in circles."

Attempting to buddy-up with the two older men, "Stupid as that Frenchman," Gore added. For him and Teller, it had been both stimulating and, in their minds, an initiation of sorts; their acceptance into an exclusive pack.

"Just remember what I told ya, boys," Farliss warned again, "Not a word 'bout it ta anyone. Not even 'tween yerselves."

Although sworn to silence, in their opinions they needed no alibi for their crime. To most cattlemen, sheepherders were considered a scourge and as unwelcome on the range as typhoid. They felt the Frenchman and his flock had been more than deserving of eradication and certainly wouldn't be missed.

"When we get in ya gonna ask the boss about the wine, Far?" Jahns asked.

"I said I'd mention it."

Jahns and Herron had found most of a case of wine in the Frenchman's cabin and they, along with Teller and Gore, now carried the liquid plunder in their saddlebags. The clinking of the bottles as they rode, kept their minds on it, whetting their thirsts for spirits. The two older riflemen hadn't drunk alcohol since the night after they'd left Cheyenne, and they were both more than ready. And though they were relatively inexperienced drinkers themselves, so too, were Gore and Teller.

Lucas and the others watched as the dark band of smoke drifted south, painting its soot-black streak along the western sky-line. They'd been preparing to set their last camp before returning to the ranch.

"Somethin's burnin up north, that's for sure," Welles said.

"Prob'ly a field and brush burn," Carl added,

"Dark smoke like that's usually a structure," Lucas said. Throughout the war he'd seen enough buildings burnt to know. He also knew better than spouting off without thinking first. He didn't want to give away anything that could possibly stir anymore curiosity connecting him to his past.

"I'm seek of beans and johnnycakes," Rocha fumed as he was building the campfire.

"Me too," Carl and Johnny simultaneously said.

"Tomorrow night we'll be eatin Wooten's chow," Welles reminded them.

Since they'd set out on the eastern patrol and restocking assignment, the days had steadily become cooler and the nights frosted. Lucas noticed how the wind, which had blown predominantly from the west, was now pushing out of the north, and was much colder. He thought how he'd probably be riding the same line soon enough in the snow. It wasn't a particularly pleasant prospect to entertain, but at least he'd be out in the open spaces and still on the payroll. *Every dollar you make will get you closer to that place in the mountains,* he repeatedly reminded himself. Keeping his sights set on that would bring him through.

Welles stood and tossed another slab of wood onto the fire. "Cain...I mean, Lucas, you're first watch," he said. He had his eyes set and leveled on Lucas, watching for his reaction. Lucas showed none, but let his own eyes bore equally into Welles'. In short time, Welles, feeling himself threatened, blinked and turned away.

That evening, after the others had turned in, Lucas twisted and lit a smoke. He shook his head thinking about Welles. He almost felt sorry for him for allowing himself to be so twisted over Katie. He had it bad. Rocha told him once how he'd heard that when Welles first went to work for Valentine, he and Katie had been sparking with one another. But then, how Katie had gone cool and left Welles pining. He considered how the smitten cowhand's hopes would likely never amount to anything other than disappointment. Then again, the way he'd increasingly hardened himself against him, things between the two of them could very well escalate. That evening he'd seen it clearly in his eyes after he'd tried baiting him with the *Cain* remark. If Welles hadn't been so afraid of him and his revolvers, he probably would've pushed things farther already. He was smart not to and, hopefully, for his own good, would keep it that way.

Augustus Valentine checked the hallway outside his den before closing the door. From the glass faced cabinet he removed two glasses and a crystal decanter of cognac. As he poured the thick mahogany-brown liqueur, he said, "Sit down, Far." Handing the foreman one of the half-filled glasses he offered, "Smoke?"

"Thanks, Augustus," Farliss said. He took the cigar and lit it by the flame also being extended to him.

Valentine eased himself into his oxblood leather chair behind his desk and peering through the curling wisps of cigar smoke, said, "Tell me about it."

"Nothin much to report. It was easy."

"You see anyone else?"

"Nope, I had Gore and Teller stationed along the upper side to keep watch. The scab-herder never knew what hit him, Augustus."

"And the wife?"

"Together forever. We drug 'em both in their shack before settin it."

"What about the sheep?"

"Vulture and cat grub."

"Good. You talk to the boys?"

"Yep, told 'em not to breathe a word to anyone, not even themselves. That reminds me, they found the Frenchman's wine stock and Herron and Jahns was wonderin—-"

"How'd they do?" Valentine interjected. He knew already what Farliss was getting at.

"Well, they obviously got no qualms 'bout killin, that's certain enough. And they're both plenty sharp with rifles. Prob'ly all the buffalo huntin they've done. But we used plenty of cartridges on them mangy sheep."

"That's a small expense that'll weigh out in the long-run, Far." Bringing the cigar to his mouth, Augustus settled back into his chair and took a deep, contemplative draw. Looking beyond the thick plume of smoke, a grin formed slowly at the corners of his mouth.

"So they want to drink the Frenchman's wine, you say."

"Yeah, I was gonna bring you a bottle, but wanted ta run it by ya first."

"Keep it. When are Welles and the others due in?"

"Likely tomorrow, I figure."

"All right, Far. Have the fellas check in their side arms and hold them till morning if they're gonna drink."

"I think it'll be good for 'em, before movin on the JK."

"Yes, I'd like that done as well. But we should wait a little to let the smoke clear, so to speak," Augustus said flashing a sinister grin. "Then I'll file the quit-and-desist claims on all three at once with Stenerson." With that, he took a sip of the rich cognac and another draw off the cigar.

"You had any thoughts on it, Far?" he asked.

"Well, Hard's started work on the brandin iron. Soon as he's done we just gotta put it to use. Still it won't be a cinch like the Frenchman's. It strikes me them JK folks got some peculiar, stubborn pride about 'em and ain't gonna just fold. And the way they're holed secure down in that gulch of theirs, we'll likely need Lucky's talents."

"No, I agree," Valentine said. He leaned forward and reflectively rubbed his chin.

"I just haven't been able to get a good read on him, Far. For a gun hand, he seems to have a lot of...I don't know...conscience about him...I guess."

"Yeah, he strikes me that way, too; a hard read. He's quiet, which is fine, but the way he keeps to himself he's hard to make. Maybe when he sees a couple of the rebranded hides, it'll convince him to throw down on 'em."

"He will if they fire on him first, remember?"

"Yeah, that's fact enough, 'specially after Hard was shot."

"How's Hard getting along, anyway?"

"He seems alright, just sore some's all. It'll be a while before he's ridin saddle. He can swing a jack with his right, but still can't get his left arm in his coat without it bitin 'em."

Augustus Valentine only half-heard what his foreman said concerning Harding's health. He was pondering something else.

"I was thinking Far...maybe you can send Herron and Jahns up ahead and have the two of them fire back towards the rest of you to make Lucas think it's coming from the JK."

Farliss took a drink of the cognac and a pull from the cigar and thought for a moment. "It's an idea that could work, but might be kind'a catchy settin up."

"Think some on it. Next summer will make five and they'll have their deeds in full. They're between us and that river and we're gonna have a lot more thirsty cattle to water come summer. We need them gone and the sooner the better."

They were back in at the ranch and Lucas was unsaddling Heston when he saw Welles and Farliss entering the Valentine house together. He knew what that meant. Soon they'd all know his old handle. He began thinking how the ramblings of that mouthy cowboy from Texas didn't make it or anything else necessarily true. What did he know? Texas was a long ways away and there were probably a hundred men with scars on their foreheads between here and there. After all, that fellow was a complete stranger and it was only his word against his own.

Realizing he was building a defense for himself, he halted it knowing full well that if anyone brought it to light and pressed him over it, he'd just cash out and ride. He wouldn't waste his breath or time denying it or anything else for that matter. Lifting the saddle from Heston's back, he turned and spat.

Lugging the saddle by its horn with bags and tack slung over his shoulder, he started for the barn. Glancing again at the Valentine house, he saw Jodie standing at her window. He was tempted to wave to her, but thinking better of it, didn't. As he was stowing the saddle and tack, he saw a piece of paper lying on the ground. He picked it up and unfolded it. It looked like the design for a cattle brand. He set it on the shelf above the tack hooks. He was tired and wanted to get cleaned up and stretch out over his bunk a spell.

When he entered the bunkhouse, he was surprised to find that Teller, Gore, Jahns and Herron were all still in their bunks. He figured they must have come in late; that, or they'd all come down sick.

Herron and Jahns had told Wooten, the bunkhouse boss, how they'd bought the wine from a traveling drummer they'd come across out on the open spread. They said he had a wagon full of it headed for Cheyenne. When Farliss informed him that he'd cleared it first with the boss, who'd given his permission for the men to drink some, Wooten, absolutely unpleased, turned and spat on the bunkhouse floor and marched off muttering to himself and scratching at his beard.

Herron, Jahns, Teller and Gore had laughed all the more throughout the night as they drank the Frenchman's private stock. But they weren't laughing today as the red wine exacted its revenge and, one after the other, they staggered from the bunkhouse. Lucas could hear Wooten adamantly directing them to go farther out into the yard, away from the buildings to puke.

"They thought they knew him, you say?" Augustus Valentine asked, focusing his attention more closely on Todd Welles.

"You betcha, I mean…yes sir. Oh, they knew him sure enough, Mister Valentine. You should'a seen the looks on their faces once they figured him out. I ain't never seen drovers so willin to turn tail and oblige. Lest off apologize."

"*Cain* was it, ya say?" Farliss asked.

"Yup, Cain's what that fella called him, Far. And he said he knowed him by his blue scar. And judgin by the way they were lookin at him, so did them other wranglers, too."

"What did Lucas have to say about it?" Valentine asked.

"Nary a word. But I'd stake a month's wages he's an outlaw or wanted somewhere, sir."

"All right, Todd. I'm glad you told us, son. But I want you to do me a favor and keep it under your hat for now, till I've had a chance to look further into it. You hear?"

"Yes sir, Mister Valentine, I won't…say nothin I mean."

"How'd the others do?" Farliss asked.

"Well, Lucas ain't any kind'a cattle hand at all, but the others done fine. That is 'cept for Rocha sayin how Mister Valentine and us was clearin everything out 'tween us and the river."

Farliss chuckled uneasily. Augustus did not.

"You did good, son. Now go get yourself something to eat and some rest," Augustus said standing.

"Thanks, Mister Valentine."

Todd Welles left the den pleased with himself that not only had he knocked Lucas' image down a notch with the bosses, but that he'd also pleased the man he still hoped would one day be not only his boss, but his father-in-law too.

"That's interesting," Farliss said after Welles had departed. He was busily twisting one side of his moustache and thinking about Welles' report.

"Well, if Lucky *is* wanted, that oughta play to our hand, wouldn't ya think?"

"Just what I was thinking, Far. If it's true, it evens the slate some, doesn't it? A past is one thing, but a known, bad reputation's another. Outside of his telling me he was from West Virginia, he didn't mention any other specifics. I asked around some back in Cheyenne and no one there knew anything about him, either. I've got a friend who works in St. Louis now who I'll write and see what I can find out about Lucas…or this *Cain* business. I'll draw up a letter tonight and we'll send one of the boys in to town to post it."

"I'll send Todd with it," Farliss said. "He's the only one who won't go gettin side-tracked or drunk and'll get straight back."

"Good idea."

"What ya make of our mouthy Mexican?" Farliss asked.

"Might be he's getting a little too smart for everyone's good about things that don't concern him, Far. But that won't be for much longer."

"He thinks he's smart all right. I'm just tired of his smart-ass mouth," Farliss grumbled. "He's a good cattle hand, but he's gotten ta be a reg'lar pain in the hind side."

Welles had made it to the gate at the end of the walkway in front of the Valentine home when Katie opened the front door and called after him. He stopped and turned as she light-footed it over. His heart went instantly on the gain.

"Hi, Katie."

"Todd, when did you get in?"

"Just a short spot ago."

"I'm glad, Todd. I've wanted to apologize for being short with you the other day."

As Todd recalled their last encounter, she could see the troubling effect it had on him by his pained expression. It was after she'd had her arms around Lucas and when, after he'd asked if she was okay, she'd snapped back telling him to mind his own business.

Just glad that she was speaking with him again now, "That's okay, Katie," he said.

"I was just upset and…friends?"

"Friends."

"Anyway, it's Jodie I was worried about. She's young and I didn't want her getting hurt."

"Hurt? How?"

"Oh nothing, just getting herself involved with—-" Katie stopped short of finishing.

"*Lucas?*" Todd half-said and asked. He recalled how Lucas and Jodie had ridden together that day as they were returning to the ranch. What he couldn't connect though, was how Katie's having her arms around Lucas that evening had to do with her concern for Jodie.

Katie turned and glanced back at Jodie's window. "Perhaps," she said. Returning her attention to him she added, "She hasn't spoken a word to me in two weeks, Todd, and she rarely comes out of her room."

"Cause of...*him*?"

"Just forget all that, Todd."

"Stay away from him is all I can say, Katie."

"Why, what happened out there?"

"Nothin, he's just—-" Todd paused, remembering what her father had just told him about not talking about it.

Taking him by the shirt sleeve, "He's just what, Todd Welles?"

"He just ain't what he seems is all," Todd said. He began gnawing at his lower lip.

"No one is, Todd. What do you mean by that?"

"I've done said too much, Katie. I ain't supposed to talk about it's all."

"I can't believe you'd keep something from *me*, Todd."

Trying to change the subject as well as seize on the opportunity at hand, "Ya wanna maybe go for a ride later, Katie?" he asked.

"I can't, Todd. I promised mother I'd help with some sewing. Another time, okay?"

"Okay, well...see ya later then, Katie."

Katie had lied about helping her mother sew. The only thing she was interested in sowing were the seeds of her own malcontent.

~ 18 ~

Wooten's beef pie and apple cobbler was extremely fine fare after eating beans, bacon and pan bread for ten days. After having his fill, Lucas went out to saddle Heston. There was an old, lone oak tree that stood on a knoll about a mile west of the ranch that he'd come across the night after having supper with the Valentines. Though dark at the time, there'd been enough moonlight that he could just make-out the outline of mountains in the distance, which, at the time, he'd found encouraging. He would go there to the oak now where it would help remind him why he was where he was and doing what he was, as well as rekindle his longing to be where the level earth broke and rose into timber. He was accustomed to being around more trees; forests of trees, and streams, lakes, fish and bountiful game. He also imagined how there would be more shelter there not just from the relentless wind, but also the peering and prying of human eyes.

Nothing further had been said to him about the Texan recognizing and calling him *Cain*. Other than Welles, for the most part the others seemed to be acting as they normally would. While he'd never expected the shadow of his past to find him so soon, he also wasn't overly surprised. Christian Jack the ex-raider was ready in his bones for the solitude of the high ground, but Lucas Jackson, the actor with the real revolvers for hire, would try and hold out on the open range and Valentine ranch hopefully until spring. He reminded himself again how with each month he did, there would be another pack mule loaded with tools and supplies trailing behind him when he set off in search of the place he'd eventually stake as his own.

Seeing that he was preparing to ride, Katie hurried from the house to the barn and suggested her possibly joining him. Without making direct eye contact, he replied, "I ain't really up for company just now." She wasn't prepared for his brusque response and before she could offer a second bid, he'd swung himself into the saddle and rode off. Having failed yet again to garner his attention, she turned and saw Todd Welles, who, as usual, was watching. Although she'd just turned down his offer to go for a ride a few hours earlier and, ignoring what her father had said concerning Lucas' being vital to the ranch's future, she asked, "You still want to ride, Todd?"

"Sure, Katie," he eagerly replied.

As the two of them rode together, she easily warmed up to him in order to find out what it was he wasn't supposed to talk about. Acting as though it was somehow relevant to her understanding Jodie's unfortunate infatuation over Lucas, she promised not to say anything if he told her about it. Then, later that evening, after their ride, Katie further fanned the flames of her discontent by turning to her greatest ally—-her mother.

Geneva Valentine, prideful woman that she was, had raised and instilled in Katie an element of lofty self-esteem, and as well, an unhealthy habit of having most anything she desired; short of her living on her own in Cheyenne, that is. She never spoke about her own childhood, and how her parents were penniless immigrants; an abysmal state she'd finally managed to marry up and away from. Assuaging her dark memories of poverty and fear of being without, she adorned herself with the finest of wardrobes and surrounded herself with objects of opulence; a practice she continued to the point where it was clear that her husband—a modest accountant at the time—would need to secure a more profitable occupation. On the verge of bankruptcy, Augustus at last discovered just such an opportunity. One that promised not only greater income and rewards in the form of sizeable bonuses, but also a secure distance away from bill collectors and the metropolitan shopping venues. Geneva was devastated at the idea of leaving New York and moving to what she called *the backwoods* to live; and where, of all things, they were to oversee a cattle ranch. But, with no other recourse, she packed up her collection of worldly possessions and climbed aboard the trains and stages with her family and migrated. She'd firmly determined, however, that her penchant for finer things would not be lost to uncivilized prairie life. If she was going to live on a cattle ranch, as much as possible, she would have the accustomed comforts of New England life to lessen her estrangement; hence, the underlying reason for her hiring Case, the family butler and cook. Her unyielding resolve in maintaining an affluent lifestyle—much to the continued monetary chagrin of her husband—she'd also imparted in full to her first daughter.

After all, Katie was being groomed for the higher circles of society, which by all indications, were just on the horizon. With the completion now of the Transcontinental Railroad and the expected declaration of Wyoming's statehood—which Cheyenne would certainly be designated the capital of—there would naturally follow some degree of wealth and aristocracy. *Who knows, perhaps your father will one day be governor and you will marry into power and prominence and we, my dear, shall be as founding royalty.* Thus, Geneva had often encouraged Katie. There was even speculation that the Wyoming territory would soon be passing an equal rights provision, giving women the right to vote. Indeed, change *was* just around the corner and, in the meantime, Geneva, in her attempt to prepare Katie for it, had in essence spoiled her, making her not only in many ways similar to, but an even more determined reflection of herself.

Katie went to her mother and complained about Lucas, accusing him of turning Jodie against her and the rest of the family. She told her how she believed he was a bad man, and so much so that he was also appropriately known as *Cain*.

"Cain and Abel, Mother," she further prompted seeing her mother hadn't made the Biblical connection.

Still not detecting the reaction she was hoping for, she said emphatically, "Cain's scar, Mother!"

"Oh, dear," Geneva gasped.

"I simply don't see how or why the security and future of our ranch should rest upon the shoulders of a man who has so much blood on his hands."

Having succeeded in convincing her mother of Lucas' uncertain, but no doubt, nefarious intentions, Geneva in turn, went to her husband, expressing her concern over Jodie.

"She rarely comes out of her room or talks to anyone," she said. "She used to be so outgoing and cheerful. Frankly, Augustus, I am most concerned about her."

She went on to tell him that she believed Jodie's depressed state and behavior was a direct result of Lucas' presence, and that if he would not dismiss the gunman, to at least keep him away from the girls and the ranch proper.

In an attempt to appease his wife, Augustus instructed Farliss to send Lucas and one of the other hands out to patrol and restock the remaining line shacks along the north side of the property.

"What about the JK?" Farliss asked.

"Tell 'em to come back in a week, Far. Those sodbusters will wait a little longer. Besides, the colder it gets, the less likely they'll be ready and expecting it."

The following day, not long after breakfast, Lucas and Rocha set out with the wagon and its load for restocking the line posts on the upper side of the Valentine spread. The farther they went, the stronger the wind gained fighting their progress until they had to pull their bandanas over their faces in order to breathe in the frigid gusts. It was bone-chilling cold and Lucas was grateful for the heavy canvas coat and thick breeches he'd purchased in Cheyenne.

It took all day to reach the first line shack and it was dark by the time they started the fire in its half-drum. Using lit branches, they scoured the shack's ceiling, walls and floor, clearing it of any potential pests. Then they sat and had supper. The small shelter, like the others, was set into the lee of a slope with a lean-to beside it, which offered some shelter from the wind for the three horses. With the fire blazing, it didn't take long for the shack to warm, even though its cowhide door, which they'd also re-hung, billowed in and out like a sail on a ship with the heaving breath of the wind. They'd scarcely spoken to one another all day since the howling bite of the norther had made it almost impossible.

"More coffee, Rocha?" Lucas offered as he poured himself a second cup.

"No, amigo. I weel be out there peeseeng all night een that weend."

Lucas smiled. Rocha was a naturally funny character and he'd come to the conclusion that if he had to be with any of the hands from the ranch, at least the Mexican was entertaining and could keep an easy attitude; even if he wasn't happy about being sent back out the following day after they'd just come in from their east side patrol. He figured Rocha was probably a few years older than himself. While he wasn't as tall, he was solid and wide at his chest and shoulders and definitely appeared capable of handling his own; even without his intimidating cartridge belt.

Lucas set the coffee pot down and for the sake of conversation asked, "Think it'll snow?"

"Eet's too damn cold, *ay*, amigo?"

"Yeah, might be the only good side of that wind."

"You know, Lucky, I reelly thought Far would cash me out for the season after we come een yesterday. He deed after fall round-ups last year."

Lucas eased his backside down onto his saddle facing the fire in the drum and considered what Rocha said about being laid off after their coming in. He'd been half-expecting the same thing after the business with those cowboys from Texas. But bad weather and wind or not, he was just glad to be away from the eyes at the ranch and still on the payroll.

"Might be there ain't enough hands left," he suggested.

"Eeven though there eez not much cattle, you are *right* about that, amigo. All but Far who eez geeteeng too old, the rest are not very good cowhands."

Lucas remembered how yesterday outside the bunkhouse, he'd overheard Wooten talking with Johnny and Carl and telling them that Rocha was probably the best all around cowboy he'd ever seen, and that by their watching him they would learn a lot. When Carl asked where Rocha was from, Wooten didn't say Mexico as Lucas expected he would. Instead, he told them how Farliss, while on a cattle buying trip in Colorado, had recognized the vaquero's skills and, at the time overlooking his nationality, wisely lured him to come to work for him and Augustus.

"And all that Far does now eez have meeteengs weeth the boss eenyway. Carl and Johnny are okay hands, just young eez all. And Hardeeng, he eez slow and shoulder-shot too, now. And Welles, he eez too——." Rocha stalled, hunting the word he wanted. "What you say amigo…no eenterested but when the bosses are watcheeng heem or that red chili pepper Katie eez around?"

"Moody?"

"That eez eet—-*moody*. Heez got too much love beezyness in heez moody *cabeza, si?*" Rocha had pointed at his own head and rolled his eyes dreamily as he'd said it causing Lucas to chuckle at both description and gesture.

"I theenk Far and the boss feel sorry for heem. But the rest are more like gun hands. No offeense to you, Lucky," he said now raising both open hands from his poncho.

Digging in his pocket for his tobacco and rolling papers Lucas asked, "What about them other two?"

"Who, Gore and Teller?"

"Yeah."

"Watch theez two, amigo. Theez got no heart. Snake-blooded, sneaky leetle punk weasels. They think they eez *hombres*. And I bet you they are on the run from sometheeng, too, and Far and the boss know eet and are covereeng for them, too."

Wondering what Rocha was implying and who he might be referring to with his *on the run from something, too* remark, Lucas shot a quick glance over. Rocha was staring blankly at the fire in the drum. *Here it comes*, he told himself expecting at any moment he'd start getting nosy and wanting to know more about him and what it was he was *running from too.*

When he'd finished twisting the cigarette and was bringing it to his mouth to seal, he looked again at Rocha. He was still staring at the fire and Lucas saw that the expression on his face was changed; like perhaps he was deeply concerned over something. Looking away, he prepared to roll a second cigarette. He was pre-rolling them to keep himself occupied and, too, so he wouldn't have to fight doing it outside in the wind tomorrow. He shook tobacco onto the paper and as he started twisting it, glanced again at Rocha to find he was still apparently consumed with whatever it was he was thinking about. He thought how whatever it was it must have been troublesome to overshadow the Mexican's usual easy going demeanor. Then he saw it in Rocha's eyes—-it was the mark. But before he could observe it further, Rocha, as though still experiencing some regret or remorse, began slowly shaking his head from side to side. Still staring at the fire before him, in a low and solemn sounding voice he mumbled aloud as though he were talking to himself:

"That eez why I am up heer een theez cold country, cause me and some of my *compadres* found trouble down een Chihuahua, and when a couple of them was keeled by those damn *Federales,* I come north over the *Rio Bravo* and have not been back home seence." With that, he blinked, disconnecting himself from the fire and, looking towards the ceiling, crossed himself.

Lucas had heard mention of the *Federales* before and assumed they were some Mexican military/police outfit, but wasn't thinking about that or them just now. What was on his mind was the mark he'd caught in Rocha's eyes. The one you get once you've crossed that certain line in life. That glint of guilt reflecting some wrong that lay hidden within. One which, upon detection, often served as an advance warning of potential unfavorable actions a man might be capable of committing. Over the years throughout and following the war, he'd instinctively learned to watch for it as a matter of self-preservation; knowing all the while of course, that he possessed it in full measure himself. And while the mark with most men was not as apparent as he reckoned his own to be, if you looked well enough, it was, without fail, in some measure almost always there. And it didn't come just from killing he'd learned. Life was full of ways a man could gain it, and once they had, they'd likely wear it like a brand forever. It was one of the reasons he tended to be suspicious of most men. In particular, those who, rather than trying to conceal it, without reservation, openly projected it as an instrument of intimidation; which in many cases, he'd also learned, was in fact only a front for masking their actual fears and weaknesses. Herron and Jahns he thought were prime examples; Herron with his unfounded, nevertheless, lofty self-appraisal and projection of himself; and Jahns, all the while insecure himself, trolling indulgently along in the inflated wake of his shallow partner.

He began rolling another smoke and thought how he'd only recognized Rocha's having the mark just before he'd made his voluntary confession. While he wasn't overly concerned, suspicious or passing judgment on him because of it, he did however, consider how if Rocha's friends had been hunted down and killed because of something they'd done south of the border, and that he'd had to come this far in order to escape a similar fate, it must have been for something serious. All this he thought to himself also suspecting there must be some other reason for his unwarranted dredging up of the past as he had.

Breaking the silence, Rocha, looking at him now said, "I do not mean geeteeng een your beezneez Lucky, but I seez some preety good *hombres* weeth *pistolas* and you are as good or eeven better than eeny of these. *Ay* amigo, I used to could see like a hawk and could shoot a rattlesnake between heez eyes while ropeeng mustang through cactus."

Thinking how Rocha had left off directly nosing into his business as he'd expected he was about to, he grinned at his humorous boasting over how well he used to see, shoot and ride.

"You learn to fight like that een that war, Lucky?" Rocha then asked.

There it was, just as he'd been expecting. Fixing his eyes firmly on Rocha's now, he thought how he'd inquired in a casual, unassuming manner. Thinking as to how he might respond, it struck him how here the two of them were, sitting essentially in a hole in the ground, each with their marks, scars and pasts. Then, too, after Rocha's revealing something of his own troubled past, who was he to lie. Saying nothing, yet saying much, he nodded.

"I knew eet, amigo. Did they ever know what they was fighteeng for een that war?"

"North and South...each side mad at the other for one reason or another. Like any other disagreement, I reckon."

"A long and bad deesagreeing no, amigo?"

"Yeah...bad enough. Care for a smoke, Rocha?" he asked changing the topic.

"*Si,* amigo why not."

Lucas handed him a cigarette and drew a lit branch from the fire drum. He held it over for Rocha then used it to light his own.

"*Gracias,*" Rocha said.

Lucas nodded.

"I reely deed theenk by now I'd be headeeng south for Pueblo or Santa Fe and een some cantina with my arms around a *bonita Mexicali señorita.*"

Lucas realized it was Rocha's usual infectious smile, which had for the most part, now returned, that had kept him from recognizing the mark earlier.

"You ever been with a Mexeecan girl, amigo?"

"I can't remember."

"That eez funny, Lucky," Rocha said. He laughed aloud, baring his teeth.

It was true, though. The women he'd been with were as drunk and wild as he was at the time and he didn't remember them or their names, let alone their nationalities. Plying their trade, they'd all been the same to him and all part of the same blur. The only thing he could remember was in the mornings—those when he was able to see—how when he'd depart, the women all had that same lost and vacant look, which always left him with something of an almost hollow feeling inside. As he thought about it now, it caused him to think of how different Jodie was. He wondered if he'd changed so much himself, or if it had just simply been something about her all along.

"*Ay*, amigo, you should try one sometime. You weell never look at a *gringo* girl again. Mexeecan girls' weell make you much happier. Those *gringo* girls love theyselves too much and there eez not enough love left een them for a man."

Lucas was thinking how when Rocha commented about *gringo* women loving themselves too much, the disquieting image of Katie came immediately to mind.

"I'll keep that in mind," he said.

The wind had cleared the clouds from the sky overnight and had let up some by morning. The sun shone piercingly bright in the cold, crisp air. Rocha and Lucas scouted above the thin, frozen trickle of the north creek and rounded up and drove down about twenty scattered head. As they broke ice in the creek so the cattle could drink, Rocha said there were two more line shacks and he figured that after spending two days at each, they'd head back for the ranch.

At the second line shack, they found the remains of a yearling in the lean-to beside it. It looked like it had been drug there by a mountain cat; probably to get out of the wind before consuming it. They found no cattle above the creek there.

On the fifth day, as they approached the last line shack, they watched as an unusually large number of vultures steadily circled an area not far from them to the northwest.

"What ya make of it, Rocha?"

"Don't know, amigo. I never deed see so meeny before. There eez a couple homesteads, and one eez a sheepherder and heez wife. Far and the boss hate heem to hell. We weel ride tomorrow and see, no?"

The following morning there were still as many vultures circling the same area, so they set off to look into it. In the half-frozen mud of the creek bed they picked up multiple sets of wolf tracks that were leading in the same direction they were. When they'd reached the top of one of the rises, they were dumbstruck over what they found. The Frenchman's house and barn was burnt to the ground. There was nothing but two piles of charred black remains, and all around the small hollow were the carcasses of dead sheep being worked by the vultures.

"Maria, mother of Jesus!" Rocha exclaimed.

A ranch fire was one thing, but all the dead sheep, another. They'd been purposely slaughtered. Then Lucas remembered the smoke they'd seen the day before their coming in from the east side patrol.

"Who ya think mighta done it?" he asked.

Without hesitation, Rocha replied, "Ranchers. *Indios* would not waste sheep or bullets like thees."

"What's the nearest ranch?"

"I theenk the JK, up at the reever."

As Lucas scanned the area, he faintly remembered Augustus' mentioning the JK before.

"They a big outfit?" he asked.

"Some homesteaders I theenk eez all I heered. Come on amigo, let's geet a better look."

On their way down the hill, they came to a pit where the Frenchman had been dumping garbage. Things like tin cans and jars that couldn't be disposed of easily by burning. Among the refuse, Lucas noticed a number of green wine bottles that reminded him of the ones he'd seen back at the ranch. The ones Herron and Jahns had bought from the traveling liquor merchant.

"Look, Lucky, *lobos*," Rocha said. He reined his horse and reached for his rifle.

"The boss pays five dollars a hide for these."

Drawing his own Winchester from its scabbard, Lucas saw across the vale there were a number of wolves working what was left of a couple of the dead sheep.

"We weel shoot together, amigo."

"What you think, Rocha…just over a hundred yards?"

"*Si*, Lucky, but eef we geet closer they weel run, no?"

"Yeah, well, I'm no rifleman, but with this wind, I'm gonna try sightin just to the right of the thick of the pack. Between the two of us, on a three count, we might wing somethin."

"Okay amigo, you count when."

As Lucas was about to start the count, two gun shots one on the back of the other cracked across the vale.

"What een the—-" Rocha exclaimed lowering his rifle.

As the wolf pack scurried a short distance away, uncertain of what happened, two that were yelping, hopped and limped awkwardly in circles before going down onto their haunches. A throng of vultures had lifted into the air and, flapping wildly, swooped about the vale.

"Must be eet's those JK hands," Rocha said disappointedly.

Then two riders emerged from the brush thicket at the far end of the ridge that rimmed the north bluff of the hollow. The other wolves dispersed. When the two horsemen reached the downed wolves, they shot them again with pistols then dismounted.

Seeing now as one of the men was pointing towards them, "We've been spotted, Rocha," Lucas said.

"And thees JK eez not going to share. *Vamonos* amigo."

~ 20 ~

The wind had completely let up during the night and a low, solid roof of clouds had formed making the morning air thick and heavy so that it felt like it was on the verge of snowing. Wanting to cover as much ground as they could before it started, it was neither dark nor light when Lucas and Rocha set out for the ranch. The sun never broke through and the snow never fell, and with every mile the breath of the north wind at their backs gradually gained momentum until it eventually felt as though they were being blown along by it. Without stopping, except midway to switch places manning the wagon, they made good time arriving at the ranch late in the afternoon.

Gore, Teller and Welles were splitting firewood behind the barn when they rolled in. It was an endless chore that could never be finished and like most of the domestic duties around the ranch, all of the hands hated it. Tonka, followed by Farliss, came out of the barn and over to greet them.

"How'd it go, boys?" the foreman asked. He was looking at Lucas with his eyes squinted over a hesitant, thin-lipped grin while working his moustache. He had a noticeable way of doing both whenever he thought someone was getting ready to unload a possible bellyaching about something.

Easing himself stiffly from the wagon-box, "Okay, Far," Lucas answered.

"Rocha?" Farliss said wearing the same loaded expression.

"Just peachy, amigo. Cold-ass peachy."

"Yeah, I thought about you two after ya left," Farliss said. "That norther kicked it up a hefty mite, heh? We thought the barn was gonna heel to it. Looks like we might be in for an early winter."

"We got good news for the boss, Far," Rocha said. He was leading his gray roan into the corral and was too tired to act or sound excited.

"Yeah, what's that?"

"Someone done burnt out that sheepherder north of the creek."

"Well I'll be——" Farliss said watching as Lucas led Heston to the corral.

"Well, come on in then and tell the boss 'bout it yerselves. Burnt his place down, ya say?"

"*Si*, to the dirt, amigo. And keeled all heez sheep, too."

"You go on, Rocha," Lucas said. He preferred not to after the way his last visit in the Valentine home turned out.

"Come on in, Lucas," Farliss said, clapping his hand on his shoulder. "Hey, Welles," he called, "You fellas see to this rig. Come on, boys."

From his den window, Augustus watched as Farliss led Lucas and Rocha up the walk to the house. So too, did Katie from her window, and Jodie from hers.

"Come in, men," Augustus said.

Tweaking his eyes in forewarning, Farliss announced, "The fellas got somethin to report, Augustus."

Lucas had never been in Valentine's office and he looked at the Indian artifacts displayed on one of the walls. In the center hung a long, feathered war bonnet surrounded with spears, bows and two quivers full of arrows. It was quite a collection.

"Have a seat, men," Augustus said. Like Farliss, his attention was focused largely on Lucas. There were only two chairs facing the desk and Farliss, standing to the side, motioned for them to sit.

"So, what you got?" Augustus asked.

Turning to Lucas, Rocha began, "What was eet...two days ago, amigo?"

"Yeah, 'bout that," Lucas said.

"We was comeeng up on the last station and we seed the most buzzards we ever deed circleeng over where that sheepherder's place eez, and so the next morneeng me and Lucky rode over and see'd that someone done burnt down heez whole place and shot all heez sheep, too."

Valentine, apparently engrossed with the news, leaned forward attentively folding his arms before him on the desk.

"Burned him out and killed the sheep, you say," he said.

"*Si* amigo, and me and Lucky were feexeeng to shoot some *lobo* when some others shot them first."

"Must be JK," Augustus said looking at his foreman.

"Sounds like it," Farliss said intently working his moustache. "Can't say as I necessarily blame 'em, though."

"Looks like the JK's getting bold these days, wouldn't you say, Far?"

"Yep, certainly does at that."

"Have you shown them the hide?"

"No, they just come in and I wanted ya ta hear about the Frenchman."

"The other day a couple of the hands came across two of our head that had been running ironed with the JK brand." As Augustus paused letting the report sink in, Lucas noted his grave expression. It was the same he'd worn before they'd made their siege against the Marsh outfit. Augustus continued:

"To be sure, we had Wooten butcher one and he's got the hide stretched out against the barn. The brand on the underside's ours." Again he paused, this time looking regretful.

"So, unfortunately, we've been planning to pay the JK a little...overdue visit, if you get my meaning."

Rocha looked at Lucas then back at Valentine and said, "When?"

"Soon as the other fellas get back in from the east side, weather permittin," Farliss answered.

"The sooner the better," Augustus added. With his eyes once more fixed on Lucas, he said, "You men go get yourselves some supper and rest. And good job up there."

"Yeah, boys, Woot's got some tasty beef stew," Farliss said. "I'll be along shortly."

Lucas and Rocha left the house and were at the front gate when Jodie came out the front door behind them. She called to Lucas and he and Rocha both turned. She had a brown paper package tucked beneath her left arm and was making her way barefooted over to them.

"Hello, Rocha," she said, smiling.

Rocha, wearing that big famous smile of his, doffed his sombrero and after deep bowing before her said, *"Buenos Dias, señorita."* Then, turning and casting Lucas a wink he said, "I weel see you een the bunkhouse, amigo."

"He's so funny," Jodie said.

"Yeah, he is. So how ya been, Jodie?"

Jodie looked down at the ground before her, then back up. "Okay," she said. She sounded reluctant while trying to be convincing. "You're growing your beard I see," she added.

Lucas brushed at his chin. "Yeah, it helps fend the wind some."

"That's why I made these for you," she said. She handed him the papered bundle.

"What's this?" he asked taking it from her.

"It's a sweater and boot stockings. I hope you don't mind."

He could see that she was as nervous giving him the gift as he was tentative about receiving it.

"Well, Jodie…thanks. Thank you very much." He was touched by the notion that she'd made something for him and he felt bad that he'd been trying to avoid and not think about her. He felt awkward, but could also tell that she was pleased about giving him the gift and that it obviously meant something to her. Though it was getting dark, they could each tell that the other was going flush.

"You're welcome," she said.

He was trying to think of what next to say.

"I miss smokin with ya," he blurted at length. He felt clumsy and dumb having said it and, looking down, saw her small and delicate feet. Raising his eyes, he dared to gaze once more into hers. They were amazingly meek and gentle, and she was more beautiful than he remembered

"Me, too," she snickered.

"Jodie" Katie called from the doorway, "Mother wants to see you."

"I'm coming," Jodie droned from over her shoulder. She sounded dispirited and Lucas felt sorry for her, having to deal with Katie on a daily basis.

"I hope they fit okay, Lucas. Well—-"

"Thank you again, Jodie," he said and smiled.

Right then the snow began falling and looking up, they both laughed.

After silently watching it fall for a moment she said, "Good night, Lucas." As she turned for the door she added, "Oh and I like your beard."

"Good night, Jodie."

He watched as she disappeared into the house before he turned away. Welles, Gore and Teller were watching from just inside the open barn, but he paid them no mind and looked at the neatly wrapped package in his hands. All he knew was, he'd never felt the touched and flustered-up way he was feeling just then.

After seeing to Heston, he went to the bunkhouse. There, he sat on his bed and carefully untied the bow of string wrapped around the package in his lap. Inside were a thick, handmade, slate-gray wool sweater and an equally thick pair of matching boot stockings. He felt the material with his rough, leathery hands and thought about how long she must have worked making them. He smiled, his heart greatly warmed, realizing how much she must truly like him.

"Oh, amigo, I seed that look before," Rocha said.

Lucas looked over at him. He was lying stretched out over his bunk with his arms folded behind his head. Lucas smiled at him and while wrapping the paper back around the gift, said, "Let's go get some of that beef stew, amigo. I'm starvin."

As he stood, it dawned on him that he'd just called Rocha, *amigo*. It sounded funny, but after receiving Jodie's gift, he felt unusually relaxed and pleased about everything.

"I am too, amigo," Rocha said swinging his legs from his bunk. "But I seed my bed and could hear she was calleeng to me."

Lucas chuckled.

After eating two bowls each of Wooten's beef stew, the two of them stepped outside and over to the side of the barn where the rebranded hide hung stretched and nailed to the wall. Lucas only looked blankly at it and its cross brands for his mind was still on Jodie. From there, he and Rocha headed around the corner to get out of the wind. Standing in the sheltered doorway of the barn, he twisted himself a cigarette and thought about the times he and Jodie had spent together.

"If eet keeps thees snoweeng, I hope we weel not be goeeng to the JK tomorrow," Rocha said.

"Yeah," Lucas said smoking and watching as Jodie's shadow moved against the curtains of her bedroom window. He didn't care just now about re-branded hides, the JK, the snow or anything else. All he could think of was her and her gift. He hadn't been given anything by anyone since he was a boy living with his folks. He felt strangely fine about everything and everything was unusually perfect. Even the mesmerizing way that the snowflakes circled and drifted slowly downward collecting on the ground was perfect.

Back in the bunkhouse, as he was showing Rocha what Jodie made for him, Jahns and Herron came in stomping and brushing off the snow that had collected upon them. They'd been out patrolling the east side.

"Where eez Johnny and Carl?" Rocha asked.

"Prob'ly in a coupl'a whores' beds in Cheyenne 'bout now," Farliss said raising a laugh among the others. "The boss laid 'em off and cashed 'em out the other day. Ya likely won't be seein 'em till next spring."

The snow let up during the night, leaving only a couple frozen inches on the ground in the morning. The north wind had begun howling again. Farliss told the men they wouldn't be leaving for another day, so in the meantime, they were to help Wooten with chores. The hands all moaned as Wooten, happily set them straight to work cleaning and straightening the bunkhouse and outbuildings. While Lucas and Rocha were straightening and cleaning the bunkhouse, Rocha came across Johnny's picture magazine that he always kept under his mattress. He used to spend every evening looking at the depictions of the fancy eastern gals portrayed in it. He was so attached to that magazine it was hard to believe he hadn't thought to pack it with him. Farliss took the magazine from Rocha and said he'd keep it till Johnny came back in the spring.

"Where are you goeeng to keep eet, Far, under your peelow?"

Everyone but Farliss laughed—-Wooten most of all. Farliss glared disapprovingly at Rocha, and shook his head mumbling to himself.

That afternoon, finished with the chores, one after another, each man scrubbed clean his clothes then, hung them to dry from a clothesline they'd strung crisscross from one wall to the other behind the potbellied stove. Later in the evening, Farliss returned from a meeting with Valentine, carrying two bottles of whisky and two decks of playing cards. Both items normally not permitted in the bunkhouse. He said that since most of the hands had been laid off, the boss had agreed to let them share the one bottle and play some cards. The actual reason for it was that before making their move against the JK, Augustus and his foreman thought it would be good for comradery letting them bend the rules a little. After all, there wasn't enough whisky to go around for anyone to get mean-drunk. Farliss told them that if they checked their side arms in, they could play a few hands of *friendly, civilized, penny-stakes poker and have a snort.*

In no time at all, they cleared the table and watched carefully as the foreman, using a shot glass, evenly rationed out one of the bottles between them. He said the second bottle was for himself, Wooten and Harding to split as they played a few hands of their own. Sitting in their long johns while their outer clothes dried, the men played penny stud poker. Even Lucas, presently in an unusually sociable mood, gregariously joined in. He didn't drink his share of the whisky, but kept it sitting beside him. He figured he could use it for collateral if his luck and pocket change didn't hold out; otherwise, he'd just give it to Rocha.

The mood in the bunkhouse was high, and it wasn't long before they could be heard all the way to the Valentine house. There,

Jodie sat in her room smiling and Katie in hers, wearing a frown. She wanted to be amid the boisterous men and join in the fun they were obviously having.

Throughout the evening, Lucas couldn't help but detect the sour disposition coming from Welles and aimed exclusively at him. It wasn't just the unfriendly looks he kept giving him, but also the subtle little verbal digs and snide jabs he kept throwing his way; not to mention his intentionally referring to him once as *Cain*. Lucas had just about had his fill of it when, while he'd paused once to consider his card hand, Welles asked him if he was going to play or wait for his whisky to evaporate. While the other men laughed, Lucas looked squarely at him and said, "What's eatin at you, Welles? If you've got a problem with me, spit it out and quit circlin the damn barn."

Welles had gone too far with his cynical charade and he knew it now. He sat looking gut-punched and speechless at Lucas, who'd called his hand.

Trying to prod him further into a fray with Lucas, Herron teased, "Ya gonna sit there and let him talk to ya like that, Welles?"

Shifting his attention now to the jaw-gaping rifleman Lucas said, "If you're so all fired interested in seein a fight, Herron, I've got one right here for ya."

"I ain't talkin to you, Lucky," Herron snubbed.

"Then you best shut your snake hole or I will."

Herron tensed and dropped his hand to his side, forgetting that Farliss had his gun belt.

"It's a good thing, Herron," Lucas said. "It would have been your last draw."

"All right, fellas break it up," Farliss said. He'd come over and was scooping up the cards.

"Save that vinegar for the JK. All of ya."

Lucas handed Rocha the tin with his share of the whisky and Rocha, famously smiling, said, "*Gracias,* amigo. *Salud,*" and tipped it back.

"That's a damn sinful waste of good liquor," Jahns fumed.

"I just hate when he don't talk American," Gore grumbled.

~ 21 ~

If there was a sun, it was hidden behind thick purple and charcoal-gray clouds that looked like a large ugly bruise covering the whole of the Wyoming territory. And the frozen air hung tensely suspended, suggesting that at any moment its menacing dark ceiling might give way releasing its gathering burden of rain or snow, or both in the dreaded form of sleet.

Augustus Valentine and his foreman's attempt to bring the men together into a more unified outfit by letting them drink a little whisky and play bunkhouse poker, had for the most part failed. Although they rode with a seemingly common objective, they did so in three distinctly frigid groups, each as unpredictable as the weather.

At point, Farliss rode abnormally quiet in deep contemplation over how to orchestrate the move against the JK. He was particularly concerned with the fact that there could be no survivors, therefore making it most difficult to know how to involve both Lucas and Rocha. In the back of his mind, he was also worried about how much they really knew about the Frenchman and if they'd been able to put any of it together. As much as he wanted to utilize Lucas' fighting skills in the hopes of its being a quick and clean sweep the way it had with the Marsh outfit, a confrontation with him was the last thing he wanted to face.

On the rewards side, he considered what awaited him at the end of next year's cattle season; the sizeable payoff that would come once he and Augustus had finished clearing the land between the ranch and the river. In light of that, he envisioned himself lounging leisurely in some high-class bordello parlor and surrounding himself by beautiful women.

Welles rode purposely close to Farliss, keeping a healthy distance from Lucas. He was still skittish after his near-miss altercation with the gunman the evening before. His unfounded, Katie-compelled dislike of Lucas was every bit as tangled as the dream he hopelessly fostered in his infatuation over a woman whom—he could not bring himself to see—he could never have.

In the second group rode Herron and Jahns side by side and closely shadowed by their two apprentices, Teller and Gore. Last night's confrontation with Lucas' gauntlet-grounding challenge with Herron, still freshly festered in all of their minds. Herron's pride in particular had been trimmed to the quick. Both Teller and Gore had overheard him earlier out in the barn swearing to Jahns how, when the moment was right, he intended to permanently settle the score between himself and Lucas. Like their reckless idols, the two younger gunmen also disliked the solitary gun hand. He was a one-man show who not only garnered the favor and respect of both Farliss and the boss, but had apparently also become good friends with Rocha, the Mexican foreigner whom they thoroughly disliked. They both eagerly anticipated the impending showdown between Lucas and Herron to come.

However distant, dreamy or unlikely, Rocha and Lucas each entertained more pleasant thoughts as they rode together.

Mexico's sunnier and warmer disposition with her beautiful, dark-haired, brown-eyed daughters, colorful fiestas and lively cantinas, beckoned to her free-spirited, wandering son. Rocha missed the land of his birth and longed for the day when he'd finally return to her.

Like his homesick friend, Lucas gave the upcoming JK confrontation little forethought. He knew that it, like the countless other skirmishes he'd ridden into, would present itself soon enough and when its time was at hand. Rather, just now, Jodie occupied his thoughts. He was wearing the sweater and stockings she'd made for him and they fit perfectly, as if she'd woven them around his person. Wearing the sweater, he could almost feel her arms wrapped around him as she had the time not so long ago when they shared the ride to the ranch together on Heston. He even found himself allowing himself to entertain the unlikely notion of her being with him in the mountains at the cabin he'd built so many times in his mind. He wasn't accustomed to entertaining such dreaminess, but found it most difficult to resist.

As the group rode on, the still air was steadily replaced by the wind which, by the time they'd reached the old Marsh ranch, had regained its full breath and was once again blowing with an arctic bite out of the north. They found the empty ranch where Lucas and Heston had made their previous decisive midnight charge just as they'd left it a few weeks earlier. They would stay there the night and in the morning, move on the JK; which, Lucas learned, was some ten to fifteen miles farther north and just beyond what was once the Frenchman's place.

With their horses in the barn, secured from the weather, they kept a fire going in the cabin's stove, made coffee and ate the cornbread and stew that Wooten sent with them. The wind blustered and moaned eerily, sounding like haunted spirits as it passed through every slat and seam of the old run-down cabin. Occasionally, an extremely violent gust would blast the house and they'd all look up expecting the roof might be torn away.

After eating, Lucas asked Farliss about what they might expect to encounter at the JK.

"Just another immigrant sodbuster and his brother," he said. Turning, he spat in the corner with disgust adding, "They both staked claims side by side, and ever since, there's been every blasted one of their relatives migratin like barn rats from Europe and movin in."

Other than his having said they were a number of European family immigrants, the foreman's answer had not been strategically beneficial with respect to their mission. It was apparent though, that the Kansan did not like them. Lucas tried conjuring what little he knew himself. For one, he'd seen the underside of the rebranded hide and that it was the Valentine brand, while on its outer side it had been recently, as well as poorly, altered to that of the JK. Short of their starving to death, the idea of family homesteaders rustling cattle from an outfit the size of Valentine's seemed inconceivable. But then there'd also been the torching of the Frenchman's place and, more than likely, not only the slaughter of his sheep, but probably the man and his wife as well. Finally, he and Rocha had seen the two suspected JK men shooting the wolves. In light of those factors, he concluded that the homesteaders could well be every bit as armed, aggressive and prepared as the Marsh outfit had been.

"What about women and kids?" he asked.

"Till we get in there and deal with the rustlers, I don't know," Farliss snapped. He was certainly annoyed discussing it, and more irritable than Lucas had ever seen him before.

"Ya ain't goin soft on us are ya, Lucky?" Herron asked. A wolfish sneer cracked at the corners of his mouth as he eyed Lucas. He was playing with his revolver, idly spinning the chamber barrel and listening to its *click- click- click*.

Dismissing the rifleman, Lucas glanced at Rocha. He could tell by his eyes there was something on his mind. The two of them had come to know each other well enough that just a look from one to the other could say a lot. Deciding to step out and take a break from present company, he knelt on one knee beside his bedroll to roll a smoke. As he did, he listened to the ghostly moan and howl of the wind. It sounded other worldly, like something one might expect to hear churning from the bowels of a deep cavern; that, or haunted battlefield graveyards at night. When he'd finished twisting the cigarette, he cast Rocha a nod and stepped out of the cabin. The wind was blustering wildly and he turned up the collar of his coat. A couple minutes later, Rocha joined him and the two strolled across the yard towards the barn.

"I don't know, Rocha. Between you and me, somethin don't feel right."

"*Si*, amigo, rustlers are one theeng, but not weemeen and *bambinos*. And theez Marsh place eez *espeluzante*."

Lucas looked at him about to ask what it was he'd said, but seeing him shiver as though he were attempting to shake something unnatural from himself, figured it probably meant something akin to being spooky or creepy.

"I know gun support's what Valentine hired me for, and much as I hate sayin it, I'm thinkin maybe he should'a brought the law in on it."

"*Ay*, and we should be south of Colorado now where eets much warmer and you and me dreenkeng *cerveza*, no, amigo?"

Lucas smiled at him as he turned his back to the wind. Sheltering the cigarette inside his coat, he struck a lucifer and lit it.

Seeing the brief flare across the yard through the wavy pane of window glass, Farliss motioned with a flip of his hand for Jahns and Herron to join him. Welles, Teller and Gore were sitting and staring at the flames in the woodstove.

"Listen up, fellas," Farliss said in a hushed voice. "Me and the boss figured Lucas and Rocha might be gettin cold feet on this thing. So we thought by sendin the two of you out early before anyone wakes, you could ride up along the east side of the JK. There's a stand of trees there, this side of the river, where you can take cover from. Then, when you see the rest of us comin, I want you to send a couple rounds over our heads to make it look like it's comin from JK hands. Then, both of ya swing wide along the river and close in on the homestead from the west as we hit 'em from the east."

Wearing a puzzled expression, Jahns turned and looked at Herron whose lower jaw hung open revealing his own lack of comprehension.

"Me and the boss figure that'll stir Lucas and Rocha into fightin," Farliss added.

"We don't need them just to take care of a bunch of filthy sod busters," Herron said.

"Keep yer voice low," Farliss warned. "No, we want Lucky's guns just in case those immigrants are dug in expectin it. They might well be on alert after the Frenchman's, ya know. Then—-" he started, but paused, looking back across the room. His hand shook as he worked his moustache.

"Then what?" Herron impatiently asked.

"Once we get things under hand, I'm gonna send 'em both up to scout the river. Then, we want the two of you to follow 'em and...finish 'em off." Farliss watched as both men seized breath, their backs going rigid and their eyes widening with renewed interest.

"You mean...kill 'em?" Jahns asked.

"Yes. Now the boss says he'll split half the wages they both got comin between the three of us, and that's a fair reward."

"Yeah, now you're talkin sense, Far," Jahns exclaimed. Turning to Herron he smiled hungrily darting his tongue over his lips as though he were preparing to feast.

"Shush down!" Farliss quietly cautioned. "So, what ya think?"

"You betcha, Far. I've been wantin a crack at that prima donna," Herron snarled.

"And that mouthy greaser friend of his, too," Jahns added.

Herron, now suspiciously scrutinizing Farliss asked, "You wouldn't be joshin' us would you, Far?"

"I ain't joshin' you, Herron," Farliss sternly replied insinuating he didn't care much for the suggestion. "I'm dead serious. Just remember, we don't finish 'em off till we get 'em away from Welles and the others and don't need 'em anymore. The less who know about it, the better. We'll report that the two JK fellas who fired on us from the trees earlier bushwhacked 'em down along the river."

~ 22 ~

In the morning, Farliss told the others that he'd sent Jahns and Herron ahead to scout and cover the west side of the JK. Between the constant racket of the wind against the cabin and his having slept soundly wrapped in the pleasant fragrance of Jodie, which still lingered on the sweater he'd worn as he slept, Lucas hadn't heard them leaving. As the six of them now left the cabin headed for their mounts in the barn, there was a faint snowfall being blown sideways by the north wind.

Trying to encourage and motivate himself, as well as them, "This weather's our edge, boys," Farliss said. "They're not likely to be expectin us in it."

After saddling Heston and before mounting, Lucas drew tight the chin cord of his hat beneath his jowls and pulled his bandana up to just below his eyes. Though reasonably warm in his new canvass coat, breeches and wool sweater, his lips and nostrils were blistered, and his cheekbones raw from windburn. Unlike the damp winters in Missouri, which were nevertheless, cold, winter in Wyoming with its accursed wind that never stopped had a different bone-chilling dryness about it.

With nothing but absolute whiteness about them and their riding straight into the windblown snow so that sight was even further diminished, trying to gauge how much ground they'd covered was difficult. It wasn't until they'd crossed the frozen north creek that he and Rocha had followed before discovering the burnt out Frenchman's place that Lucas recognized how far they'd come. Finally, about an hour and a half later, Farliss waved his arm in a wide circle over his head and pointed to the northwest, apparently indicating they were nearing the JK.

Lucas searched the direction he'd pointed through squinted eyes but could see no sign of anything. Just then, Heston jerked his head and whinnied. Then came the muffled report of two gunshots, the second right on the back of the first, signaling more than one shooter. He instinctively bent forward clipping Heston to a charge passing Teller, Gore, Welles and Farliss. Yanking down his bandana, he shoved the reins in his mouth, bit hard and drew both revolvers. He could just make out a stand of trees growing visible in the blurred-white distance straight ahead. He figured more than likely it was where the snipers were firing from. Glancing quickly behind him, he saw that Rocha was following but that Farliss and the others had broken left.

Heston thundered forward and Lucas, with revolvers ready, scoured the tree line expecting a second volley and hoping to catch sign of the muzzle flashes. The icy, windblown snow stung his eyes making them tear up, so that he had to keep blinking them clear in order to see. Fortunately, there was no more gunfire. It was odd there'd only been the two single rounds. There were only the sounds of his and Rocha's mounts blowing hard clouds of steamed breath and their pounding hooves as they crushed through the frozen layer of ground snow. As they charged into the forward line of the trees, he expected to catch fire at any moment from either side, but there was nothing; only spinning snow devils and the furious howl of the wind whipping at the branches of the trees overhead. Slowing Heston, Rocha rode past. A moment later, from the backside of the shallow wood he called, "Tracks, amigo, two riders!"

There were two sets of freshly punched horse tracks in the crusted snow leading west from the grove of trees. As he and Rocha set out cautiously following them, they studied the surroundings. There was the churning river below the steep cutbank to their right. To their left was a dense thicket of shrubs interspersed with scrub oak, pine and cottonwood trees. Then they heard the deadened cracking of multiple gunshots being fired from over the ridge beyond the thicket of shrubs. Leaving the tracks and ridge, they headed for an opening in the brushwood. Winding their way in, one behind the other, they came to a partial clearing where they could just see over and beyond the bramble.

Herron and Jahns were firing from horseback onto one of the two cabins while, some fifty yards to the left, Farliss, Teller and Gore had surrounded and were firing on the other. Lucas continued working Heston through the dense tangle only to find that they'd reached an impasse and could proceed no further. The undergrowth, although not high, was too thick to traverse even for a man on foot. As Rocha began backing his mount so they could turn, Lucas saw that there were now men with their hands over their heads emerging from both cabins.

"They're surrendering, Rocha," he called. Rocha stopped and stood in his stirrups to see.

Herron and Jahns had dismounted and with guns raised, were milling the surrendered homesteaders in the open area of the yard. Lucas saw as Farliss was directing Gore and Teller each to one of the cabins. Then he noticed two bodies lying face down on the ground not far from the barn. He thought they might have been the snipers who'd fired on them from the grove earlier and who, in all likelihood, had probably run unexpectedly into Herron and Jahns as the two riflemen were moving in from the west. Now he saw that Welles was exiting the barn. Apparently the situation was already well in hand.

"Hey, Far!" Rocha shouted.

Twisting in his saddle, the foreman spotted the two of them amid the wooded bank. Pivoting his mount, he started up towards them. When he'd gone as far as he could, he shouted across the bramble, "Go search this north side for anymore of 'em."

"We peeked up tracks, Far," Rocha yelled back. Swinging his mount, he said, "Come on, amigo."

They left the brushwood and picked up the top of the ridge and continued following the hoof tracks in the hard snow. They'd only gone a few minutes when, despite the rush of the river below and the blast of wind against their faces, Rocha raised his hand and halted. He motioned having heard something and pointed towards the brush line. Then, Lucas thought he heard something, too. It sounded almost like coyote crying. With revolvers drawn, they dismounted and securely wrapped their reins around the trunk of a swaying pine. Working their way on foot into the hedge-row and out of the immediate brunt of the wind, the sound was growing clearer.

"Eet eez a baby, amigo," Rocha said.

Just beyond the tree and brush line, they found freshly hewn tree boughs lying scattered about on the snow. Then they saw amid the severed boughs that there were human tracks which they then discovered, led to a wooden hatch set an angle against the side of an earthen berm. It looked to be some kind of root cellar. As they approached, it was obvious that Rocha was right, and that it was the sound of at least one infant crying. With both revolvers ready, Lucas nodded and Rocha yanked open the hatch.

Huddled tightly together in the small cave and staring at them in utter terror, were four women, two of whom held crying babies. There were also a number of young children. There was a dimly lit lantern on the ground before them and by its flickering light Lucas could see they were wearing bedding clothes beneath the blankets they held wrapped about them.

"What we do weeth these, Lucky?"

"I think they're better off in there…for now, anyway," Lucas said. "But don't say anything about it to the others, all right?"

Rocha nodded.

Bringing a finger to his mouth, Lucas gave an urgent *shhhh!* Rocha did the same. Then they closed the hatch and recovered it with the cut boughs, leaving it concealed better than they'd found it. Scanning the immediate area, they saw in the dense tangle of brushwood there was a narrow foot path that apparently led to the homesteads. But it was much too tight for leading horses. Not wanting to draw any unnecessary attention to the location of the cellar, they decided that for the time being, it would be best if they returned to their mounts.

Now, back on the open ridge, the wind was gusting even more violently than before. The frozen snow stung their faces like the points of pine needles. As they were mounting their restless horses, there was the barely audible report of a single gunshot coming from the direction of the homestead cabins. Sitting still in their saddles, backs and shoulders hunched against the wind, they looked at one another, each uncertain as to what they should do next. Then, a minute later, there was the popping report of another round being discharged.

"Let's go see what's going on, Rocha. We'll tell 'em we searched and the area's clear."

"My hands and feet are freezeeng, amigo."

"Yeah, mine too."

As they headed back, all the while searching for an accessible route through the brushwood, there was the continued, odd and intermittent discharge of single shots. There would be a couple minutes pause, followed by a single shot, then another pause, followed by another shot.

When they'd reached an opening that looked like it might possibly lead through, they followed it until they'd come to a clearing where they could see the cabins below. From there, they saw that all of the men who'd surrendered earlier were now lying face down on the ground. Squinting to better focus through the flurry of snow, Lucas saw that some of the bodies appeared to have what looked to be arrows standing in them. He nudged Heston on.

Farliss, having seen them approaching, cut a quick path up to meet them.

"You find anything?" he asked. He'd positioned himself and his mount sideways on the path blocking both it and the scene below. He was extremely tense and wouldn't sit still and kept frantically looking about.

"Just some old tracks headed up alongside the river's all," Lucas replied.

"What eez goeeng on, Far?" Rocha asked. He was stretching to look around him at the scene below.

"Just coverin our tracks, fellas. Insurance is all. Anyone comes 'round they'll think it was Cheyenne done it."

"I thought they surrendered," Lucas said.

"Two of 'em had pistols and tried usin 'em. Look, all of 'em said the same thing 'bout their womenfolk and kids bein gone. I want you fellas to go down and scout along the river for 'em just ta be sure."

"Gone…where?" Lucas asked.

"They said Denver, but never mind that now. Just go check along the river, anyway."

Lucas looked hard at Farliss, but he was fidgety and wouldn't make direct eye contact. Beyond the aching pain of his face, feet and hands, he tried to fathom what Farliss said concerning the homesteaders having guns and the business with the arrows and insurance. But it was all too much to negotiate presently. All he could think about was that the women and children he was sending them to locate were for the most part safe where they were.

"Okay, Far. But we've done scouted this whole wooded side along here and there's no one. Come on, Rocha, we'll check the river."

"When we geeteeng out of here, Far? I am wet and freezeeng to death."

"We're fixin to pull out soon as we mop up and you fellas finish scoutin the river."

Once more out in the open at the top of the ridge, the wind was ripping with so much force they had to ride folded forward holding their hat cords tight to their necks. Shards of frozen snow were being lifted from the ground and blasted like shot from a scatter gun. It was difficult to breathe, let alone talk, and they both shivered as they forced their reluctant mounts once again into the brunt of the storm. Earlier, they'd seen a banked access that sloped gradually down to the river and they headed for it. Once they'd dropped down the cutbank alongside the racing river, they turned their backs to the wind and rode slowly side by side.

Shouting to be heard over the howling wind and rush of the river, Rocha said, "When we geet een, I am casheeng out, amigo and queeteeng."

"If it weren't for those women and kids——" Lucas started saying but left off as his jaw had begun quaking too hard to continue.

"Collect your stake and we weel ride south, amigo."

As Lucas nodded, he had the strange sensation of having been there beside the river before.

"*Jesucristo y María, esto es del Diablo!*"

"What?" Lucas said.

"Jesus and Mary. Thees eez of the Devil."

~ 23 ~

Shouting against the wind, Jahns said, "They ain't movin, they're dead, Herron." Then, turning stiffly as though some part of him might by any sudden movement snap off, he hobbled on his deadened feet towards the wailing grove of wind-whipped trees. He could no longer distinguish individual parts of himself; all was but one large aching throughout and he was rapidly succumbing.

Herron shivered uncontrollably as he ratcheted and raised the rifle again, trying to seat its stock to his numb shoulder. He had to force his senseless finger into the trigger guard and it was all he could do to tighten his jaw from quaking as he pumped a second round into one of the two bodies lying beside the river below. Ratcheting the rifle once more, he awkwardly raised it to sight and drew in as deep a frigid breath as he could tolerate. Then, when he'd exhaled, emptying himself completely of it and was the most steadied, he squeezed, shooting the other.

The elevated cutbank had served as a perfect vantage point looking down onto the backs of Lucas and Rocha. The nearest river access was an incline too far upstream to venture now in the raging blizzard, otherwise he and Jahns would have gone down after the two men's guns and scattered mounts. But it was out of the question now. Frozen range snow that had been swept up and gathered for miles, was being hurled like glass nails blasting against his face. As he staggered back towards the wind-lashed stand of trees, through the white blur of driven snow he could just make out Jahns struggling to steady his agitated mount. Both horses had been tethered to the skeletons of the swaying cottonwoods and as they fought to free themselves from the howling tempest, they'd cinched tight the now frozen knots in their reins. With fingers useless, the two riflemen were unable to pick apart the knotted leather straps and had to cut the reins free.

Once he'd managed to pull himself up into the saddle, Herron shouted, "They're dead."

Frosted to the marrow and crimson-faced from the concentration of freezing blood, the remaining six Valentine men fell back into the shelter of the old Marsh cabin. Once they'd finally managed to get the fire in the stove stoked, it hurt to be near it. They would wind up staying there at the cabin two nights before the driving ground blizzard would let up enough for them to return to the Valentine ranch.

Farliss had developed a bad throat and could barely speak. He, Herron, Jahns and Welles were all suffering colds with all the usual symptoms of coughing and snotty, runny noses. Although not as directly affected by the weather itself, the spirits of Teller and Gore had been considerably shaken as well. That was because of the coldblooded initiations they'd undergone at the JK. Both Herron and Jahns had insisted they take a personal hand in the executions, having each kill one of the surrendered homestead men. Shooting someone point-blank who was lying face down on the ground at your feet while sobbing and begging for mercy, wasn't the same as seeing it done from a distance the way the Frenchman and his wife were killed. Nevertheless, by the time they were back in at the home ranch, the reason given for their abnormally subdued demeanors was accredited to the savage blizzard.

Before the questioning and execution of the surrendered JK boys and men, Farliss had sent Welles off to search the southwest corner of the property for any signs of the missing women and children. Therefore, he hadn't witnessed the heinous massacre and was told the same lie that Farliss told Lucas and Rocha; that being that two of the surrendered men had guns which they'd tried using.

As for Augustus Valentine's initial concern over the absent women and children, Farliss personally assured him that all of the German men said the same thing concerning their whereabouts, even after watching each of the other men in their family being individually questioned then shot. *Nein, fraulein und kinder gehen Denver,* is what they'd each professed, he reported. He didn't bother to mention how four of the seven had wept bitterly, begging for their lives as they, too, repeated the same thing before being executed.

"We checked every inch of those cabins and their barn from the floors and walls to their roofs for any places where they might have been holed up, Augustus. Even the two ground lockers outside. One a vegetable keep and the other where they stored their salted meat. We checked the whole surroundings and the woods and the river, and they ain't there."

Augustus Valentine did not bother to summon any mental vision of the homestead slaughter; he only saw the potential figures amassing at the accounting ledger's bottom line; those eventual black ink results that would spell not only profit, but his continued good standing with the investors. Power-wielding men whose financial support and political influence he also envisioned having in the future. Yes, he'd clearly seen the threatening financial forecast looming on the horizon, as well as the opportunity to avoid its potential outcome. And he'd chosen to cross that threshold and seize upon it. Now the chess pieces were lining up perfectly. Soon the newly acquired riverfront properties would be filed under both his and Farliss' names and by the end of the upcoming cattle season, the proven benefits of the new holdings would compel the investors to purchase the valuable properties from them. They would be must-have acquisitions and the transactions would be made at a fair, yet favorable sum for both parties. All of that, in his ultimate strategy, was just another of the necessary stepping stones being set on the path to his greater ambition of one day obtaining political office. It was all manifest destiny and might-makes-right; the hard law of nature. The dead were the insignificant and unavoidable results incurred in the building of a greater purpose and legacy. Success was attained and measured with money and, without it, everything else was pointless.

"We've only one left, Far, and that'll be easier than the Frenchman. Lucas served his purpose, and besides, there was no guarantee we could trust him or what liabilities his past might have eventually presented; and for that matter, Rocha and his careless mouth, either. He's replaceable. We'll wait towards spring and finish up before the new herd arrives. By end of next summer, our stock will be watered and grazed cash-fat. Better years are ahead my friend."

While Farliss was yet under the weather, he sat with a very satisfied grin etched beneath his red, sniffling nose. He envisioned himself stepping from a train car onto the warm, golden streets of San Francisco, holding in each of his hands a valise full of cash, insuring the future of his greatly anticipated retirement. He'd be living in the finest hotels, dining on the finest fare, and being attended to by the fairest of female creatures.

Geneva Valentine was particularly pleased that her husband was no longer as beleaguered over the ranch's financial uncertainties. Especially since, according to him, by this time next year they should finally be living in Cheyenne. Besides the many fine things she longed to add to her collection of possessions, none was more eagerly anticipated than her long awaited dream of having her own private castle built in which to properly display them, her and her daughters.

Katie was pleased as well. Not only for the encouraging prospects concerning the family's financial future, but because Lucas was no longer an annoying reminder of her slighted pride. Although she knew not the actual circumstances behind his demise, she considered his end a matter of justice having been perfectly well served.

With the exception of Case and Wooten who had no particular reasons for disliking Lucas, and, who knew nothing about Valentine and Farliss' ultimate plans, all of the other hands in the bunkhouse were satisfied with his death as well. They'd quite honestly all been afraid of him. He was standoffish and never really tried to fit in with them. And, too, with the lingering *Cain* issue, there'd been plenty of suspicious speculation concerning him and his mysterious past. Then of course, based on what Katie had insinuated about Lucas' having hurt Jodie, Welles certainly hadn't liked him. But without doubt, the most pleased of all in the bunkhouse were Herron and Jahns. They'd be evenly splitting with Farliss, half of what Lucas and Rocha had earned. Plus, there was the personal satisfaction they each enjoyed, having been the ones to finally eliminate the two disliked hands. On top of all that, they were also each fully aware of their timing being in hand with the aggressively expanding Valentine operation. Now, being fully embedded, they were counting on it to provide the two of them security and position for some time to come. They knew it was highly unlikely that Valentine or Farliss would be cutting them free any time soon; not with the implicating cards they held. Their game hands were pat.

Finally, there was an end to Rocha. He was only a Mexican, making him in their minds, a creature of lesser breeding and standing. His failure to accept and yield to his proper social status among them was a generally shared point of detraction. As entertaining as he could be at times, in their minds it had only been his amusing way of gaining their acceptance. An acceptance which they'd granted out of their gracious tolerance, but had suffered long enough.

Jodie was the only one at the ranch distraught. And while she inwardly refused to believe it was actually so, she mourned deeply and wept for both Lucas and Rocha; praying through tears to the God she'd learned about when she was younger attending school in the east, that somehow, none of it was true. Against all reason, she alone clung to that thread of hope and, once again, began keeping to herself in her room, rarely coming out or speaking.

On one occasion, attempting to console her, Katie expressed her sentiments, but added, "After all, Jodie, he dealt in death, and now, death has dealt unto him." She'd even gone on to add how Jodie would eventually get over him and find a more suitable friend. Jodie promptly directed Katie out of the bedroom, shut the door and cast herself onto her bed and sobbed.

PART TWO

~ 24 ~

I *once was lost, but now am found. Was blind, but now I see...*
Surfacing partially to consciousness, Lucas could hear his
mother's rich singing. His eyelids fluttered weakly.

"Mama?" he muttered.

"Heaven's sakes look who's come to join us," she said.

Glad of his being home and hearing the happy ring of her
voice he smiled parting his eyes. But the light was yet too bright
and so they closed. As she laid her open hand gently upon his forehead, he contentedly drifted off. Two young boys rose from their
breakfast table and came over to the bedside.

"Is he awake, Mama?" the younger boy asked.

"He was a mite, Samuel, but's done gone back ta sleep agin.
Least he ain't feverin no more. Guess the Lord ain't done with 'em
yet, unh-unh."

The older of the two boys frowned at the stranger lying in his
and his brother's bed. He'd been hoping he would pass and not
wake at all.

Noting the disappointment on his face, the woman asked,
"Nathan, why you so angry child, 'bout what the Lord's done?"

In a way that made him appear much older than his twelve
years, he looked at her and said, "He's one of them, Mama—-a
killer." With that, he turned and headed towards the door of the
cabin. There, he snatched a coat from the wall, pulled it on and
dashed out leaving the door open behind him. A draft of cold air
rushed in, filling the small, warm home.

"Close that door, Samuel," the woman said shaking her head.

"Is he a killer, Mama?" Samuel asked after he'd closed the
door. He was seven and didn't understand such things.

"Son, whatever he is, he's a child'a God, too. And God brought
'em through that storm to our step. If we didn't help 'em then we'd
be same as killers wouldn't we?"

Samuel looked at the smiling stranger asleep in the bed he and his big brother had always shared and nodding said, "Unh-huh."

"That man woke, Pa," Nathan glumly reported as he entered the barn.

His father was forking fresh straw into a crowded stall that now held along with their draft horse, the stranger's large dark mount. The thin-framed man slowly straightened his long back and, looking at his son, coughed a couple of times.

"That's good, son," he said when he was able.

Again openly revealing his consternation, Nathan grumbled, "Why's it good, Pa?"

His father rested against the handle of the pitchfork and coughed again. He was sick and every time he coughed, it shook his whole being, inside and out. "Cause—-" he started his breath catching as he succumbed to another cough. "Cause when he's mended, he'll be able to go back where he's from. He might have hisself a family. Maybe a boy your age. Toss a couple of them sugar beets in ta them hogs, son."

Nathan growled within as he carelessly slung the sugar beets into the winter hog pen.

"What if he's one of them...those men?"

"That's 'tween him and God, son."

Nathan growled again. He was angry. Life for their family had been hard enough without being frightened and threatened by the armed and bandana wearing men, who would occasionally appear on the hill and from there, sit on their horses looking down upon them. It was obvious they were trying to frighten them off their own land. And now, in his mind, he was certain that the heavily armed stranger who'd come to their home in the blizzard—shot or not—was one of those same men. And the fact that he was now lying in his own bed, was a further injustice in every possible way he could imagine. Then, on top of all that, since the blizzard, his father's condition had grown worse. More than ever he felt tempted to curse God for the hardships his family suffered. He wondered how there could even be such a thing as a god.

The woman dipped a rag into a bowl of cool water, lightly wrung it out and began dabbing the stranger's forehead, cheeks and closed eyelids. She'd been doing it repeatedly over the past few days, trying to keep the fever in check.

"Heston," he stirred and mumbled.

"What's he sayin, Mama?" Samuel asked.

"I don't know, son. But he's sure a smilin, ain't he?"

Smiling himself, "Unh-huh," Samuel said.

Lucas could feel Heston's large wet muzzle nudging at his face, trying to wake him. Again he tried opening his eyes, but there was only the piercing light forcing them shut.

As the woman continued dabbing his face with the wet cloth, again he mumbled, "Heston."

"What's yer name, son?" she asked.

He moved his swollen tongue slowly over his parched and wind-blistered lips and thought it odd her asking.

"Christian, Mama," he said just loud enough to be heard.

"Christian's a fine name," she said. "Ain't ya hungry, none? Ya needs ta eat somethin so ya can get mended, Christian." Whether he understood her yet or not, she was just glad that he'd at last awakened. Outside of some fevered and fitful outbursts, he'd been unconscious going on four days since his arriving in the storm.

Lucas' stomach told him he was hungry as the aroma of food triggered his sense of smell. "Yes, ma'am," he mumbled.

"Here, try sippin a touch'a this."

Supporting his head with one hand, she tipped the warm cup of light chicken broth to his cracked lips. The broth smelled and tasted good and one small taste after another became small sips, and sips, small swallows. At the same time, his eyes had parted a little and were beginning to adapt to the light shining through the small window before him. Life and his senses were slowly returning. He saw a blurred and darkened face beside him, but was yet too far away to clearly consider anything. Before the woman had lowered his head back onto the makeshift pillow, he was again fast asleep.

It was later that same day when he awoke next. The sun had passed and the sky outside had gone overcast so that there wasn't the piercing light shining through the window. As he lay there in a haze yet unaware of what had happened or even who he truly was, the inner fog began to dissipate and the sense of his self-being gradually returned. Upon recognizing that he wasn't in the bunk-house, he tried placing the surroundings. They weren't familiar and neither were the voices he heard speaking behind him. Nothing was familiar and he wondered how he'd come to be there—wherever it was he was. There was a small window pane edged with ice, set in a mud-chinked, plank board wall before him which he also couldn't recall having ever seen. Beyond its glass was empty gray sky. He tried sitting up and felt a sharp pain in his right side and upper left leg and hip.

What's happened and where's Heston?

Hadn't he just been nudging him awake? Or had he only been dreaming it?

As he lay there confused and trying to further gather his bearings, it came back to him that Heston *had* awakened him. And that it had been dark and very windy and cold. Then he remembered that he and Rocha had both been…*asleep? Asleep and beside… a river?*

Then it struck him like a shotgun blast, jarring his senses and shocking every nerve in his being. There'd been blood! Frozen blood crusted over Rocha's face and eyes. His recollection of the alarming image made him dizzy and, trembling, he broke instantly into a dank sweat. Panting hard now, he tried swallowing, but could not. His tongue was swollen to the roof of his mouth and his throat was as dry as ash.

What's happened?
Am I dreaming?
Is Rocha really dead?
Am…I?

There was the deep throbbing in his left upper leg again suggesting he wasn't dead, but quite painfully alive. Blinking nervously, he drew and held his breath and, bracing himself against the pain of movement, trembled as he lifted his head and the unfamiliar blanket and looked down. He was wearing some sort of nightgown and his gun belt was missing. He slowly drew up the skirt of the gown and saw that his left thigh was bandaged and that the dressing was stained red with blood. Staggered, he eased back his addled head and sank into the realization that he, too, like Rocha, must have been shot; and judging by the biting pain just now in his right shoulder and side, there as well. Yes, whatever was left of him was very much painfully alive.

Trying to think clearly beyond the pain now coursing throughout his entire body, he remembered his falling and spinning. Of being caught up in the dark tunnel of some kind of twister and falling helplessly through a dark, empty and silent void with nothing to take hold of and helpless to stop the endless falling and spinning—falling and spinning.

What's happened and where am I?

While pain, confusion and questions permeated his blurred consciousness, he was again jolted to see there was a Negro boy standing nearby.

"Hello," the boy said.

Lucas stared wide-eyed in absolute shock wondering: *Is this—-? Am I...in hell?*

"Mama, Daddy, the man's awake," the boy called.

Then a tall, slender Negro man with a short bushy beard streaked with gray and wearing overalls that had many patches on them, followed by an equally tall Negro woman wearing a flour sack dress and a cloth rag on her head appeared. They all had very dark faces and concerned, white eyes.

"Hello," the Negro man said.

Lucas could only manage a choked grunt in response.

"My name's Joshua Smith and this is my wife, Grace," the man said. "And this here's our youngest son, Samuel."

Lucas blinked and blinked again, but the vision of the Negroes remained unchanged. He was dumbfounded and wondered again if it weren't all just a nightmare he was having.

"Grace sez yer name's Christian. It's a fine name there yer folks give ya," the man said.

"Unh-huh," the smiling woman said.

Lucas could only gawk at the Negro people who somehow knew his real name. Then he thought about his parents. He remembered his being home and his mother being there and that she'd been singing. Or had it only been a memory? It was extremely disturbing to him that not only was he in pain, no doubt from having been shot, but somehow also somewhere in the company of Negroes. He felt panicked, but was barely able to fathom his dilemma, let alone do anything about it. His thoughts turned instinctively to the prospect of his escaping.

"Heston?" he muttered.

The man and woman looked curiously at one another.

Finally, the man said, "Your hoss?"

Blinking his eyes, Lucas nodded.

"Oh, he's okay," the man said smiling. "He's out in the barn there, 'long wid Ol Mare. Sure's a fine lookin hoss, too."

Lucas nodded, somewhat relieved over Heston's at least being nearby and apparently okay. Then, in a dry, throaty whisper he asked, "My guns?"

The man turned to the woman, now clutching at his arm, and Lucas saw as their smiles turned worrisome.

"I got 'em put up safe 'till you're well enough and ready ta go," the man said. Then he bent forward and began coughing.

When he'd finished, the woman told him and the boy, "Go and eat your suppers afore it gets cold and let Mister Christian wake hisself up." Speaking to him now she said, "I'll be back in but a mite, unh huh."

A moment later, through the frantic spinning of his mind, he could hear the man behind him offering a supper blessing and in particular, the words:

"...and we thank ya for Mister Christian's health and comin 'round, Lord. In the name of Jesus. Amen."

Again he thought about his mother and father. They, too, used to give thanks before meals.

Soon, the woman returned and, bending over him, put her hand beneath his head and said as she lifted, "Let's get ya tilted up some so's ya can try eatin and gettin yerself mended."

He stared nervously at her as she bunched a rolled blanket behind his head. It hurt being jostled, but he kept his lips sealed so that he barely emitted a sound. Then the woman set a stool beside the bed and sat down.

"Ya wanna try sippin some water first afore ya try eatin?" she asked.

He didn't respond and tried keeping his heavy eyes trained on her as best he could. She brought the cup of water to his mouth, and though tempted to refuse it, he knew he needed it. He tried lifting his hands to take it from her, but was seized by a painful stabbing in his right side causing him to yelp sharply.

"I'll help ya with it, Christian," she said.

She brought the cup closer and tilted it to his mouth. The water was good, wet and cool. After he'd sipped and swallowed more of it, she offered him a spoon of something that smelled inviting. Again he was tempted to refuse it, but once more found himself unable. The one sense of his that wasn't impaired was his sense of smell, and it told him now that what the woman was offering was good. He'd always trusted his nose implicitly when it came to food. As the Negro woman patiently proceeded to spoon-feed the warm chicken broth to him, and he took it, he never stopped staring nervously at her.

"I know ya doesn't likes bein here none," she said. "I kin see it in yer eyes plain, unh-huh. But Good Lord knows, Christian, we ain't done no wrong to ya, unh-unh." Then, turning, she looked towards the small window in the wall and he heard her saying quietly to herself, "I s'pose it's all but a testin, Lord."

"Testin?" he muttered.

Turning back to him, she smiled and said, "I s'pose for us all, unh-huh."

"Testin…what?"

"Why, doin for others as we'd want 'em doin us, nat'rally."

Although extremely unusual, it was clear the Negro woman was trying to help him. And his being tense and on edge had been quickly wearing on what little strength he had. He couldn't hold up any longer and it felt better letting go. As he lay back, he thought how she reminded him some of his own mother. Not in the way she looked or spoke, but by what she'd said about *doin unto others.* Yes, he ate the soup because he was hungry and knew she was right about his needing it if he was going to heal. But he could only smell not taste it over his present state and confusion; that, and the thought of his being fed by a Negro. Thoroughly exhausted, he surrendered to sleep.

~ 25 ~

It was better his being asleep, which he did a lot of. Awake, his whole body it seemed throbbed with pain that dominated consciousness. Then, by his having wounds on both sides, he was restricted to lying on his back. The added pain and amount of effort it took trying to move, even in order to relieve himself, was excruciating and exhausting. Thankfully, afterwards, it usually put him right back under. Time was no longer divided or measured by days or nights, just one long drawn out and helpless existence between waking, pain and sleep.

Then there were the times when his body and mind would not submit to sleep, and he was able only to lie there awake in his pain and frustration till he was even nearer the brink of madness. Times when had he had his revolvers, he seriously might have ended it all. Times when, unconcerned whether or not he might be heard by his hosts, he'd sometimes growl and curse fiercely, sounding as though he were demon-possessed; and that not just because of his physical state, but the seemingly senseless absurdity of life as a whole.

Following one particularly ugly eruption, he overheard the following conversation of the Smiths who were at their supper table behind him.

"Why's he do that, Daddy?" Samuel, the youngest boy sounding frightened asked.

"He's hurtin, son, he cain't help it," his father explained.

"I hate it and him," Nathan, the older boy said.

"Nathan!" his mother exclaimed. "You jes 'member yerself, that yer mouth speaks from the 'bundance of yer heart."

"That's right," his father said. "Now eat and let Mister Christian rest."

Amid the simmering dross of his self-pity and anger, Lucas remembered having heard something similar before concerning the *mouth speaking of the abundance of the heart.* No sooner had he begun to reflect on it then it clearly came to him how it had been his own mother who'd said it. Then, too, the circumstances in which she had.

There'd been a neighbor who had an extremely bad temper and who would sometimes get drunk and go into a rage cursing and shouting at his wife and children. He remembered how it had always been unsettling for both him and his parents. And just as Samuel just had, he'd asked his parents the same thing—*Why's he do that?* To which his father replied—*He's a lost man without any self-control, son.* That was when his mother said, *The mouth speaks of the abundance of the heart,* which, at the time, he'd been too young to understand.

As he lay there now, mindful of both it and his own abundant bitterness, he felt the strong urge to break welling up within him. But before surrendering himself to it, he succumbed to sleep. And while there were many times afterwards when he felt like letting himself go and openly cursing aloud, he never did, keeping it always inside to himself or at least beneath his breath. Nevertheless, even then, he'd still find himself not only reminded of both the Smith's and his own parents' explanations for it, but subsequently being convicted by it as well.

While the permanent scowl etched on Lucas' face was initially seen by the Smiths as being due to his physical suffering, eventually Joshua and Grace could tell it was also a reflection of his reservations over their being Negro. But with time and their continued compassion and patience with him, in spite of his bitterness, he gradually began developing an appreciation of the fact that he was extremely fortunate to be alive at all. And that, he knew, was only because of his unlikely hosts—-Negro or not. Except for Nathan, the oldest boy, whom it was obvious, thoroughly disliked him, the concept of the willingness of the Smiths to bring in a white stranger and to care for him as they had and were, was nothing short of amazing. This was a hard and unforgiving world and having as little as the Smiths had, for them to put an injured white stranger up in their small, already cramped cabin, was equally inexplicable.

And not only did they feed him and redress his bandages, but they even emptied his slop basin, which for him, invalid or not, was unbearably humbling. The non-begrudging way in which Grace and Joshua waited upon him without the least show of displeasure, he found not just uncanny, but, once again, extremely self-convicting. He often wondered what it mattered to them whether or not he lived. The only answer he could come up with was that it had something to do with their religion, which it was obvious, they had; and that, not just because of their giving thanks before meals, but because they would also occasionally read aloud from the Bible. They didn't need him. Outside of Heston and his revolvers, he had nothing of value to offer in exchange. He was incapacitated and nothing short of an added burden for them. Like a lame and injured horse; and those you just shoot and put down.

Equally strange was the Smiths never once asking him how it was he'd come to be shot in the first place. And though he'd initially resented the fact that they somehow knew his real name, which he came to assume they'd learned while he was semi-unconscious, they'd never even asked him what his full name was—-that, or where he was from.

All in all, as much as he hated his situation, he was being humbled. As a result, he found himself with no choice but to face the fact that he actually had no legitimate or truly personal reasons for disliking Negroes. He realized that the basis for his adopted prejudice had been purely the result of his acquaintance with most of the other bushwhackers and raiders; men who generally fostered an intense dislike for Negroes considering them only fit to be slaves and to serve the white man. He'd started riding with the bushwhackers before the War Between the States was declared, and that to avenge the death of his father, not because of the slavery issue. Although he was aware that it was a major point of contention between the two warring sides, he'd never really seriously considered or questioned the matter. He'd simply and ignorantly accepted it. Therefore, and, too, in light of Grace and Joshua's kindness towards himself, his baseless grounds for disliking Negroes simply because of the color of their skin was no longer a viable part of him. In fact, it strongly reminded him of the way most of the Valentine crew had disliked Rocha because of his being Mexican.

While having come to terms with himself over his unfounded racial prejudice, there was, however, a smoldering caldron of venom brewing within him. One expressly reserved for all of those responsible for what happened to himself and Rocha. It was a hellish hatred fueling a consuming desire for revenge; one even greater than that which had possessed him after his father's murder. He spent many waking hours relishing his eventual retaliation and, at times, even found it almost intoxicating; so much so that it even seemed to lessen the presence of his physical pain. He'd concluded that starting with Valentine himself, each of the men who'd ridden in the siege against the JK would pay with their lives. His desire to kill them became the single motivating reason not only for him to recover, but bothering to live at all, and he anxiously awaited its fulfillment.

Not only had he been shot twice, but he also had a sizeable gash on the right side of his scalp, no doubt from his being thrown from Heston. Once, while she was examining the wound, which she'd stitched closed when he'd first arrived and was unconscious, Grace noted that the hair might not grow back there. But he wasn't concerned about that, nor the fact that there were now four more scars on his person to go with the blue one above his left eyebrow. Inside and out, his body and soul was a growing collection of scars.

The first shot had struck and tore clean through the lateral muscle beside his right shoulder blade and exited along his rib cage just below his armpit. A few inches left and it probably would have hit his lung or heart and killed him. The force of the slug had no doubt thrown him headlong onto the rocks, and either the impact of the bullet itself or the fall had rendered him unconscious. He couldn't remember either. But there was now a purple and green bruising over half of his back and the whole of his right side. The second bullet, the one Grace and Joshua dug out of his upper left, rear thigh, had entered the part of his leg that would have been inaccessible had he still been in the saddle. That area, too, was dark and discolored with bruising. He was certain that soon afterwards, Heston had awakened him, and that then, although his recollection of it was hazy, he'd discovered Rocha's being dead. Beyond that, he couldn't recall his own climbing back into the saddle, let alone Heston's somehow finding his way through the blizzard to the Smith's doorstep. Grace repeatedly contended that only an angel of the Lord could have delivered him. *Your mama or someone must'a been a prayin mighty for ya, Christian, unh-huh,* she'd say.

Each time she did, it would remind him of the time when the raiders were near his hometown and he'd gone to visit his mother only to discover that she'd recently passed. And he could hear the pastor's wife saying what a gentle and God-fearing woman his mother had been. That and how she'd prayed for him daily. And she would have, too. She loved the church and her religion and could never have too much of it. As a child he'd figured church was simply what older folks did. Then he remembered how, while riding with the raiders, he'd come to the conclusion that the reason people had religion and went to church was because of their getting old and facing the inevitable certainty of their mortality. He'd always reckoned the business of God and religion as being similar to snake oil; that and a salve for their fear of dying.

Bit by bit, lying there on his back in bed, he began to connect the fractured pieces and troubling images leading up to his and Rocha's bushwhacking. Peculiar and disturbing things that needed understood. Like the pushing of arrows into dead men and Farliss' odd explanation about *insurance*; a hidden door to a darkened pit where children cried and frightened women stared; the charred remnants of a cabin surrounded by vultures and wolves devouring the countless carcasses of slaughtered sheep; the same empty green wine bottles lying scattered about the Frenchman's and Valentine ranch; all the brands and rebrands on hides, inside and out, and even sketched onto paper. Finally, there was Farliss' sending him and Rocha to search the river for the JK women and children. It had all begun taking its ugly shape and making its sinister sense. And he felt absolutely stupid for having not seen through Valentine's intentions from the start, as well as for allowing himself to be so easily deceived. How had he let his normal vigilance slip? If he'd kept his senses, Rocha would still be alive and he wouldn't be in the state he was in now. He'd been duped by Valentine and his Kansan foreman because he'd been too busy trying to conceal his own identity and past, all the while making money and dreaming of that imaginary place of his somewhere in the mountains. *Yes,* he repeatedly chided himself, *you'd completely let your guard down.*

No—-he and Rocha hadn't fit in with Valentine's scheme the way the other snakes did. So the ranchers had attempted to eliminate them both by shooting them in the back. While he could still hear Augustus saying things at the hotel in Cheyenne like *having the law on his side* and *the right to protect what was his,* he believed now that he'd been planning it all even then. That way he wouldn't have to worry about his or Rocha's witness to his crimes, let alone pay them what they had coming. On that count, since he'd had no use for money while on the range, he'd even entrusted Valentine to hold in his safe his remaining funds from Cheyenne.

The more he thought about it all, the angrier it made him. Only his witnessing of his father's senseless murder came close to the intense desire for revenge that gripped him now. While his ultimate goal then had been to kill the Kansas jayhawker known as The Grim Chieftain, riding with the raiders had never afforded him the opportunity and satisfaction of confronting him face on. But the Valentine crew would not be so fortunate as to escape his wrath. Looking back now, in comparison to Valentine, he had to admit that at least the jayhawker had openly declared his heinous intentions, while Valentine conducted his murderous campaign from behind a mask of deceit, making the Grim Chieftain's role almost pale in contrast. Yes, Valentine and his ploy going even so far as to use his own daughter as a distraction.

Yes, Jodie. He couldn't summon her name or face without feeling the pang of it. And he found it particularly disturbing trying to understand and separate her role in it all. How does someone spend their whole life beneath the same roof with another person without knowing the kind of person they really are, or, at least what they're actually up to? Had that been why she tended not to take sides on issues? That or to ask him potentially compromising questions, knowing all along that in the end it wouldn't matter? Could it actually be possible she hadn't known? Besides Rocha, she'd been the only seemingly bright spot in his memory. Then, too, in light of that, if he hadn't been so consumed with his thoughts over her during those last couple days leading up to their moving against the JK, he might have seen what was about to happen and been able to prevent it. As upsetting as it was, on that account he couldn't bring himself to actually blame her, only himself. And while he'd never intentionally hurt her, he *was* going to kill her father. This was war, and there was no place in it for things like relationships. War and killing was what he understood and was good at. It was futile thinking of his no longer fighting or being about it and its business. No matter where he went, there was war. War and killing. It was his fate. He was made, quartered and marked for it.

Finally, as if he needed anything more to feed the flames of his wrath, there was one other thing which had lodged itself firmly in his craw. Something perhaps insignificant by contrast, but which, nevertheless, he couldn't quite spit free or swallow. It festered like an annoying foxtail sticker that won't be found to be removed from a boot and it nettled and gnawed at him continuously. It was the loss of his new hat. So new it hadn't even been broken in. He figured it probably blown or washed clear to Missouri by now.

~ 26 ~

Todd Welles often stood alone and from the shadows, watched uncomfortably as Katie and Herron carried on laughing and flirting and having a grand time with one another. He didn't like the cocky and boisterous gun hand and could not understand what it was Katie saw in him. And he was certain Herron didn't care for her the genuine way he did. What he could not bring himself to see, however, was how much alike the two of them were.

Todd was in love with Katie and had been ever since he first came to work at the ranch, and the two of them had, for a season, been close to one another; sneaking around the barn, necking and kissing close. Then, for some reason, right after he'd told her he wanted to marry her, she quit coming out to meet him. He'd always figured it was because her mother had found out and put a stop to it. Geneva Valentine never seemed to think highly of him or any of the other working hands for that matter. Nevertheless, he'd vowed to himself that he would wait until the day she and her family realized that the two of them were meant to be together, no matter how long it took. Therefore, in the meantime, as difficult as it was, keeping true to his personal pledge, he steadfastly remained devoted to her. What he thought was genuine, dedicated love waiting to be recognized and fulfilled Katie considered a pitifully childish and amusing infatuation. And albeit at times annoying—entertaining and ennobling nonetheless.

It was a cold December night, and unable to sleep, Todd restlessly tossed from side to side in his bunk. As he lay there thinking about Katie and his latest ploy for regaining her favor, he observed Herron leaving the bunkhouse, likely headed for the privy. A little later, he heard the familiar sound of the Valentine's front gate clang shut. Standing on his bunk, he unhooked and raised the hinged cover over the high window and saw Katie in the light of the full moon, making her way across the yard towards the barn.

She had a shawl wrapped about her shoulders and as it flapped in the wind, he saw she was cradling what looked to be a bottle to her breast. His first thought was to go out to see her, but not wanting to make her angry by his being overly persistent, decided against it and laid back down on his bunk.

She'd spoken little more than a word or two to him since they'd last rode together and he'd shared with her how Lucas had been recognized by the Texans. Mindful of his latest plan—-*Stick to your guns,* he coached himself. He'd recently begun the new strategy of trying to act unconcerned about her whenever she was about. And he really thought he was on to something with it because it fit hand in hand with the other notion he'd also had of late. Thinking that it might somehow, one day help impress her, he'd also begun going off away from the ranch to perfect his pistol draw and marksmanship.

As he lay there pondering his predicament, he was overcome with a spirit of devil-may-care and, for the moment disregarding his strategy of acting unconcerned, decided to go out and see her anyway. He could simply say that he'd suspected something was going on and that wanting to protect her father's interest had come to check it out. Confident with the excuse, he sprang up, spun his legs from the bed, and pulled on his breeches and boots. Out of recent habit, as well as also wanting to appear manly and prepared, he strapped on his gun belt, grabbed his jacket, and left the snoring bunkhouse.

Through the brisk night air, he headed across the yard for the barn. When he heard a trace of Katie's familiar laughter coming from inside, he smiled. Seeing that the barn door was slightly ajar, he quietly eased it open and poked his head in and looked about. There was the faint glow of lantern light coming from one of the stalls at the far back corner.

I bet that pregnant cat's givin birth, he thought to himself. *And Katie's probably with her and has warm milk in that bottle for the kittens.*

Stepping past the barn door, he took a few steps towards the light then balked. Katie had made another sound, but he couldn't discern if it was a giggle or sound of distress. A sudden, strong urge to turn and leave rushed over him, but he ignored it, compelled by his overwhelming determination. He was tired of being timid. He had to see her. He'd come this far now and maybe it was the moment he'd so long awaited. As he was thinking these things, he recalled what Lucas had said to him the night when they'd played poker—*Stop circlin the damn barn.*

Todd Welles drew a deep breath and stepped boldly into the opening of the corner stall and there, saw that Katie was naked and straddling Herron who was also naked and lying on his back beneath her.

Katie, startled by Todd's presence, gasped and dove straight for her clothing which lay strewn between her and Todd's feet.

Todd, equally stunned, stood in a shocked stupor unable to think or move. Then, realizing Herron was reaching towards his gun belt, he instinctively went for his side arm also. Seeing as he was about to draw, Herron swung and fired first, hitting Todd square in the chest with so much force that it lifted him from his feet, causing him to discharge his half-drawn revolver.

The searing hot lead from Todd's gun ripped along the right side of Katie's face, grazing the flesh from the corner of her mouth to the back of her jaw and sent her sprawling senseless across the stall onto her back.

Todd Welles lay dead, shot through the heart.

Katie lay naked and quaking in the straw.

Herron had just pulled on his breeches before Harding and Wooten rushed in.

In self-defense he exclaimed, "He drew on me first . . . and he shot Katie!"

The blacksmith and bunkhouse foreman wrapped a saddle blanket about Katie and as they were about to lift her, Farliss arrived. The three of them rushed her to the Valentine house. Everyone at the ranch had been awakened by the gunfire and there was no more sleeping to be had that night as Katie came to and total hysteria reigned. Her blood curdling shrieking went on throughout much of the night until she'd finally howled herself unconscious.

Todd Welles had worked four years for Augustus Valentine, and though the boss had liked him, he now paid no concern over his sudden and unlikely death. He was however, because of what happened to Katie, angrier than anyone, including Geneva, had ever seen him before. He wanted to fire Herron on the spot. But Farliss finally settled him down, allowing him to more clearly consider the sensitivity of the situation.

In his deep, calm voice, the foreman rehearsed the score, which Augustus knew only too well already. Nevertheless, he reminded him of how much Herron knew about what they'd been doing, as well as the resulting and, therefore, incriminating casualties. That and what could possibly result from a hasty decision now on their parts. He went on to diplomatically suggest that it might be best to send both Herron and Jahns to Cheyenne for the remainder of the winter, then, have them return in the spring to assist with the last homestead.

"We can station 'em up at one of the empty posts, then. That way they won't be around to cause any more trouble or grief for Geneva and Katie."

Having somewhat regained his self-composure, Augustus contemplated Farliss' advice and suggestion. His foreman was right and he knew it. That was why he was his right-arm man. He was smart, as well as a good cattleman and ramrod. And more than all of that, he was now an equally invested partner having an interest of his own also to protect.

"Speakin of Cheyenne, think maybe we oughta take Katie in ta see the doc?"

"No, Far, Geneva, Case and Jodie are looking after her. Case says it's a flesh wound and that it's not deep, and that it'll heal here just as quickly as it will in town. And besides, Katie won't hear of it. She doesn't want anyone outside the family seeing her like that. And of course that's why Geneva's so upset. She's worried she'll wear scarring from it. You know how women are about those things. But whether Katie knows it or not, she's fortunate. It could have been a whole lot worse."

"Yep, it certainly could'a at that."

Standing now with his back to his foreman, Augustus Valentine stared blankly beyond his den window. The night sky was ashen by the approaching dawn. It had been an extremely tense, nerve racking and exhausting night. He drew a deep, labored breath and slowly exhaled himself to resignation.

"All right, Far. Go tell them, then."

"It's a sight of a thing, I know——" Farliss began then paused, "but maybe we oughta pay 'em what they got comin so they don't go gettin all pissy an runnin at the mouth. If ya know what I mean."

Outside the bunkhouse, Farliss took Herron and Jahns aside. He explained to them that it would be best if they took some time off to let the boss and the situation simmer some.

"Hell, Far, Welles slapped leather first. What was I supposed to do...let the stupid hayseed shoot me?"

"What's done is done, Herron. Now you fellas take your pay and have a good time in Cheyenne. And like I said, come back end'a winter. We got one last homestead ta deal with and after that, there'll be plenty more work."

"Another homesteader, ya say?" Jahns queried.

"Yeah, an African sodbuster and his tribe," Farliss said.

Looking at one another, Jahns and Herron both drew sadistic grins.

"Ya know we'll be here for that," Herron said.

After counting out and handing them each their stakes, Farliss said, "All right, boys, just remember...not a word about what's been goin on, ya hear?"

"Got ya, Far. Come on, Jahns, I've been ready for a town visit anyway."

The following afternoon when she learned of Todd's death, Katie exclaimed, "Good!" Then she growled, "If he weren't dead, I swear I'd kill him myself."

Jodie shuddered at both the malicious remark as well as the demonic look in Katie's eyes when she'd said it.

Katie then adamantly insisted that Todd's remains be disposed of as far from the ranch as possible. She didn't know that Wooten had already taken the body in the morning and buried it.

It soon became apparent that the daughter Augustus Valentine once called his *Fiery Little Mustang*, might now be more appropriately called his *Furious Bitter Storm*. If she'd been demanding before, she was absolutely unappeasable now. She began throwing tantrums daily and snapping viciously at her family and Case with unbridled profanity. Her fits of rage could often be heard all the way from the barn and bunkhouse. Then, when she'd learned that Herron had left for Cheyenne, once again the injustice was too much to bear and in an especially agitated state, she all but destroyed everything in her bedroom. Though she and Herron's relationship had been purely physical, she now cursed him as well for having not been shot also.

No matter how many hours she and Geneva sat before the mirror trying to mask her blemished cheek, it would not be concealed. Her dreams of one day being the beautiful woman at the center of the circles of the social elite had been forever dashed. In that same light, she also absolutely refused to allow anyone outside of the immediate household to see her; and even then, in the privacy of the house, she habitually kept a kerchief up, veiling the right side of her face.

Jodie felt sorry for her sister. Not so much because of her scarring, but because of the aberrant state to which she'd descended. She couldn't even glance at her without Katie angrily growling— *What are you looking at?* She, having spent the remainder of fall and the start of winter in her own room mourning over Lucas, now found herself fleeing Katie's incessant, nerve-shattering tirades, and frequently going for rides alone. The icy winter winds outside were numbing, but the hellish flames of Katie's torment inside were torturous.

~ 27 ~

At Lucas' request, Joshua made him a pair of crutches using slat boards. With great determination, along with both Joshua and Grace's assistance, he used them to hobble from the cabin and over the frozen snow to the outhouse. Initially the venture was excruciatingly painful and thoroughly exhausting, but with each following attempt, it became more bearable. Within three weeks of his returning to life, he was stick-limping on his own about the immediate cabin and, depending on the weather and how able he was feeling, occasionally as far as out to the barn to visit Heston. He'd even begun joining the Smiths at their family table and eating alongside them.

Following one particularly active day of hobbling about, he awoke late the next morning in considerable pain. He'd unintentionally slept on his right side and was barely able to raise himself in the bed. Needing to visit the privy, he saw that his crutches had been moved across the room to where he could not reach them. Also seeing that Nathan was in the kitchen stocking firewood, he asked him if he'd fetch them for him. Nathan, knowing the rest of his family was busy outside, turned and displaying his usual contempt, sneered at him and left the cabin. Lucas wound up crawling on his hands and knees across the floor to retrieve them.

Later that afternoon, while Joshua and the boys were outside, he hobbled over to the supper table where Grace sat knitting.

"Am I interruptin?" he asked.

"You ain't interruptin, Christian. Sit yerself down."

As he sat, she chuckled as she often did and said, "I reckon that's in part what livin is, one big interruptin 'long wid a bunch'a littler ones."

Lucas thought she was referring to his coming into their lives as being the *big interruptin* and, looking down, stared self-consciously into the rough wood grain of the table.

"Sorry 'bout all that, Grace," he said.

"No need ta be sorry 'bout nothin, Christian," she said busily working the knitting needles. "That's what it's all about...life I mean. How we deals with that what comes 'long the way. Ya know, like the testin we talked on 'afore. And it'd be an awful thing if there weren't no other folks from time to time ta jostle us out'a our sets and ruts. I reckon it helps keep a soul balanced, else none of us would ever learn nothin 'bout livin and lovin how the Lord wants. I s'pose we'd all be nothin but the likes of critters, rocks and trees then, unh-unh."

As Grace chuckled again to herself, Lucas thought how it sounded like she was describing the life he'd always imagined having at that place of his alone in the mountains; the one without any people interrupting, and with only the trees, wildlife and seasons. He'd never thought of it in terms of its being possibly selfish or unbalanced.

"Truth be told, I miss havin other folks about...'specially other women ta talk wid. Like my lady friends in the Bible study back home. But I ain't complainin, unh-unh. I s'pose in a way, Joshua's bringin us all the way out here ta this country was somethin mindful of that Mister Moses and his lookin for that promise land'a his. A place where he figured no one could look down on him and his own...'ceptin the Lord of course. And since it's what Joshua always wanted and what the Lord's give to us, I was willin and gladful of it, unh-huh."

While some of what Grace said sounded completely foreign, Lucas *was* aware of her willingness to submit her own preferences in order that Joshua's desires would be fulfilled. Meanwhile, thinking of what he'd originally intended to ask her, he decided to go ahead with it.

"Grace, why you suppose Nathan dislikes me so?"

She stopped her knitting now and gave him a long, penetrating look, the likes of which he'd never really seen her do before. She seemed to be giving both him and his question serious consideration.

"Not that I'm 'scusin his un-Christian-like manners, Christian, 'cause I ain't——" She paused and, chuckling awkwardly said, "I didn't mean *you* personal, Christian. It was just a manner of speakin's all."

"I know," he said.

"Anyhow, a coupl'a times now over the past year, there's been armed white men wearin scarves over their faces and sittin on horses on the hilltop there just watchin and sizin up over us. And when we tries wavin neighborly to 'em, they doesn't wave back so that it feels Cold and sort'a . . . threatenin like. And besides bein troublin enough for me and Joshua, it's always been somethin frightful for Nathan and Samuel, unh-huh."

Lucas saw as her hands had begun trembling so that she set her knitting onto the table. Then she folded them together in her lap and, bowing her head, closed her eyes. He figured she was praying. A moment later, when she looked up at him, he again sensed the serious reservation in her eyes as she looked into his own.

"So, 'course when you showed up, and armed with all them guns you was wearin, Nathan figured you was one of them same men."

Lucas exhaled deeply and slowly thinking how not only had she explained the reason for Nathan's not liking him, but had also suggested to him how the Smith homestead, being as near the river as it was, could very well be one of Valentine's future targets. Not wanting to further frighten or concern her, he did not disclose the possibility.

"Well, I'm not one of 'em, Grace," he said.

"Joshua didn't think so, neither."

As she took up her knitting and resumed it, he sensed her relief in her smile. Returning his thoughts to what she'd told him about the masked riders, the thought of Joshua and Grace trying to defend themselves from the likes of someone like the murderous Valentine crew was pitiful to say the least. It would be a slaughter. And the possibility of its actually occurring before he was back in the saddle and able to fight was equally troubling. At the same time, wanting to change the topic, he attempted to shift trails.

"How long has Joshua had that cough of his, Grace?" he asked.

Again she stopped her knitting, this time projecting a concern of a deeper and more personal nature. Looking beyond him towards the kitchen window she said, "It started back just after that first winter we come out. But I doesn't believe it's just no cold, unh-unh. I think he's got too much of that coal dust still in his lungs from workin them mines back in Kentucky where we——" She paused and blinking away from the window, looked down at her knitting, then back at him.

"That was when we was slaves and 'afore Union soldiers come and give us our 'mancipation." Pausing again, she chuckled awkwardly and said, "It's a big word for freedom——'mancipation. Anyhow, ever since that first winter, Joshua got ta coughin and ain't been able ta shake it clear. And 'tween all this wind and weather and the way he works day in and out, the consumption's just hung on ta him like he hangs on ta this blessed dirt'a his. And he won't hear no talk of leavin it, neither. So I doesn't say nothin more 'bout it, unh-unh."

Lucas sat silent considering Grace's explanation for Joshua's health. He'd come to respect the two of them a great deal. In particular their coming out to this hard country with two boys and trying to scratch out a living; whether it made sense or not. He figured Joshua had probably brought them this far in order to insure no one ever tried making him or his family slaves again. That much made sense and, in an offhanded way, reminded him of his own reasons for coming west; at least in as far as wanting to shake off the past and find a place where he could breathe in peace. He sat there thinking to himself about things like slavery and hopes and dreams, and how pitifully absurd life and the world really was.

"Ya know, Christian, I don't know if yer wedded or not, but I knows ya gots yourself a girlfriend."

He was stunned and tried masking his surprise at Grace's odd and unexpected remark.

"What makes ya say that, Grace?"

"Cause of that nice hand-wove sweater and boot stockins yer wearin. They ain't store bought, unh-unh. There's too much work and love wove in 'em."

Lucas said nothing and stared blankly at his folded hands on the table before him. Grace had darned the bullet holes in his breeches, coat, shirt and sweater, and she knew better than he did how well or not the sweater had been made.

"Well ya does, don't ya?" she asked.

"Huh?" he said looking up.

She was looking directly at him as though expecting him to answer.

"Jodie," she said before he could summon what to say.

Again he was dumbstruck.

"What'd ya say, Grace?"

"Jodie. That's her name, ain't it?"

"Well, yeah, but...how'd you—-"

"Cause ya said it out loud agin and agin while ya was toppin that fever. So's I knowed ya had yerself a galfriend, unh-huh."

Lucas eased a bewildered smile. Thinking about Jodie always troubled both his heart and mind, and, although he tried not to, he couldn't help thinking of her often.

"Ya love her don't ya?"

Grace was being unusually pointed and the way in which she was studying him now reminded him of how his own mother might have once questioned him over something he'd been involved with when he was a boy. He stared blankly into the rough grain of the table again, feeling his face going warm and flush.

"I suppose," he mumbled.

"Well, she surely does you spendin all that time knittin ya them clothes. And they prob'ly kept ya from freezin yerself solid in that blizzard, unh-huh."

~ 28 ~

Keeping in mind what Grace had told him about Nathan's suspecting his being *one of those men* Lucas began making more of an effort to befriend him. But Nathan remained resistant avoiding his attempts. Then one afternoon while in the barn with Joshua and the boys, Joshua noticeably detecting Nathan's coarse indifference towards Lucas, stopped what he was doing and in a particularly uncharacteristic manner issued a very stern and blunt warning:

"Watch what side yer heart's ridin, son. Good or bad—-God's or the Devil's!" Then, looking directly at Lucas he added, "A man can't serve both, and'll only come to no good tryin."

Now what's that supposed to mean? Lucas asked himself setting his eyes hard on Joshua's. While his warning to Nathan had been justifiable enough, the way he'd then looked at him struck him as being an indictment of sorts also. He'd only been trying to be friendly with Nathan and was tempted to take exception with Joshua and ask what it was he was insinuating. But, just as he was about to defensively respond, still looking into Joshua's eyes, he was suddenly struck with the question of *who* in fact it was he *was serving.* It was undeniable that his time being with the Smiths had been ultimately about one thing and one thing only—-that being his recovering so he could exact his revenge on Valentine and company. Turning his eyes away from Joshua's now, he also found himself being confronted by his hair-triggered propensity to take offense and be angered to the point of almost takling Joshua to task over it. *And that after all he's done for you—-even saving your life?* It was further validation of who he had and hadn't been serving. And Joshua's having pointed it out as he had, now seemed to him to sound almost like something his own father might have once said, being at the same time firmly corrective yet sincerely concerned. He wasn't accustomed to being shamed or apologizing for anything and, standing there now, felt himself guilty and appropriately judged.

Tucking the crutches beneath his arms, he turned and hobbled from the barn wondering as he went if his feeding of the dark fire within had been that obvious to the Smiths, and if so, how much it might actually be affecting them. In any case, he felt extremely selfish and self-conscious about it. Was that really all his life was about—one long continual ride on the side of dispensing what he considered to be justice served? Raid after raid, killing after killing, year after year, over and over again? And in so serving that seemingly insatiable end, just *who* was he actually serving? As odd as it was for him posing those kinds of questions, he knew without doubt that the answer certainly wasn't the God whom Joshua served.

Over the following days, he consciously began to remove—at least from the forefront of his mind—the dominating burden of his desire for revenge. After all, there was nothing he could do about it yet. He could scarcely get around, let alone mount, ride and fight. As a result, he found himself taking more of an interest in the Smiths and who they were as individuals, each with their own personalities, cares and feelings. At any rate, either because of that, or, Joshua's earlier warning to him, Nathan had even begun speaking respectfully and regularly to him; even addressing him as *Mister Christian*. Then, too, on top of all that, he'd found himself feeling noticeably much better, smiling and occasionally laughing, as well.

Nathan had begun asking a lot of questions about Heston, horses in general and riding. He liked the large stallion and had a genuine interest in horsemanship that reminded Lucas of himself when he was young. One afternoon after Nathan had finished his chores and he and Lucas were in the barn alone, talking about horses and riding, Lucas showed him how to check Heston's legs and hooves and how to properly prepare him for riding.

When Heston was saddled, he asked, "You ready to ride, Nate?"

With eyes as large as Heston's, "Yes sir," Nathan eagerly responded.

After attaching a guide rope to the cheek strap of Heston's bridle, Lucas had Nathan mount Heston and he, with both crutches beneath one arm, led them from the barn. There, standing in the open yard and holding the guide rope, he let Nathan ride slowly in circles feeding out the rope farther with each pass.

Seeing how his brother was having such a swell time, Samuel asked if he could ride also. So Lucas helped him onto the saddle behind Nathan and instructed him to hold on tightly about his brother's waist. Round and round in circles on Heston they rode, laughing and having a grand time. Then, when he was certain Nathan was in capable control, he removed the guide rope altogether and they continued going round the yard on their own. Samuel was hanging on to his brother's midsection and squealing with joy. Lucas thought how while it was good for the boys it was also for Heston, who whinnied and snorted, tossing his head as he strutted proudly about.

Hearing Samuel's squeals of laughter, Joshua and Grace, having finished their bathing in the cabin, came out to see what was going on. Standing together hand in hand they watched, and before long, were laughing much like children themselves.

Lucas awoke the following morning sore from head to toe as a result of having been so long on his feet with all the activity the day before. As he lay there trying to muster the strength to rise, he heard Joshua and Grace coming out of their bedroom.

"Merry Christmas, everyone!" they cheerily announced.

The boys, who were asleep at the foot of the bed, sprang to their feet and bolted past. Lucas hadn't thought about Christmas in years, and the way that Nathan and Samuel's faces were lit, strongly reminded him of when he was their age. It gave him the added motivation to rise.

Grace had knitted red woolen sweaters, stockings and caps for the boys, and Lucas watched as they eagerly tried them on. Then Grace came over and handed him a red cap for himself. She told him that she'd started knitting it for Joshua, but since he had his favorite old felt hat which she knew he'd never give up, the two of them decided he should have it since he had none.

He thanked them for it and at the boy's urging, pulled it onto his head. They all laughed at how he looked, and he didn't mind at all and laughed along with them. Still, he felt empty not having anything to give the Smiths who'd shared so much with him. All he had was Heston, a saddle, his revolvers and rifle, a gun cleaning kit, skinning blade, jackknife, whetstone, a striking flint, two canteens and a drinking cup. Then he remembered the mouth harp he'd once found at a battle site and kept.

After pulling on his boots and coat, he excused himself and hobbled on his crutches first to the outhouse, then to the barn. There, he dug the harp from the bottom of one of his saddle bags. He rapped it against his healthy thigh knocking free the trail dust that had settled in it. Then he lightly blew into it checking to see that it still functioned which it did. Using a damp cloth, he polished it bringing back to life some of its silver luster. He took it back to the house and presented it to Nathan and Samuel to share. You would have thought he'd given them a valuable treasure the way the two boys reacted. And they took turns blowing on that mouth harp for the following two hours until Grace finally ushered them into her and Joshua's bedroom to play.

"Sorry I didn't run it by you folks first," Lucas said.

"Oh, that's fine. But ya didn't have ta do that, Christian," Joshua said.

"No, ya didn't have to, unh-unh," Grace said as she poured coffee for the three of them. "I'm just hopin they can find some better soundin notes than some they been makin from it. Some sounds more like they're skinnin wildcats wid a rusty can lid."

The three of them sat at the table laughing and visiting as they had their coffee and ate hot, freshly baked biscuits with strawberry preserves.

It was about an hour later when Nathan and Samuel came out of the bedroom into the kitchen. Both boys wearing anxious expressions and their new red sweaters and caps, stood patient and silent not wanting to interrupt the adults. Finally, Joshua asked them what they were doing.

"I wanna play you the new song I made," Nathan said.

"New song already?" Grace declared.

"Yes, Ma'am, and it's good, huh, Sam?"

"Unh-huh," Samuel said nodding.

"Okay, Nate, let's hear yer song," Joshua said.

Preparing himself, Nathan donned a serious expression and drew in a couple deep breaths of air. Then, starting from the high-sounding scale of the harp, he blew slowly into it creating a long sustained note, followed by another long and drawn note as he drew his breath in. And thus he continued until he'd worked his way to the opposite end of the harp, slowly blowing out and drawing in. By the time he finished, he looked like he was about to pass out.

"Is that it, son?" Joshua asked.

"Yessir," Nathan replied panting.

"What's the name of yer song?" Grace asked.

"The Wind," Samuel said.

"No, it's *The* Wind *Song*," Nathan said correcting him.

"Yeah," Samuel said and snickered, "*The* Wind *Song*."

"Well, son, it certainly do go on like the wind, sure enough," Grace said smiling. "An it's a right fine enough song, unh-huh."

"Let me do it now, Nathan," Samuel said.

Nathan handed the harp to his brother and Samuel, drawing deep breaths like Nathan had, began blowing into it. But its reeds had gotten damp now and so it wasn't making much sound other than a muffled splutter. The stunned look on Samuel's face was priceless.

"You broked it, Nathan," he said.

"It ain't broke, Samuel," Grace said. "It's just gotten wet and needs dryin out some's all." Taking the harp, she placed it on the mantle behind the stove to dry.

"You can play yer song when it's rested itself, son."

Like they normally would on Sundays, but because it was Christmas, Joshua and Grace limited their chores. Like Lucas' mother used to do, Grace baked and prepared a special ham supper. Then, after they'd eaten, Joshua and Grace, working at it together, read slowly from their Bible.

Grace once told Lucas that she'd learned to read from a white woman named Lois who lived near their old home. It was clear that both she and Joshua thought very highly of the woman. Grace said Lois had allowed her to attend the women's weekly Bible readings and had given her the Bible and taught her how to read from it. And now, using the same Bible, Grace was teaching Joshua and the boys.

Many of the stories that they'd read from it, Lucas remembered hearing when he was younger but had long since forgotten. Then, too, like his own parents, following each reading, Joshua and Grace would discuss with the boys what they'd read and ultimately wind up talking about Jesus and what the meaning behind his surrender and sacrifice on the cross was.

He'd never forget how tickled they'd all gotten that Christmas evening after Joshua, with Grace's help, had read from the Book of Luke. It was the story about Mary who was pregnant at the time with Jesus, and how she'd gone to visit her aunt Elizabeth who, at the same time, was pregnant with John the Baptist. When the story told about John sensing Jesus' presence, and how he began kicking excitedly in his mother's womb, Samuel said—*He could see him through her stomach, huh, Mama?* Because of the absolutely confident way in which he'd expressed it, he, Grace and Joshua couldn't help laughing. Then Grace told Samuel, *Yes, they could, son.* It reminded Lucas of how his own mother had always told him that he'd been a feisty kicker, too.

Later that evening, the boys, each with their own sack of marbles, engaged in one of their favorite pastimes. Grace spread an old blanket on the floor and then laid out a length of yarn in a circle over it. The boys played, taking turns trying to shoot and knock the marbles from the ring of yarn. Lucas always noticed how it didn't matter to Samuel that Nathan, being the older and, therefore, better shooter, typically wound up with most of the marbles. If Samuel had but a few, he was every bit as content as if he'd won them all. And the next time they wanted to play, Nathan would gladly share with Samuel some of his previous winnings so that they could. Watching as they played always reminded him of times when he was happy and life was carefree. Times before his father's murder and he'd ridden off to avenge it.

The following day, Joshua brought a cloth bundle with him out to the barn and handed it to Lucas.

"I removed the cartridges and tried dryin the pistols 'fore I wrapped and stored 'em," he said. "But it was sometime after you'd showed up till I could get to 'em. I hope they're okay and ain't rusted none."

"Thanks Josh, I'm sure they'll be fine," Lucas said.

Later that afternoon, after helping with chores, he unwrapped and spread the four revolvers out onto Joshua's workbench. They were clean and he could see no traces of rust, but after rubbing the more sensitive backside of his fingers over their steel, he could feel the rough trace of rust beginning to form. In the process of his drying them, Joshua had inadvertently removed most of their protective oil. From his saddle bags, he took a small tin box that held his cleaning kit of wiping pads, bore brush and a small tin of gun oil and began cleaning and re-oiling them. Nathan and Samuel came into the barn and soon, were standing alongside him watching.

As his father was coughing, Nathan asked, "Why ya got so many guns, Mister Christian?"

Lucas had never said anything about his past, and Joshua and Grace had never once asked. Turning, he saw by Nathan's expression that he'd only asked out of youthful curiosity.

"I found a couple of 'em on a fella I come across on the prairie once," he said. He'd lied, and was immediately sorry for it. And looking now at Joshua, no longer coughing, could tell he knew he had. He hadn't wanted to say that he'd been one of Quantrill's Raiders fighting for the Confederacy, or, one of Valentine's gun hands running folks off their land; whether he'd been aware of the truth of it at the time or not. Feeling the heat of shame as it swept over him, he thought how his whole life was only a lie. He could never tell the truth about whom he really was or what he'd once been. He shook it off the best he could with no recourse other than to accept it. As unpleasant as it was in contrast to the open lives of the Smiths, that was just the way it was.

"Was that man...dead?" Samuel asked.

Lucas saw his eyes were wide with concern.

"Yeah," he said lying again.

"Boys, it ain't polite diggin into other folk's business," Joshua said.

"Sorry, Mister Christian," both boys said together.

"It's okay, fellas."

"How'd that fella die, though, Mister Christian?" Nathan, still naturally curious, asked.

"Don't know," Lucas said lying again.

"That 'minds me," Joshua said. "Back 'bout hog killin time and just 'afore that blizzard hit, I was out south'a here rabbit and bird huntin and come 'cross a coupl'a young, dead fellas. They was froze and had arrows in 'em, but weren't scalped. Nope. Still had their hair, clothes and boots. I didn't have no spade with me or I mighta buried 'em decent. But seein 'em like that shook me so it made me hurry back home."

Lucas figured Joshua had changed the subject for his own benefit, and was thankful he had. On the other hand, his story reminded him of the arrows and the dead men at the JK homestead.

"Young fellas, ya say?"

"Yep, just boys, not even twenty on, I'd reckon. And they weren't dead long neither 'cause the vultures and other varmints hadn't found 'em yet."

~ 29 ~

Augustus Valentine and Farliss had sent Harding on a business errand to Cheyenne to file claims on the now vacant Marsh, Frenchman and JK spreads. Following his return, a stir went through the ranch over one of the letters he'd brought back with him for the boss. It was from St. Louis and pertained to Lucas and his questionable past. Jodie, unwilling to believe what she'd gleaned being shared between the men here and there around the barn, decided to confront her father about it. Augustus, thinking if she were to know the truth about the deceased gunman it would help in her getting over him, consented.

Sitting together in his den, he explained to her how after Lucas had been recognized by a group of cowboys from Texas and, who'd addressed him as *Cain,* he felt it was his responsibility to find out if there was anything in his past that might possibly bring any unfavorable attention on the ranch. Therefore, he'd written a friend of his in St. Louis requesting any known background information on him. He added that he'd also included in the letter a brief description of Lucas.

"Well, dear, my friend wrote back and—-" pausing, Augustus scanned the letter for the relevant portion. "Oh yes, here we are. He says that:

"'I could uncover nothing on any *Lucas Jackson,* however, the moniker *Cain,* as well as the description you sent—in particular the blue scar over the left eyebrow and aggressive horseback-fighting ability—strongly suggest a man named *Christian Jack,* alias *Cain.* A known member of a group of outlaw renegades during the war known as Quantrill's Raiders. A lawless gang of murderers and bandits comprised largely of former members of smaller guerilla bands called Missouri bushwhackers. Both groups of which it has now been determined—not without considerable objection by many, I might add—operated independent of the Confederate command. While the records availed to me show no reference of there ever being any actual official arrest warrants or death certificates filed on Jack's behalf, it is strongly suspected that he may yet be an actively resistant threat against the Union.'"

Augustus broke from the letter and looked up at Jodie. She hadn't drawn a breath from the moment he'd begun reading. Her face was stoically blank and her eyes hollow, showing no visible trace of emotion. He continued:

"And, he goes on further to say, 'Jack is considered dangerous——' and that, 'other notorious members of the outlaw bands include the likes of the brothers Frank and Jessie James as well as Cole and Jim Younger, to cite but a few. '"

Folding the letter, he looked sympathetically at his youngest daughter. What he saw in her contemplative expression as the news settled within her, he took to be an encouraging sign.

"Unfortunately, dear, that certainly sounds like our own Lucas Jackson, only his real name was Christian Jack. I know how hard it is to learn you've been deceived. I was stunned myself to learn of it. At any rate, he's no longer a threat or danger to the ranch or anyone else. Now, your mother and I truly hope you can put all of this behind you and move on."

Jodie said, "Thank you," stood, and left her father's den. The gravity of the report weighed heavy in her heart and it felt as though her feet were sinking through the floorboards with each condemned step she took. In the hallway, just outside her bedroom, she could hear her sister from inside her own room telling her mother how she wished she could have died rather than being scarred the way she had, and that she didn't see how she could possibly live any longer looking the way she did. Jodie shook her head pitifully from side to side as she pulled on her coat and headed for the front door. She needed desperately to get away and be alone.

Leaving the house, she thought how Lucas hadn't been officially wanted by the law. Only that he was considered dangerous, comparing him to others who'd gone on to become known criminals. But she knew it was pointless trying to defend his honor to anyone else; their minds were made up. They hadn't known him like she had. Compared to most of the men who'd ever worked at the ranch, and who frequently hung about ogling both her and Katie, Lucas had been nothing short of a true, even valiant, gentleman. *After all,* she thought, telling herself, *people could change for the better, could they not?* Whatever he'd been in the past, she believed with all of her heart that he *had* changed, and therefore, she was not ashamed of the fact that he'd been the man whom she'd truly come to love.

Jodie was not one given over easily to impulse or swayed by the opinions of others. The purest womanly virtues within her, however young she and they may yet be, were every bit as real and trustworthy as she was alive and breathing. And so long as her heart might still beat and she drew her next breath, she and they were one and the same and would always be inseparable. Nothing in the world to her was more true, precious and valuable than love, and in her mind, God would never have allowed the eyes of her heart to be deceived. Broken perhaps, but never deceived.

She went to the barn to saddle her horse, intending to go to the lone oak on the hill where Lucas sometimes went. There, she too would sit alongside Tonka with her back to the same tree, wishing also on things seemingly impossible. Like that he was actually still alive and somewhere safe and okay. Sometimes she wished that she could be a thousand miles away, but that too, would only remind her of the time when she'd asked him if he had any dreams and he'd told her that he sometimes dreamt of having a place of his own somewhere in the mountains with only the silence and seasons. How many times she'd repeated those very words to herself and, in dreams, been there with him.

~ 30 ~

"Ya know, Christian, 'cept that early blizzard blowed through, it ain't been a hard winter," Joshua said. "But there's plenty time yet for changin its mind," he added with a chuckle, thereby triggering another cough.

It was Lucas' first winter in that country and other than the blizzard and relentless wind he had no way of gauging it. He said nothing and as he continued forking manure from the empty stall shared by Heston and Old Mare, he reflected on Joshua's appraisal of the season with respect to Augustus Valentine's repeated concerns over the lack of water.

Once Joshua was recovered from his coughing, he asked, "Have you folks had enough water here, Josh?"

"Even though there ain't been as much snow or rain as there was when we first come out, the garden and well's been doin just fine. I s'pect it's cause of the river's bein close by, that and the Lord's blessins of course."

Lucas smiled at the notion of the Smiths having enough water while Valentine didn't. As for the rivers being nearby, once while they were discussing how Heston had found their place in the blizzard, Joshua told him that since they were less than a half-mile from it, Heston might have been able to hear some of the racket the wind was creating as it was slapping loose the roof shingles and siding boards on both the cabin and barn. He'd said it sounded like the whole place was being hammered on and about to buckle.

Joshua, sitting on the milking stool beside Milky the she-goat, smiled and said, "It'll be spring and plantin time 'afore we know it. Yep, good Lord willin, and if me and Ol Mare there hold up, we'll be turnin dirt and gettin seed planted soon as the ground thaws."

"And strawberries too, huh?" Samuel said as he watched his father.

Lucas smiled at Samuel licking his lips, no doubt thinking how fine strawberries tasted.

"Yessuh, and strawberries, too, son," Joshua said.

"Pa, the coal bin's gettin' down," Nathan announced as he entered the barn.

"I seen that, son. I reckon we'll be okay for a spell yet then we'll make us a run."

"Where ya get it, Cheyenne?" Lucas asked. He'd just stood the pitchfork in the corner and, conscious of how well his right shoulder was healing, flexed his arm back and forth and from side to side.

"Heavens no," Joshua said standing. "Nathan, take this pail of milk in to your ma, son."

"Yessir, Pa."

"Ya better step out and shake some of that dust off ya first, though."

"Oh yeah," Nathan said. He'd been stocking the coal box in the house and had it on the front of his coveralls. Bringing in the coal and firewood was one of his many daily chores.

"The Lord's somethin else, Christian. I guess all those years I spent workin in them coal mines, He saw fit to give us a patch'a land with its own seam sittin right out on top of it. We jes gotta go up with the wagon, chisel and break it out and load it up. Don't gotta go down no shafts or nothin. No suh, it's sittin right out just as easy as pickin strawberries, ain't it, Sam?"

Samuel, smiling once more large for strawberries nodded and said, "Unh-huh."

"Late summer, when the river's down, I takes a few wagon-loads of it up to Fort Laramie and trade for supplies. That's how I bartered most the lumber for the house and barn."

"And Miss Milky, too," Samuel said.

"Yep, Miss Milky and Billy there, too," Joshua said as he led Miss Milky the female goat into the pen where Billy the male goat stood guardedly watching.

Joshua's bartering his coal reminded Lucas of how his father had been a carpenter and his mother a seamstress, and how they also traded services with other folks where they lived. They bartered for everything from tools and foods to lamp oil and the cloth material his mother would use for making more clothes. Even occasional doctor visits were paid for through trade.

As Lucas was healing and, too, being reintroduced to many things from his forgotten pre-war past, consequently, the intense desire for retribution that had gripped him initially had greatly subsided. He found himself being more compelled to be healthy enough to defend the Smiths—should it be necessary—than to fulfill his own personal vendetta. He knew full well what he intended to do once he was able and the time was right; and, too, that it would not be godly. But, in the meantime, dwelling too much on that he'd learned, was a hindrance not only to his recovery, but his presence among the Smiths.

From the moment he felt able, he was back in the saddle. Early mornings and late afternoons, before and after helping with chores, his rides patrolling and watching for any possible threats to the Smiths grew longer and Heston's pace faster. When he was well out of view of the homestead, he would practice standing with his weight in the stirrups testing the stamina of his left leg. And as Heston galloped over the frozen fields where the layers of crusted snow were not deep, he'd lift a revolver in his right hand trying to retrain his shoulder and arm to be steady. Though much improved, shoulder, arm, leg and hip were still on the weak side, shaky and sore.

One afternoon, while riding beyond the southeast corner of the Smith's parcel, he came across the skeletal remains of two humans. They were in a small, natural depression alongside a snowdrift and not easily seen until he was almost upon them. Lying askance among each set of exposed bones and the remnants of shredded clothing, were single arrows. It dawned on him that these were probably the same young fellows Joshua had spoken of his having come across before the blizzard.

Then, after nudging Heston closer, he didn't have to dismount to know who they once were. He recognized what was left of the clothing and both pairs of boots. It was Johnny and Carl.

He'd spent enough time with the young hands to know their leathers. He recalled the night when Herron and Jahns, returning from their east side patrol, came into the bunkhouse covered with snow, and how when Rocha asked where Johnny and Carl were, Farliss answered saying they'd been laid off. They hadn't been laid off, they'd been laid down. Probably shot in the back the way Valentine and Farliss had everyone removed once they were done with them and their services. No wonder Rocha found Johnny's picture magazine under his mattress. Johnny hadn't known he wasn't coming back. But Valentine, Farliss, Herron and Jahns all knew.

While it made him angry, it also made him sad. Unlike most of the other men back at the Valentine ranch, Johnny and Carl— he now perceived—did not have that tell-tale mark in their eyes. They hadn't gained that dark distinction in life yet; hadn't crossed that line. They were innocent and trusting. Just a couple of good-natured boys who'd staked out together looking for a life beyond their family farms. But just like all of the victims of Valentine's avidity, no one was likely to miss them. They hadn't deserved having their lives cut short like that.

Deserve?

"What the hell's deserve got to do with anything?" he angrily grumbled aloud.

Had his father deserved to be killed as he had, simply because of where their family happened to be living? Thereby also ushering the subsequent, pre-mature death of his mother? And too, what about Rocha? Or those surrendered JK boys and men? Had they all been deserving of their fates? Had Joshua and Grace deserved to be made slaves because of the color of their skin? Or Joshua forced to work in coal mines until his lungs were full of its death? Unlike him, those people hadn't deserved their fates. How had he, he wondered, after as many men as he'd shot and killed, managed to survive the war, and now, a bushwhacking in a blizzard to boot? The justice and meting out of what's fair in this life was as willy-nilly and random as which way the wind would blow next.

He thought how Joshua and Grace, like his own mother and father, believed that God kept tally of the intentions in everyone's heart. He'd been raised to believe that also, but as a kid those concepts were foreign and meaningless. He remembered how much he'd hated hearing his mother say that she forgave the jayhawkers who'd killed his father. Then, in that same light, he thought how he'd never once heard the Smiths blame or curse the man who'd kept them bound in slavery. Somewhere between the *turning of the other cheek* and *an eye for an eye*, he always got confused. In any case, he was still glad there would be a final and higher settling of accounts; and that, being said in full recognition of how his own judgment and sentencing before God was likely to weigh out. If it's true that the rewards and punishment come later, then that makes this senseless life only the proving grounds, or more aptly put— the battlefield. That had been his life and he was still very much quite alive, and to think that life would actually change was futile. He was different, battlefield made and marked. War quartered no compromise and he would be helping God when Valentine and company got what they deserved.

After all he'd been through and seen he couldn't shake what happened to Carl and Johnny from his mind. A few days later, he rode up to the river and west along it, all the way to where he figured he and Rocha were shot. He kept a watchful eye for riders and studied the river banks as he went. Finding no trace of Rocha's remains, he figured that he, like his new hat, had been swept away by the river's storm-swollen current. He was half-tempted to go on to the nearby JK homestead to try and see if those women and kids were there, but he knew it was a foolish notion. If they'd survived, they would have fled after finding all of their menfolk slaughtered.

Still, one way or another, sooner than later, he knew Valentine and his crew would face his reckoning, and not because of revenge only, but as a plain matter of principle. Yes, they would face it and they would see clearly who it was passing the judgment. It would not come from behind as it had with him, Rocha, Carl and Johnny and all the others.

Then the thought occurred to him of whether or not it mattered if you saw who it was that was killing you.

What you going to do, wait around in Hell to give them more of it when they arrive?

~ 31 ~

One afternoon as Joshua and Lucas were in the barn working, Joshua was stricken with a severe bout of coughing. Seeing that he'd begun bringing up blood, Lucas cradled his arm about his midsection, attempting to lessen the severity of the body-jarring convulsions. When the attack finally subsided, he helped ease him back onto the sugar beet bin. He was very weak and drained from the battering he'd just taken.

"Want me to get Grace?" he asked.

Joshua took him by the coat sleeve and shook his head *no*. Lucas waited for him to regain himself.

"Don't…Grace," he said. He shook his head *no* again releasing his hold on Lucas' sleeve.

"I'll fetch some water," Lucas said.

As he was drawing the water at the well, he thought how he wished there was some way he could share with Joshua some of his own improved health. But he knew that even if such a thing were possible, Joshua, not wanting to put anyone out, would never accept it. Back in the barn, he found a rag and dampened it to wipe the bloody spittle from Joshua's mouth and beard.

"Christian."

"Yeah, Josh?"

"If you're still 'round, and should somethin happen to me—-" Pausing to catch his breath, he looked into Lucas' eyes to see if he'd understood what he meant. Sensing he had, he continued speaking slowly, gaining short breaths between his every three or four words.

"I'd like ya ta take Grace and the boys ta town with the papers and see what ya can get for this place. Then see 'em safe on the train for Denver. Grace has an older brother who run off and joined the Union Army and now works for his old commander there."

Joshua, on in his forties, was a silent man whom Lucas had come to learn, did much of his speaking with his eyes which were always so clear and forthright that it was easy enough to tell what he was thinking. Although his physical health was evidence of the hard life he'd lived, and his request just now revealed his concern over Grace and the boys, the contented resolve he saw in his eyes, made it hard to take what he was suggesting seriously.

Bearing a fatherly smile, Joshua said, "Okay, son?"

"Yes, sir, but you—-"

Joshua took hold of his sleeve again, stopping him short. "She never wanted this. I did, lookin ta be free. But it ain't no place for her and the boys. Like I said, if you're still 'round, just try and get enough for her ta make a start."

"Yes, sir," Lucas said.

"Don't say nothin ta Grace 'bout all this, though. It'll only trouble her."

"You got it, Josh, and don't worry, I ain't goin anywhere. But now, I want you to go in and rest some. I'll see ta things out here."

"Yes suh," Joshua said preparing to stand. He smiled at Lucas in a way that reminded him of how his own father sometimes would. That smile that his young heart had once known and naturally recognized as being the unbreakable seal of the father-and-son bond they shared between them.

"Ya know, Christian, it don't matter how far a man runs, he cain't no more get away from truth than he can his own shadow and self. It's likely easier tryin ta stop the wind from blowin. But through believin in God and the gift of Jesus, He sets us free and makes us all able ministers of His grace."

Initially, Lucas thought Joshua was referring solely to his own life and past having brought his family west, but on further reflection, couldn't help thinking it intended for him personally. The running from *truth, shadow and self* thing, he knew first hand was true. You can't. And as for the *God, ministering and grace* business—-the very fact that he was alive at all was evidence of that truth through the compassion and rich faith Joshua and Grace held in God. A gift he knew without any shadow of doubt, he'd been most undeserving of. As his thoughts turned to the business concerning the *gift of Jesus,* he experienced at that moment a wonderful sensation of lightness and clarity. And outside of Joshua's physical health of course, everything seemed perfectly clear. Looking again into Joshua's eyes, it struck him once more how in spite of all his life's hardships and injustices, as well as his body's present weakened state, there was no discernible trace of fear or self-pity whatsoever. Rather, what he saw was an abiding peace which seemed to speak of a far greater understanding and wisdom than all of the pulpit-ranting sermons and soapbox speeches he'd ever heard.

As they walked side by side and were nearing the open doorway of the barn, Lucas saw Nathan and Samuel were racing across the yard towards them.

"Pa...it's those men!" Nathan gasped pointing towards the hill.

From the shadow of the barn's doorway, Lucas cast a quick glance around the corner and saw two mounted riders sitting at the top of the hill.

"Boys, go with your pa into the house. Bar the door and stay there."

As Joshua and the boys started over the open yard for the cabin, his first thought was to saddle and mount Heston. But he knew that by the time he could catch them, they'd likely be half-way to Valentine's; if indeed that was who they were and where they were from. As he strapped on his gun belt, he felt unusually composed, and he told himself to stop fooling himself. *You know well enough where they're from and what they're up to.*

He drew his rifle from its scabbard and saw that Joshua and the boys were just entering the cabin. Moving to the west wall, he peered through the cracks of the slats at the two horsemen. Sure enough, they were both wearing bandanas over their faces making it impossible from that distance to accurately identify them. It struck him then that they were only scouting otherwise they would have attacked already. He also knew that if he was to chase or even catch them, it would only intensify any plans Valentine and Farliss might have already made for moving against the Smiths.

"Moving against the Smiths?" he mumbled. A shiver coursed through his whole being and he whispered solemnly, "Moving against me and *mine,* now."

He felt as part of the old him desperately wanted to throb back to life. And while the instinct to confront them was overwhelming, he remained tempered keeping a level head. He continued watching and thought how their size and hats suggested they might be Teller and Gore. *No, you don't want to tip your hand for these two,* his inner voice instructed. He knew the type of attack Farliss was most likely to use, striking early when it was least expected. As he considered his options for dealing with them before such time should arise, he thought how with Joshua's health the way it was he could no longer entertain the notion of taking the battle to them; not just yet, anyway. If something happened to him and he couldn't make it back, it would leave Grace and the boys defenseless. No, he'd have to wait for the whole greedy crew to assemble, once and for all, and then, God willing, he'd be ready to respond—-once and for all.

As he continued watching, he shook his head over the blatantly bold way in which they casually sat there in broad, open daylight in the obvious knowledge that the Smiths were an easy mark who posed no threat to them whatsoever. Then, along that same disturbing note, he found their appearing as they had right on the heels of Joshua's debilitating coughing attack even further unsettling. It struck him how like predators in a pack on the prowl for weaker prey, they could somehow sense it and were taking full advantage. Then, too, in that same dim light of opportunity, their forcing him to focus on their darkness just as he'd been experiencing the illuminating moment with Joshua in the barn that he was. At any rate, he thought the coincidence of their timing most uncanny.

Finally, after maybe fifteen minutes, which seemed more like an hour, the two riders turned and rode off.

Over the following week, Joshua stayed inside the cabin and for the most part, in bed. He couldn't stop coughing. Grace suspected that besides the consumption, he might have a touch of pneumonia. She would hear no argument from him about his going out, other than to use the privy. And Joshua was too weak to offer up his usual protest. Not wanting to leave her and the boys alone at the cabin, Lucas suggested all of them going to Cheyenne so Joshua could see a doctor. Grace was willing, but Joshua insisted he was on the mend and that besides their not being able to afford it, all the traveling in the wagon, there and back, would probably do him in faster than the pneumonia or consumption.

"Besides," as he'd repeatedly said, "I got seeds ta get plantin."

With Joshua down, Lucas had no choice but to limit his early morning and evening patrols in order to attend to the many routine daily chores at the home front. However, he was always looking over his shoulder and scanning the horizon, fully expecting that one day he would look, and they would be there. If they didn't know he was there already, he imagined that in their minds, moving against the Smiths would be simple and easy, and therefore, an engagement they might take lightly. As much as possible, he kept Heston loosely saddled and tethered out of sight in or closely along the back and east side of the barn. All he had to do was slip on the bridle then cinch tight the saddle straps and he was mobile. For the sake of not alarming the Smiths, as inconspicuously as possible, he also kept his rifle and revolvers loaded and close at hand.

Nestled intentionally in a swale between sloping knolls in the hopes of gaining some shelter from the full brunt of the wind, the homestead offered a limited view at best of its surroundings. Trying to establish any tactical offense combined with defense was virtually impossible there. Nevertheless, in an attempt to do just that, one afternoon at the straw shed behind the barn, Lucas began squaring and binding bales of straw. The boys who'd come with him with the intentions of helping, never asked why he was doing it and soon became sidetracked enjoying a much needed romp in the straw pile.

When he'd finished squaring and binding six of the bales, he said, "Help me carry and stack these bales, fellas."

After helping lug out the first, "What we want puttin it over here for, Mister Christian?" Nathan asked. They were in the open area of the yard midways between the cabin and barn, off to the side near the base of the west hill.

"It's a skunk trap," Lucas replied.

Nathan made a peculiar face and looked at Samuel.

"Skunk trap? What ya want trappin skunks for, Mister Christian?" he asked.

"Cause I don't like the way they smell," Lucas said half-smiling.

"Me, too," Samuel said scrunching his nose.

"Well, why we doin it over here?"

"Cause skunks'll see it and think it's a good place to hide," Lucas explained.

"But how's it gonna trap 'em?"

"They'll jus fall down on 'em, huh, Mister Christian," Samuel said.

"Sure will, Sam. It'll all fall down on 'em and they won't know what hit 'em." Having said that, for some reason, part of a Bible verse he'd heard when he was a boy came to mind. It was something having to do with having the faith of a child.

Yet puzzled, Nathan's facial expression showed his bewilderment over the bales of straw somehow functioning as skunk traps.

When they'd finished with the first four bales, two upon two, Lucas said, pointing back along the base of the hill, "Now we'll go set the last two over yonder."

After stacking the last two, with Nathan still perplexed by it all, they started for the barn.

"All right, fellas, you're daddy's gonna be proud we took care of everything like he would'a wanted."

"And them stinky skunks, too," Samuel added.

Lucas scuffed his hand over Samuel's head and said, "Especially them stinky skunks."

Workdays were long and sleep short with the early pre-dawn and late evening patrols Lucas vigilantly maintained. Whenever the hours of watching began to wear particularly heavy on him, he had only to remember Rocha, Carl and Johnny, and that, along with his dedication to protecting the Smiths, and he'd find himself reinvigorated.

Grace, aware of what he was doing, never said anything directly to him about it. She did, however, pray about it throughout each day.

"He's like a guardian angel," she once said to Joshua, in the hearing of the boys.

~ 32 ~

Herron and Jahns, half-pickled and broke after a winter full of Cheyenne saloons and brothels, were practically asleep in their saddles as their mounts plodded over the crest of the trail to the Valentine ranch. The cool west wind that blew them along like tumbleweeds paid no heed to the almanac marking it was now spring.

Harding saw them approaching and alerted Farliss who slyly ushered them in around the backside of the bunkhouse. The two riflemen looked and smelled rough, like they'd just crawled out of a bottle of rotgut whisky freshly fished from the basement of an outhouse. Wasting no time, the ranch foreman updated them on the still sensitive situation concerning Katie, and reminded them about keeping out of sight of the Valentine home.

"You mean she ain't over it yet?" Herron asked.

"Nope, she ain't, and she ain't let no one else, neither."

"I know what she needs," Herron said drawing a wicked grin.

Harding, Teller, Gore and Jahns all laughed over the assessment.

"That may well be," Farliss affably remarked, "but you'd have to go through Geneva first."

Repulsed by the notion, Herron now twisted his face painfully and groaned, "Oh Gawd!"

The bunkhouse erupted in laughter.

"So when we goin Coon huntin, Far?" Jahns asked.

Like two small black marbles, his porcine eyes darted hungrily from side to side behind his dumpling-plump cheeks that were checked with a web of thin red veins. Like Herron's, the once whites of his eyes were now bloodshot pink, and not from being out in the wind, but as a result of the long drinking binge he'd been on in Cheyenne. At the same time, unlike most men who drank as much as he did, and who'd eventually begin to neglect their diets,

Jahns hadn't, and the way his bountiful midsection swelled over the sides of his gun belt was proof.

"We've been waitin on you two to show before we set plans for that," Farliss said, working both ends of his moustache. "Much as we knew, the both of ya could'a been in the Cheyenne poke; that or rolled up dead under some whore's bed."

Again the men all laughed. It had been a while since they'd had their blood stirred. They'd been for the most part relegated to ranch duties and were more than ready to get away and roust up some real action.

"Tell 'em 'bout the letter the boss got 'bout Lucas, Far," Gore said.

Farliss shared with them the report how Lucas, alias *Cain*, had been a member with the infamous Quantrill's Raiders during the war.

"I'll be damned!" Herron exclaimed. He stood for a moment looking stunned, his lower jaw gaping as though it had come unhinged. Then, turning wonder-struck to Jahns, he said, "You mean I done killed me a Ma-zur-eye raider?" Shuffling in a foot jig, he hooted and howled like a prospector having just struck the mother lode.

Teller clapped him on the shoulder and said, "Ain't that somethin?"

"I knew he weren't just no cowpoke after watchin how he rode through that Marsh crew," Jahns gargled.

"Yeah, and he done it just like one of them Missouri raiders would'a, too," Farliss added.

Before he and Harding left Kansas to come to work at the ranch, he'd heard about the trouble the bushwhackers were raising along the border between the two states. But he'd never put it together that Lucas might have been one. When Augustus received the letter confirming that he'd once been a bushwhacker and raider, the Kansas born ramrod was quite pleased with himself over his part in the Missouri gunman's demise.

Chest pumped high with a fresh batch of renewed self-esteem and confidence, Herron boasted, "Well, this ain't Missouri, Mister

Cain. It's Wyomin. And I reckon he's tasted enough dirt to know it by now, boys."

The others unanimously seconded Herron's declaration and as they continued visiting, Jodie stood outside the backdoor listening. She'd been preparing to go for her usual afternoon ride and saw the group of men as they were entering the bunkhouse. She was amazed that Herron had the audacity to return to the ranch after what happened to Todd Welles and her sister. While she rarely came around the bunkhouse where the men lived, compelled by her curiosity, she'd made the exception. She told herself that should someone see she was there, she would tell them she was looking for Wooten to ask if he'd fed Tonka.

As she listened to what was being shared by the men inside, she could scarcely believe her ears. With her mind racing to comprehend, she shuddered as it all became tragically clear and the truth, stabbed, plunging like a rusted blade again and again into her heart.

This man…these men…killed Lucas!

She wanted to scream, but didn't have the breath. Both of her fists had clenched so tightly that the nails dug deeply into the flesh of her palms. Tempted to confront them, she tried mustering some semblance of fortitude first. As she did, it dawned on her that she should go tell her father what she'd learned. But before she could move, she found herself suddenly stricken again. This time with the realization that the implications must surely also reach to him; meaning he already knew. Now, completely stunned and uncertain what to do, she wisely retreated to the barn.

There, lightheaded and trying not to blackout and collapse, she frantically finished saddling her horse. Her head was spinning and her knees wanted to buckle beneath her. She wept as she rode away from the ranch with Tonka trotting alongside. When she was safely out of earshot, exerting every ounce of her being, she let out with a desperate, piercing scream. It was so loud and sudden that Tonka was almost bowled over by it as he ran.

At the oak tree, she paced aimlessly in circles until she thought she might be ill. She couldn't help thinking back to the time when her father had read the letter to her about Lucas, and how he'd mentioned his being stunned over finding out that he'd been deceived.

Deceived?

Deceived, knowing all along that Lucas had been intentionally murdered? Murdered as intentionally as how he'd lied and intentionally deceived her himself? That was it. She'd had it. She hated them all and especially him. Devastated and feeling again that she might collapse, she pressed her back hard against the rough-barked trunk of the oak. She swore to herself that she would somehow come up with a plan to leave and follow it through. Then, they would never see her again, and she would never have to see any of them as well.

"Never, by God, I swear it," she pledged. Then, dropping to her knees, she tottered and fell face first to the ground where she wept until she passed out.

Before reporting to Augustus that Herron and Jahns had returned, Farliss assured Wooten that the two would only be around the ranch a day or two at most, and that then they were being posted permanently up at the old Marsh ranch. After what happened with Herron killing Todd Welles, Wooten was highly resistant about his being there. After all, he'd been the one, the only one at the ranch for that matter, who'd taken Welles' body, dug his grave and buried him. He didn't like Herron *or* Jahns, and he wasn't the kind of man to go out of his way pretending he did. Having somewhat settled that business, Farliss then went to inform Augustus that the two had returned.

"...and the rest of the fellas are anxious to ride and finish up, too," he added.

"Good, Far. I'm tired of waiting as well," Augustus said.

"Yu ruukun wu'll bu uuudin them?" Farliss asked gesturing to the Sioux arrows in the one full quiver that hung from the office wall. The one that once held the Cheyenne arrows now hung limp and empty.

"Who do you think is going to lose sleep over some African sodbusters, Far?" Augustus replied.

"That's true enough. Well, at any rate, I talked to Herron and Jahns and told 'em to keep scarce, so I don't expect we'll be havin any trouble there."

"Good. They're ready?"

"Yeah, a day's rest'll dry 'em out and do 'em good. They'll be ready fine."

"We'll set out day after tomorrow, then," Augustus said.

Two days later, Farliss had the men assemble out beyond the barn.

"All right, fellas, listen up. The boss is comin along, so you'll wanna keep a rein on what ya say and do. And don't say nothin 'bout it to Woot or anyone else where we're goin or why. Just like before, we're keepin low on it. We'll be settin out shortly, soon as Augustus is ready."

"What's he comin for?" Harding asked.

"He wants ta ride his new riverfront holdings," Farliss said. Turning, he leveled his attention on Herron.

Herron, aware of what Farliss was about to say spoke first, "I know, Far, I won't say nothin about nothin."

"So, what's the plan, Far?" Harding asked.

"Hard, you'll be stayin behind to keep over things around here."

"Hell, I'm fit to ride," Harding asserted.

"I know, Hard. But the boss trusts ya and wants ya around and it's his call."

"Gawd almighty," Harding grumbled. He turned and dejectedly ground off towards the bunkhouse.

Returning his attention to the others, Farliss said, "We'll be settin camp up there tonight boys and movin in at first light. It'll be a cinch and over 'afore it's started. I had Gore and Teller up there scoutin 'em out a coupl'a weeks back, and there's only the old man, his bitch and a coupl'a their young litter."

Augustus, glad to be getting away from the house and women for a spell, was looking forward with great anticipation to finally claiming the last remaining property between him and the river. As they were all preparing to ride, Farliss took him aside and told him he'd like to have Harding come along also. He explained how he thought it would be good for his morale.

"Besides, Wooten and Case'll be here and havin another gun along can't hurt."

Augustus, like Farliss, wanting to avoid any disgruntled personnel who could possibly prove detrimental at this, the final stage of their land-clearing operation, judiciously consented.

Just before noon, with the absolute confidence of an uncontestable army, Valentine and Farliss, like a couple of generals, along with a happy Harding, the younger and ever-eager Gore and Teller, and a most unusually subdued Herron and grunting sidekick, Jahns, set out to deliver their final blow. The group was in no hurry as their mounts ambled casually along, they, all listening as the boss and Farliss outlined their plans for the future. They explained how they and the investors were purchasing two thousand head of new cattle, which, in fact, were due to arrive very soon.

"Our cattle will have no shortage of water and plenty of green pasture to graze plump and fat on, men," Augustus said.

Farliss went on to outline their strategy for utilizing the two northern ranch posts, having both the vacant JK structures, as well as the African's cabin and barn at their disposal. Then, too, how at each of the two northern corners, they would be posting teams and assigning lead men and backup foremen.

Honing his political oratory and sounding as though he were giving a campaign speech, Augustus addressed them, "Gentlemen, each and every one of you are the working ground level foundation of our ranch's future. A future that, along with each and every man's hard work, full dedication and commitment, is certain to be bright and lucratively rewarding."

The hands were visibly giddy with the prospects of the financial promises that the boss was suggesting awaited them in the not-so-distant future. The challenge he was proposing was easily attainable and well within each man's unscrupulous ability and ambitious desire. Even Harding was grinning with reinvigorated purpose and a positive outlook. Augustus Valentine had successfully delivered his first motivational address and could vividly picture his riding the wave of a landslide into political office.

With great temerity, between himself and Farliss, he'd already coined the future holdings. Glancing now at his foreman, he smiled and with a clandestine blink of an eye, proudly announced: "I feel it's only fitting that you men be the first to hear this. Far and I have decided to call our new holdings the North Valentine Range."

"And besides the grass being greener, fellas," Farliss added with a chuckle, "There's rainbows up there jumpin in the river, too."

The marauders hadn't covered much ground that day when they stopped to make camp. That evening, sitting around the campfire, theirs was an air of absolute confidence without the slightest concern over the task that lay before them. They were more like a group of happy-go-lucky boys who were on their way fishing.

~ 33 ~

Grace passed beside the bed Nathan and Samuel shared. It was the one Lucas used while he was recovering from his wounds. She looked at their beautiful sleeping faces and thought how much they resembled their father.

Lucas was asleep on the floor at the foot of their bed, beneath the small east window. Grace bent over him and lightly squeezed his shoulder. He opened his eyes and she raised a finger to her mouth letting him know to be quiet. Thinking something might be wrong, he sat up quickly and looked around, then back at Grace. She said nothing, blinked and left. Standing, he pulled on his breeches, sweater and boot stockings.

At the open door to Joshua and Grace's small bedroom, Lucas saw that Grace was sitting on the edge of her bed holding Joshua's hand. On their homemade night stand a candle was lit and its flame burned smoothly, long and thin without a flicker. He stepped respectfully into the room beside Grace. She looked up at him with tears streaming down her cheeks. He hunched over a little and put his arms around her.

"He ain't dead, he's just gone ta be with his Lord's all," she said.

Joshua had a peaceful smile on his face as he lay there no longer straining for his every breath. It struck Lucas how, on the faces of all the dead men he'd ever seen, none had ever been so content and peaceful looking. He felt the overwhelming urge to break mounting within, but he hugged Grace more tightly and resisted trying to even his deep, painful breaths.

Turning to Joshua, Grace said, "Ya ain't sufferin no more is ya, honey. Yer with yer Lord Jesus in heaven. Praise God, unh-huh."

Though Joshua had been ill, his passing was completely unexpected. And even though he'd mentioned it himself not so long ago, Lucas never imagined it might actually come to pass so soon.

Clutching tightly to his arms in much the same way Joshua had that day out in the barn following his severe coughing attack, Grace said, "I'm glad yer here, Christian." Sensing the slack in her grip, and thinking she was on the verge of collapsing, he drew her more tightly to himself.

"Grace——-" he began, but stopped. He couldn't find the words, let alone the ability to speak them. Through tear-filled eyes, Grace, looking up, acknowledged him knowingly and grateful.

After she'd somewhat regained her composure, Lucas left the room to let her be alone with Joshua. As he entered the kitchen, he felt strangely outside of himself. It was as though he might still be asleep or dreaming the way his senses were stunned and his mind randomly wandered. He picked up Joshua's worn, brass pocket watch, which always sat on the rock mantle behind the stove. It was always wound, warm and ticking, just like how he'd never known the stove not to be lit and warm also. Joshua's watch read 4:14. He stood there for a moment staring blankly at its dial as though looking for some significance other than the time.

After stoking the fire and setting the coffee pot on, he pulled on his boots and coat. Disregarding gun belt and rifle, he eased himself out the front door to go to the privy. The crisp night air was still and without breath, but he neither felt nor thought about it.

Back inside the cabin, waiting for the coffee to brew, he stood facing the small kitchen window trying to think what needed to be done. Instead, he found himself thinking for some odd reason, how it was the other of the two windows in the Smith cabin, and how Joshua had told him how he and Grace had removed them from their old cabin in Kentucky and packed them in their wagon all the way out. He could still hear him saying—*You would'a thought 'em eggs the way we was so careful in not breakin 'em*. He'd then gone on to tell how the windows in their younger years had always represented a kind of freedom to them.

Shaking his head, he wondered why of all things, he was thinking about the Smith's windows and all of that business now. It was like his mind was in a trance and purposely trying to avoid having to face the reality at hand. He had to force himself to clear the mental fog and think about Grace and the boys and what Joshua had asked him to do in the event this day should come.

Attempting to concentrate and focus his thoughts, he began wondering whether or not Joshua had truly known that his time was so close at hand. Finding himself sidetracked again, he tried forcibly redirecting his attention to the business ahead.

"Stop and think," he said sternly under his breath.

He had no idea what the Smith homestead was actually worth, or what he might expect to get from it. To Joshua, of course, it was priceless. But would it bring enough to stake Grace and the boys an adequate start in Denver? That was the question before him now. Then he began to wonder if he would have to deal with the Stenerson fellow's father in Cheyenne in order to sell it. Shaking his head over the troubling prospect he wondered, *What if the father's like his son.*

Looking up and beyond the ceiling, he said, "God, help me to help Grace and the boys, please."

Returning again to the thin pane of glass and his own wavy reflection within it, he had the sudden strange and overwhelming sensation of being drawn tightly within himself; as though his whole being were imploding and being tightly bound by a force far greater than his own ability to resist. He thought it almost similar to the experience of his falling helplessly through the dark tunnel after he'd been shot. Only now, he was unconcerned and did not resist, letting go as though he were completely unstrung.

The next thing he knew, he found himself vividly reminded of the time when his father was murdered, and how, although he'd been devastated, he hadn't allowed himself room or time for mourning. Instead, he'd resisted and dammed-up the sorrow and plugged the painful hole in his heart with anger and hatred. He'd blocked it fast with the desire for revenge and couldn't wait to retaliate and kill.

No sooner had that realization come over him when he found himself confronted with the time he went to pay his mother a visit, only to learn she'd died three months prior. Then, too, how the old pastor's wife had said that his mother, being the good, faithful woman she was, had prayed for him daily. But death being the norm and constant in his life that it was then, he'd once again, just as he'd done with his father, callously refused to succumb to sorrow. Instead, he'd gotten viciously drunk and stayed that way for the following two weeks, hating most anyone or thing in life unfortunate enough to cross his path.

And it was right then, at that moment, that the blinders he'd unknowingly worn for so long, fell from his eyes so that he was quite literally jarred by the stark realization of how he'd himself, in essence, become the very thing he despised and hated most of all—-another *Grim Chieftain.*

Shaken by the startling revelation, he realized what a fool he'd been to leave his mother alone in the first place, and at a time like that. What had it proven and what had he accomplished? And now, who was he to have received the caring he had, when he, of all people, deserved to be dead? Caring and loving he could clearly see, were not burdens or weaknesses; nor were they the sources or results of fear. They were the richest gifts in life, and were one and the same; each evidence of the other. Finally, overcome as though being filled by a torrent to overflowing, the hard, brittle walls of the dam in his heart burst and he let the pent-up tears of his life stream freely.

From the moment Joshua and Grace carried him in to their home and saved his life, they'd been nothing short of compassionate and kind. And it hadn't taken long for him to be impressed over how the two of them were always able to keep their spirits up, regardless of the many hardships and discomforts they faced. Troubles and setbacks were just that, and they never seemed to affect or change their spirits of graciousness. They never flew into fits of rage or sank to the depths of discouragement. They simply seemed immune to moodiness and self-pity. Joshua had never once in his presence, complained about his physical condition or his undeserved, regretful past. And Grace always seemed to have a song to sing or hum, even as she went about the most unpleasant and tedious of tasks. There was no doubt in his mind that the unnatural calm and subtle strength they possessed, arose from their faith in God. Time and again, he'd heard them both telling Nathan and Samuel about the victory they shared in Jesus, and how He'd already fought and overcome the battle against the darkness in the world. A lesson he'd heard when he was a boy, but had to come to the absolute end of himself first before he could see or understand; and now that he had, his own soul testified to the power and truth of it as well. It was right and it was good. The true meaning of life quartered no space for pride and selfishness. The simple and meager lives that Joshua and Grace shared were rich and abundant with that faith, hope and love, and he knew that the living example of their humble, Christ-likeness would always remain with him.

Through streaming tears, he looked beyond his own image in the window glass and could see clearly how we are all, after all, either the reflections of light, or the shadows of darkness. And he could hear Joshua's saying—*Watch what side yer heart's ridin, son. Good or bad, or God's or the Devil's. A man can't serve both and'll only come to no good tryin.* He wanted with all his heart to serve that good and right side and no longer his own or the Devil's. And as he wept, he heard the small, silent voice within his heart asking— *What man wouldn't choose pure water over tainted, freedom over bondage, pardon over judgment, and heaven over hell?*

He heard Grace behind him closing the door to her and Joshua's bedroom and he quickly swiped the sleeves of Jodie's sweater over his cheeks and eyes before turning to her.

"I don't know why I woke ya so early, Christian, I just—-"

"No, I'm fine ya did, Grace. I was thinkin I'd take a ride here shortly anyway. Then we'll talk some...'bout things...later."

Looking across the room to where the boys slept peacefully side by side, she said, "Those poor boys are gonna be heartbroke 'bout their daddy, unh-huh."

Lucas wasn't sure she'd heard him, but it didn't matter. She was considering Nathan and Samuel and he fully sympathized with her. It was all the more reason for him to step out a spell so they could be alone together and he could try to collect his own bearings as well as dislodge his heart from his throat.

Turning back to the window, he blankly traced over the dark yard and the huddled shapes of the bales of straw that he and the boys had stacked. He thought about how he'd told them they were skunk traps when he thought he saw an orange glow in the air above them. He hadn't seen any lightning bugs there in Wyoming territory, and the ones back in Missouri had bluish, white lamps, not orange. He blinked and stared into the darkness and saw it again, at the top of the hill. Realizing it was the glow at the end of a cigarette or cigar and that someone was up there, he turned to Grace.

"I know it's a bad time, Grace, but I think we got company."

"Huh?" she said unaware of what he'd said.

"Maybe they're only scoutin, but this early, I don't know. You and the boys stay put here, all right?"

"Okay, Christian," she said. She sounded unconcerned and miles away.

Lucas turned and looked back through the window. The darkness was softening and he could just make out what he thought was the shadowy outline of men on horseback at the crest of the hill. As he reached for his coat hanging from a nail beside the door, a thought came to his mind. Strapping on his gun belt, he turned and said, "I'm gonna borrow Joshua's coat and hat, Grace."

She sat looking blankly through him and nodded.

Lucas pulled on Joshua's long wool coat, and though he'd never worn another man's, donned his old floppy felt hat too. He grabbed a chunk of coal that lay beside the stove and quickly began smearing it over his cheeks, above his beard and nose and forehead. Turning up the collar of the coat he said, "Listen, Grace, bar this door and you and the boys stay in. Don't come out."

If Grace hadn't been attentive before, she was now, and she stared curiously at Lucas' blackened face. He grabbed Joshua's old single-barreled scattergun, which hung on the wall, and opened its breech. The chamber was empty. He grabbed the box of shells from the shelf and slid one into the chamber and closed it.

"You ever use this?" he asked.

As she nodded her head *yes,* he saw her eyes had widened, but were still vacant and far away. With his own rifle tucked within the right side of Joshua's coat, he said quietly, but sharply, trying to get her attention and not wake the boys, "Grace! Bar this door and stay away from it and the windows. If anyone tries comin in...ya gotta shoot, okay?"

"Unh-huh, be careful, Christian," she said.

~ 34 ~

"There he comes now," Teller said pulling his revolver.

"He's movin slow enough I bet I can drop him from here," Jahns said raising his rifle as the dark figure emerged from the cabin.

"Hold on," Farliss said. "Let him get in the barn first. We'll move in on foot and catch him sloppin his hogs."

"Yeah, I wanna see the surprise in his eyes and his black face up close," Herron snarled. "Come on Jahns, we'll take him in the barn."

"Let's skin and dress 'em then," Jahns said dropping with a thud from the saddle.

"All right, Gore, you and Teller get yerselves down to those straw bales to the right there and cover that cabin. Anyone comes out, drop 'em. Me and Hard'll cover from those just below there. Augustus, we'll line-string the mounts and you can keep watch from here. This shouldn't take but a few minutes."

"Okay, Far. It's him, sure enough," Augustus said lowering the field glass he held in the same hand as his cigar.

Lucas kept his face down and tilted as he headed for the barn, not wanting them to see who he was or that he was aware of their presence. He was just able to see the outline of their shadowy figures from the corner of his left eye. He wondered what kind of charge they would make and hoped it would be by foot. He also half-expected at any moment one might try taking a shot, yet, at the same time, felt strangely unconcerned about it.

Here you go again, he thought. *Lord, if there was any other way.* But he knew, short of God's intervening, there wasn't and that it couldn't be prevented. He had to protect Grace and the boys and there was only one language the Valentine crew understood; and he knew how to speak it, and speak it fluently. *And so I shall,* he thought to himself. *If ever you had cause Christian Jack, you do now.*

As he swung the barn door open against the face of the barn, he was able to catch a better glimpse of them. It looked like they were maybe six or seven strong, and too, he noticed, they'd begun dismounting and appeared to be securing their mounts. It was a very good sign.

Inside the barn, he set down the rifle and opened the stall where Heston was and quickly saddled him. At the west wall he peeked through the slats. They'd begun moving in. Two were scurrying down towards the larger stack of straw nearest the cabin, and two more were hunched and headed for the stack closest to the barn. Off to the right, moving down towards the backside of the barn, were two more. There was one who'd remained at the top of the hill.

Fortunately, he'd played it right. He'd hoped by placing the bales out in the open it might offer ambush positions too tempting for them to pass up, thereby increasing the likelihood that they might split into groups and come in by foot; and, too, so that they wouldn't risk having any of their mounts hit by any return fire. It was a gamble he knew would only pay off if he were able to mount and fight on the move. Now he was mobile and they were committed.

He removed Joshua's coat and hat, then pulled the two extra revolvers from his saddlebags and shoved them into the front of his gun belt. Taking a cloth rag, he dipped it into the pail of water and wiped the charcoal from his face. *Now,* he was ready for them to see *who* he *really* was.

He mounted Heston and dug his boots securely into the stirrups. After placing the reins into his mouth and clamping them tightly between his teeth, he drew his two side arms and thumbed back their hammers. With a Colt in his left hand, and one in his right, he sat silent, listening intently for the sound of the two approaching the rear of the barn. Looking back over his right shoulder, he saw through the cracks a darkened figure moving east along the back wall coming around his left. The other was advancing to the right. If they were still killing for Valentine, he figured it a safe bet that after having seen his entering the barn, these two were more than likely Herron and Jahns wanting to be the first in on the kill.

The one to his right had advanced faster than the other, and had now reached the front corner at the face of the barn. Turning, Lucas leveled his left revolver and followed the form moving against the receding darkness to the east. He pulled the trigger shooting the man through the wood planking startling the chickens, goats and hogs so that they began squawking, bleating and squealing.

Thinking he'd reached the sodbuster first, Herron paused in his tracks and cursed under his breath, "Damn you, Jahns."

Over the commotion of the frightened animals, Lucas heard as the heavy body outside dropped. Folding himself forward, he jabbed his boot heels hard to Heston's flanks and the mount bolted, leaping through the open barn doors. The moment he'd cleared the threshold, he fired with his right, seeing at the same time it was Herron.

It hadn't been but a breath following what he thought was Jahns' shooting the sodbuster when the dark mount suddenly flew from the open barn. And then, for him to clearly see that it was Lucas who was upon it, and *he*, riding dead and looking him straight in the eyes. Then came the blinding bolt of white flame and his whole regrettable life flashing before his eyes and his not being able to stop the endless falling forever.

As Heston's hooves hit dirt, Lucas shifted right and the mount responded, thundering towards the straw bales directly ahead.

Just like Farliss and Harding, Gore and Teller found themselves momentarily stunned by the sudden and unexpected events. There'd been what they thought was Jahns' shooting the Negro sodbuster, then the sudden appearance of a large, dark and apparently riderless horse flying from the barn, followed by the flashing roar of a long spitting tongue of flame. Then, what appeared to be Herron's flying backwards through the air with both of his feet off the ground. Before any of the gunmen could respond, the two younger of the four realized that the charging steed had left the ground and was now leaping straight at them. It sent them both flat onto their backs yelping in fright.

Firing with both revolvers trained downward, Lucas saw who they were.

Again, this time with more emphasis, he leaned right and, Heston veering, charged straight for the hill. The whiz of bullets drilled past and the air was filled with the cracking reports of gunfire. He replied, sending three rapid rounds at the gunmen behind the straw bales to his right.

As Heston surged the hill, Lucas shoved the empty right into its holster and pulled another from his waist. Raising the fresh revolver, he saw as fire burped from the straw and that one of the two was now scrambling up the hill. He triggered two rapid rounds and the man collapsed face forward into the bank.

As Heston reached the crest of the hill where the string of horses were the firing from below stopped. Then Lucas saw Valentine, and that he was attempting to mount. But the horse, skittered by all the commotion, was sidestepping backwards in a circle. Lucas lifted his left and fired once. Valentine hit the dirt spinning with an anguished cry and the frightened mount trampled him as it broke free.

Pulling the reins from his mouth, and Heston sharply back down the hill, more shots drilled the air about him. Lucas emptied his left, squeezing two rounds at the gunman behind the straw. Clipping his heels to Heston's flanks, he holstered the empty left and pulled for the last fresh revolver. Heston thundered down.

In the brief moment it took him to rearm, he saw that it was Farliss, and that he was now breaking for the barn. Lucas pulled twice with his right. The large foreman had just made it to the front corner when he crashed face first into the ground.

Sensing no sign of movement from him or any of the others, Lucas wheeled Heston around once more and with a clip of his heels, the mount charged the top of the hill again. There, Valentine was again frantically trying to hoist himself onto another mount.

When he saw that Lucas had returned, he clumsily dropped the rifle from his right hand over the saddle.

Swinging free of his own saddle before Heston had fully stopped, Lucas called, "Leavin, Augustus?" When he hit the ground feet first, the jarring caused his left thigh and hip to stab sharply, reminding him that the old wound was still very much there.

Valentine's face was stricken with fright.

"What's the matter, Augustus? Ya look like you've seen a ghost."

The rancher staggered away from the horse and fell back over his own heels. He looked up at Lucas, his eyes filled with dread knowing his life was about to end.

"Don't, Lucas...please."

"Don't what...kill you like you did me, Rocha, Carl and Johnny and all the others?"

"Yes, please, I beg you. Have mercy."

"You mean *you* value life?"

"Yes, please. I beseech you."

"I see...long as it's *your* life."

With a wild look in his eyes, using both hands, he grabbed Valentine by the front of his coat and yanked him to his feet. Then he buried a hand into the pocket of his breeches and retrieved his jackknife. Unfolding and revealing its raised blade, he started for the rancher. Augustus' eyes bulged in terror as Lucas quickly thrust the knife blade into the shoulder at the arm of his coat. The rancher nearly fainted, expecting his throat to be cut. He was a frazzled mess. With one hard jerk, Lucas ripped the severed coat sleeve free from his arm.

"I'll pay you whatever, just please...don't."

"Shut up!" Lucas growled sickened by his pleading.

After twisting the coat sleeve till it was hard as rope, he drew it over the rancher's open mouth gagging him so that he could only be heard moaning. Then he tightly knotted it behind his head.

"The innocent people you killed would laugh to hear you wallowin, Augustus. Maybe they are. They probably begged for their lives, too, but you and yours quartered no mercy."

~ 35 ~

At the sound of the first blast, Nathan sprang up and flew from his bed. No sooner had his feet hit the floor when a second shot roared. When he'd reached the kitchen window, he saw a horse and its rider flying through the air with flames spitting beneath them. Then there was the flashing and blasting of many more gunshots. His mother had tried pulling him away from the window, but he'd wrested himself free, anxious to see what was going on outside. She now sat praying at the supper table behind him, her arms wrapped tightly about Samuel, who was frightened and crying.

Nathan watched Mister Christian, the white stranger with all the revolvers who'd come to their home shot and bloodied in the middle of a raging blizzard, and saw now as he moved like the wind of a raging blizzard himself, killing the killers who'd come to kill his family. This, the same gunman whom he'd once wished would die. His knees trembled beneath him and his heart raced as the reality of what he'd just partially witnessed, settled into his young mind.

When the shooting stopped, he watched as Mister Christian stood with another man at the top of the hill. Hoping he was okay, Nathan searched the yard and open barn for his father. In all of the commotion, he'd forgotten he was ill and staying in bed.

Turning from the window he asked, "Where's daddy, Mama?"

Valentine moaned through the gag as Lucas ripped open his pant leg to check the wound.

"You're lucky, Augustus," he said. "It went through. I had one near the same spot in my leg that had to be dug out. And there's the holes from another that went through my back from your having me killed."

After reloading one of his revolvers, he gathered the reins of the second horse which Valentine had been attempting to mount. Slapping his open hand twice against his right thigh, he signaled Heston to follow. Then, giving the cattleman a shove down the hill, he said, "Move."

Halfway down they came to where Harding lay. He'd been hit rib side and in the left shoulder near the same spot where he'd been shot by the Marsh gang. Lucas saw that his missing hat had tumbled all the way to the base of the hill.

At the side of the barn, he let Heston and the other horse into the small hold and closed the gate. He pushed his limping prisoner on.

"Looks like your foreman, Augustus," he said as they approached the large hatless body lying face down near the front corner of the barn. He'd been hit square between the shoulder blades and likely through the spine and heart since it appeared he hadn't budged from where he'd fallen.

Herron lay on his back and crushed hat only a few feet from Farliss. With his eyelashes and brows having been singed by the point-blank muzzle flash and powder burn, his face, with his mouth wide open, was hideous looking. There was a small, dark-crimson hole in his charred forehead above his left eye, which like the right, was wide open and staring frightfully skyward.

Taking hold of the back of Valentine's coat and twisting him to a full stop, Lucas said, "Go on...look at 'em, Augustus. Looks like maybe he'd seen the same ghost, too, ya reckon?"

As the rancher looked down on the gruesome sight, he trembled shaking the long snot that had run from his nose and was now dangling from his chin.

"That one's for you, Rocha," Lucas said.

Inside the barn, he folded Valentine down against the corner of the winter hog pen. After securely binding his hands behind him, he tied a strip of cloth around his wounded leg and proceeded to lash him to the post where the hogs could just get their curious wet snouts to the trim of his ears.

Standing and looking his prisoner sternly in the eyes he said, "I'll be back, Augustus. In the meantime you'd be wise to carefully consider a couple of things: one—-the value of your life; and two—-the value of this spread that you and your dead crew were trying to steal. Otherwise, I'll feed ya to them hogs and you can join the rest of 'em in hell."

The rancher groaned through the coat sleeve tied across his mouth as he strained to twist away from the inquisitive snorting of the hogs. There was a time not so long ago when in a case as particularly loathsome as Valentine's, Lucas might have considered shooting him in the other leg also, then throwing him into the hogs, but not anymore. He'd said it because he wanted Augustus to take seriously what he'd suggested about his purchasing the Smith homestead.

At the east side of the barn, he found Jahns. He'd been shot in the right temple. Shattered fragments of barn wood stood speared in the side of his blubbery face and neck. Closer to the cabin, behind the four bales of straw, Teller and Gore lay dead on their back, each in shock, looking frightfully skyward. They'd both been hit chest center. Heading for the well, Lucas remembered Todd Welles and figured he was probably back at the Valentine ranch, that or hightailing it back now as fast as he could.

At the well, he dropped the empty bucket in and cranked the windlass bringing it up. After he'd splashed a few handfuls of the icy water across his face and head, he used it to rinse his mouth. He could smell and taste the sulfurous residue of gunpowder. It never bothered him before, but did now. Its bitter taste and smell meant only one thing—-killing and death.

After reloading his other revolvers, he went for Joshua's hat and coat in the barn. The hogs were still welcoming their bound visitor. Then he ambled over to the cabin and, at the kitchen window, peered in. He saw Grace with her arms around the boys at the supper table. Seeing he was there, she sent Nathan to unbar the door.

"Thanks, Nate," he said. He looked with empathy at the teary-eyed youngster thinking of his father's passing. Nathan, with downcast eyes trembled as he nodded. He was shattered, stunned, ashamed and speechless, all at once.

After he'd hung Joshua's hat and coat on the same nail where they'd been before, Lucas removed the two back-up revolvers from his belt and placed them into the pockets of his own winter coat that hung beside Joshua's. Then he unbuckled his gun belt and as he was hanging it, thought he should cover it so it wasn't in open sight. Taking his own coat from its nail, he hung it over the set. Turning, he awkwardly half-smiled at Grace.

"Is it done?" she asked.

He nodded.

At the table he took the scattergun, opened its breech and removed the shell from its chamber. After putting the shell back into the box, he put both away.

"Ya knowed 'em, didn't ya?" Grace said.

"Yes."

"Sit yerself down, Christian. I'll pour ya some coffee."

Lucas sat down at the table and looked at Nathan and Samuel. Their eyes were red and cheeks wet from crying.

"Sorry 'bout all the...commotion, Grace."

"Not yer fault or timin, Christian."

"Daddy's gone to heaven, Mister Christian," Samuel said.

Lucas could see that Samuel hadn't really grasped the full measure or weight of it yet. He was too young. He could tell that Nathan, on the other hand, knew what it meant, but that it was still sinking in. He hadn't clearly separated his father's passing from the battle just waged in the yard outside his family's home.

Sitting there looking blankly into the wood grain of the table, Lucas tried to fathom the coincidence of Joshua's passing coming just before Valentine's intended attack. He wondered if it had somehow been Joshua's, or, even God's way of warning them in advance of it. Then, he was reminded of the time when, after Joshua's violent coughing attack in the barn, the two riders had appeared on the hill scouting. He wondered if it wasn't the way the Devil always worked, taking advantage of people when they were the most susceptible and at their weakest. Then, too, he thought of how the intended attack came right on the heels of his own soul-stirring revelation. He reminded himself of how they'd forced his hand, leaving him no alternative. Then the notion of his possibly never being able to change sent a cold shiver through him. Shaking it off and looking up from the table, he refocused his attention on the boys.

"I bet you fellas' berries and cream, he's done got all them angels up there in heaven all a workin, too," he said.

With the faint hint of a smile breaking through his state of bewilderment, Nathan said, "Yeah."

Grace set the cup of coffee down before Lucas.

Samuel, rubbing his eyes with his small fists smiled a little and said, "Unh-huh."

"Thanks Grace," Lucas said.

"Unh-huh," she said. He could see how she'd aged as she forced a smile over the strain.

"Ya caught some skunks, huh, Mister Christian?" Nathan said.

"Yep, we got 'em all."

The two boys dove into him and wrapping their arms tightly about him, started crying. Lucas could feel the tears welling in his own eyes. Grace came over and put her arms around them all. They stayed like that for a good long spell and they all wept.

When he'd finished his coffee, he asked Grace if she or the boys needed to go to the privy, and Samuel said, "We done peed in the pot, Mister Christian." Grace nodded. He told her it'd be better if they didn't come outside just yet until he'd had a chance to clear things up. She agreed and asked him if he was hungry. He shook his head *no*. His blood was still coursing with adrenaline and he didn't want food on his belly while he was dealing with the bodies. That was something he'd never allowed to bother him before, or for that matter, even considered. Many times he and the raiders had scavenged the rations of dead men, and, with their bodies lying in open sight, sat down to eat. Just like everything else then, he'd blotted it out, without the least bit of consideration.

"Who's that man?" Nathan asked referring to Valentine.

Looking at Grace, Lucas answered, "A fella who I got a hunch might be interested in buyin your spread."

"Thank you, Christian. Joshua would'a wanted you to know that," she said.

"I know. In a little I'll get the wagon hitched and…when you're…we'll——"

Saving him from saying it, she said, "We'll be ready."

After he'd rounded up Valentine's spooked horse and the others that were line-strung at the top of the hill, he led them into the small, now crowded, corral and tossed in a couple arm loads of hay. Then he gathered up all of the dead men's weapons. Four of the men's revolvers were fully loaded and hadn't been fired. Though tempted, he didn't bother going through their pockets to see if they had any money. After retrieving Heston, he used him and rope to drag the bodies by their ankles out beyond the barn, leaving them alongside the compost pile that was a mixture of manure and straw that Joshua used for fertilizer. When he'd done that, he spread dirt over the ground where blood had spilled.

In the barn, using two planks of wood, he made a simple, but sturdy cross. Joshua had a small can of red paint and he figured he'd ask Grace first what she wanted printed on the cross, and if she wanted to do it. On his way to the house, he thought how he'd never made a grave marker before.

Grace told him that putting Joshua's name on it using the red paint would be fine.

"He ain't here no more, anyway…'cept in our hearts," she added, her voice breaking as she spoke. "He's done gone on…and's… up in heaven."

Back in the barn, using his jackknife, Lucas shaved a feathered tip at the end of a thin branch to use for a scribing brush. Then, onto its nicer looking side and as neatly as he could, he printed JOSHUA SMITH, and below the name—1869. He placed it along with a shovel and mattocks into the bed of the wagon.

As he went about harnessing Old Mare and hitching her to the wagon, from the corner of his eye he could see Valentine straining to keep his ears from the hogs. They'd already begun tearing at the sides of his coat. He preferred not to deal with him just yet and kept from looking directly at him. He wasn't sure his old nature wouldn't return, that, or he'd be tempted to take mercy on the pitiful-looking creature. When he'd finished, before returning to the house, he went to the well again to wash his face and hands.

Although it seemed much later, Joshua's watch read only 12 o'clock. As he sat at the table preparing to eat a couple of the biscuits with strawberry preserves that Grace had set out, Nathan and Samuel came over and stood closely beside him. Feeling the weight of their watchful eyes, he put his hands together before him and said, "Thank you, Lord." The two boys shared needed smiles between themselves. As he ate, he thought how he hadn't voluntarily given thanks before eating since he was probably Nathan's age.

When Grace told him they were ready, Lucas went into the bedroom and carefully lifted Joshua's body from the bed. Grace had dressed him in his best work shirt and overalls and she'd neatly wrapped about him, her finest handmade quilt. Lucas carried Joshua's body from the cabin and laid it gently into the bed of the wagon. It was possibly the most painful thing he'd ever done and it was all he could do to maintain his composure. Grace and the boys were crying again as he helped them up into the wagon. There, with her arms around Nathan and Samuel, they huddled together alongside Joshua's draped form. With Heston in tow, Lucas manned the wagon reins and they set out. The wind was not blowing, but no one noticed.

On the highest knoll at the north side of the Smith property, Lucas brought Old Mare and the wagon to a stop. In all directions, the vast and waking earth spread out to open blue sky. Red and orange first spring blossoms of Indian paintbrush splattered the supple, blue-green fields. Everywhere, yellow-breasted meadowlarks and redwing blackbirds flitted busily about. Honey bees buzzed in the clover. Sliding unheard in the distance, the river shimmered, refracting rays of sunlight as it ribboned its way eastward.

Lucas climbed down from the bench and took the shovel from the bed of the wagon. Where the ground was highest, he set its blade and looked back at Grace still seated in the back of the wagon with her arms around the boys. She nodded. With his foot on the shoulder of the shovel, he stood his weight upon it and sank the blade to its hilt. It felt as though he were sinking it into himself. He'd never dug a grave before, only sent men to fill them. Here he was now, a man of blood, burying a man of peace; wolf burying the shepherd. With each plunge of the shovel there was confession; with each blade of earth, a lessening of self. He knew that while he was burying Joshua, he was also burying his own mother and father; burying a war; burying a raider. When he crawled from the pit, he knew he was no longer the same man.

After he'd placed the body into the grave, Grace opened her Bible.

"This was one of yer favorite scriptures," she said, "From 1st Corinthians." And with heavy heart, she proceeded to read it bravely, her voice breaking and choking throughout:

"Charity suffereth long, and is kind; charity envieth not; charity vaunteth not itself, is not puffed up. Doth not behave itself unseemly, seeketh not her own, is not easily provoked, thinketh no evil; rejoiceth not in iniquity, but rejoiceth in the truth; beareth all things, believeth all things, hopeth all things, endureth all things. Charity never faileth."

When she'd finished, Lucas, whose head was bowed, lifted it, cleared his knotted throat and said, "Wish I could'a known ya longer, Josh. In one season I learned more from ya 'bout what's important than my whole life. You were the best...'long with my own ma and pa. Thank you."

After he'd filled the grave, he set the cross in the ground at its head.

"It ain't much of a marker," he said to Grace.

"It'll do just fine. Thank you, Christian."

Holding the boys firmly at her sides, she sang Amazing Grace. Of all the songs she sang, it was always Joshua's favorite. And it had grown strongly with Lucas, as well.

After he'd gathered enough field stones to adequately cover the grave and reinforce the cross, he helped Grace and the boys onto the front bench of the wagon. She said she would pilot. The ride back to the cabin was quiet and Lucas noticed that the wind, oddly enough, was also. It dawned on him then that it hadn't blown all day. Meanwhile, the song Grace sang still echoed in his ears and mind.

"I remember my mother singin that song when I was young," he said breaking the silence.

"Did ya ever hear the story 'bout the man who made it?" Grace asked.

"No."

"How I heard it was, his name was Mister Newton and he was a slave trader on one of them ships bringin African folks 'cross the ocean. Well, they was caught-up in a bad storm once and it looked like they was gonna sink and drown. So Mister Newton prayed to God to save them and confessed he'd stop his slavin trade. And God did, unh-huh. And He changed Mister Newton's heart and the ways of his life after that. Then Mister Newton made that song."

"So how come God didn't save daddy?" Nathan asked. He was curious, not bitter.

"Your daddy *was* saved, son. I reckon God wanted him ta be… with Him now," she said, her voice breaking just as the last words were out.

"Your pa was the bravest man I ever knew," Lucas said. "Brave enough to challenge this hard country and want freedom for himself and his family. And brave enough to forgive them that tried to keep him from it, too."

A proud smile for his father broke over Nathan's face.

With a note of absolute certainty in it Samuel said, "Unh-huh."

Grace smiled at Lucas and said, "Nathan son, long as you walk and breathe on this Earth, the only true freedom is the freedom your soul has in the Lord."

As they neared the cabin, Lucas shared with Grace and the boys what Joshua had asked him to do in the event of his passing. Grace said nothing, but solemnly nodded her head. He then told her that the sooner they could set out for Cheyenne, the better.

"We'll be ready come mornin, Christian," she said.

~ 36 ~

In at the cabin, Grace said she would make some cornbread and potato soup for supper. Lucas unhitched Old Mare and spread hay for her, Heston and the other horses, then fed the goats, hogs and chickens even though the chickens had begun free-ranging now that the snow was gone. He'd noticed some squeaking in the wagon's hubs earlier and went for Joshua's tub of axle grease. In the barn he saw that Valentine was spent from trying to distance himself from the hogs and that the back of his coat was now shredded to the shoulders. He'd also soiled himself. He was tempted to untie him, but still couldn't bring himself to deal with him just yet. He couldn't help thinking there was no place for the likes of Augustus Valentine in the same day as that of a good man's passing.

Once he'd finished greasing the wagon hubs, going against his druthers, he went to his prisoner and removed the tourniquet he'd wrapped around his leg earlier. Augustus moaned through the gag and his eyes were wide, pleading for mercy. Lucas forced himself to ignore him. He smeared a dab of the axle grease across the entry and exit wounds of his thigh, re-wrapped it and left the barn. At the well, he washed his face and hands. He was exhausted.

Grace gave thanks and the four of them picked slowly at their food. The supper table was somber and the cabin empty without Joshua. Reality was still setting in and every strained breath and heavy heartbeat was a blink of an eye from breaking. After eating, Lucas carried a lantern, a bowl of soup and a square of the cornbread out to the barn. There, he removed the gag from Augustus' mouth.

The cattleman drew a couple of deep breaths and flaring his nostrils and setting his eyes, angrily snarled, "You're nothing but a murdering Missouri bushwhacker, Lucas, or should I say…Cain?"

Unfazed by his prisoner's opinion or knowledge of himself, Lucas responded, "And you're soon to be nothin but hog slop, Augustus. And you of all people should know—-hogs are always hungry."

"You won't, because you wouldn't get a cent, then. I know your kind."

"My kind? You said yerself I'm a murderin bushwhacker. So what makes you think I won't feed you to them hogs, go kill your family, then take all your money and burn your place to the ground? Just like ya done the Frenchman." Up till then, he'd only assumed Valentine and Farliss had burned out and killed the Frenchman, but seeing now that the rancher wasn't denying it, he knew it was true. As true as the reason behind the five of them being sent out together on the east side patrol, which Johnny and Carl had mentioned being unusual. As true as the long streak of smoke they'd all seen that day against the western skyline. As true as the Frenchman's green wine bottles that lay scattered about the Valentine ranch while Herron and Jahns, and Teller and Gore were in their bunks sick and nursing hangovers.

Augustus shrunk back into the reality of his abysmal state. He'd been spouting out of desperation, clutching at the smoke of his smoldering dreams. His words were meaningless blather and he knew it. For the time being, at least, Lucas held the cards to his fate.

"Did ya think on what I told ya, Augustus? What's your life and this spread worth to ya?"

"Untie me, please," he pleaded.

"Well, did ya?" Lucas barked sharply.

"Ya...yes...anything...please."

Lucas raised the lantern and looking sternly into the eyes of his prisoner said, "You will pay along with every cent you owe me, this family two-thousand dollars for their spread. You understand?"

Valentine nodded and Lucas untied him. Pulling him to his unstable feet, he sent him hobbling off to the privy. He didn't know where he came up with the two-thousand, but figured if Valentine had the money it should provide Grace and the boys a decent enough start. Then he thought about Augustus' knowing about his past and wondered how he'd come to put it all together, as well as how many other people at the ranch or in Cheyenne knew. He was too tired now to care. Besides, it really only mattered until he'd seen Grace and the boys safely off to Denver; after that—come what may.

Back in the barn, this time away from the hog pen, he had Augustus squat on the ground against a different post. He offered the bowl of soup and cornbread to him, but the cattleman refused it.

"You'll wish you'd eaten when the chill sets in," he said.

"I wouldn't *touch* that," Augustus brazenly replied. He was obviously repulsed at the notion of eating food prepared by a Negro. Lucas could feel the old flames of temptation wanting to flare and strike at Valentine's arrogance, but, reminded of how he'd once been as ignorant himself, he dismissed it.

Having sensed the flash of fire in his captor's eyes, Augustus began trembling again. Lucas dumped the soup into the hog's pen and they, snorting wildly, wasted no time in devouring it and the mud where it splattered. Then he securely rebound his captive for the night; this time away from the hogs. On his way out, he tossed a few of the sugar beets in to them.

Except for the faint sound of Grace's sobbing coming from inside her closed bedroom, and Nathan and Samuel's deep, heavy breathing as they slept back to back in their bed, it was silent in the cabin. Too tired to bother undressing, he only pulled off his boots and lay back onto his bedding that Grace had already laid out for him on the floor beneath the foot of the boy's bed. Beneath his blanket, beneath the east window, beneath the stars he saw twinkling above from it, he tried to assimilate the events of the day behind and the daunting burden of the day that lie yet ahead. But he could only think of Joshua. With the last ounce left of his being, half-calling and half-sighing, he uttered, "Lord," then yawned and surrendered to sleep.

The morning sun had just cleared the horizon when Lucas, Grace and the boys left the homestead. With little recourse but to leave them behind, he'd opened all the pens, feed and storage bins for the goats, chickens and hogs.

Alongside Lucas, behind the wagon that Grace piloted, Valentine rode half-asleep and hunched over with fatigue. His hands were lashed to the pommel of the saddle and the coat sleeve was still bound across his mouth. Lucas didn't want to hear him and didn't want the Smiths having to, either. The horses belonging to the Valentine crew were strung out and tethered to the back of the wagon. The boys were huddled beside their mother, each clutching a corner of the blanket that was stretched across their backs. Like her, they were silent and dazed. He knew she hadn't slept. She'd been up throughout the night preparing to leave. She probably couldn't have slept even if she'd wanted. When he'd awakened, he'd found she was prepared to go. Later, as he sat at the table drinking his coffee, she'd asked if he'd do her a favor.

"Sure, Grace, anything," he said.

"Ya might think I done loss my mind, and maybe I has, but would ya mind takin one of the windows outta the wall so's we can take wid us?"

"Of course, Grace. I'll pull 'em both."

In the bed of the wagon, along with the two small windows, were a couple sacks of clothing, folded blankets and a kindling box which held the Bible and some of the small knick-knacks that Grace wanted to keep. Beneath a spread tarp were Joshua's scattergun and the rifles and gun belts he'd gathered from the Valentine crew. On top of the tarp, to secure it from the wind, he'd placed an assortment of Joshua's tools and an armload of firewood should they need any. But just like yesterday, there was no trace of wind at all. Not a breath. It was as highly unusual as it was greatly appreciated.

Chewing on bacon biscuits as they rode, stopping only briefly for nature, it was late afternoon with the sun nearing the horizon when they arrived at the Valentine ranch. Lucas led Old Mare up to the water trough where she could drink.

Wooten, who rarely showed any sign of emotion, and whom Lucas, had never seen armed, stepped out of the barn and stared in obvious disbelief at the unexpected company of visitors. The Negroes in the wagon were a surprise to say the least, and Augustus, bound and gagged, and looking like he'd been rope-drug across Wyoming, was another sight indeed. But seeing Lucas there, one might have thought by Wooten's expression he was seeing a ghost.

As Lucas dismounted, he scrutinized the older man and said, "Wooten, take the Valentine mounts to the corral. Leave Jahns and Herron's there. See ta them and mine and that draft mare there, too."

Wooten didn't move. Lucas, too tired for reasoning, brought his right hand across to his left revolver. The bunkhouse boss and cook reluctantly started forward to do as he'd been instructed.

Lucas unlashed Valentine's hands from the pommel of the saddle and pulled him to the ground. Augustus yelped and winced at the shock of landing on his gunshot leg. Taking him by the scruff of his coat, he shoved him on limping towards the gate to the house.

Inside, Case was just walking up the hallway. The white-haired family butler stalled and looked incredulously at the two of them.

"Case, I got nothin against ya, so do what I say. I want you to put together whatever rations you've got ready for eatin, enough for four or five folks for a day. Ya hear?"

"Yes, Lucas," Case said. He was still trying to get over seeing them both, and especially Augustus, gagged and in his disheveled state.

"Well, go on then and be quick about it," Lucas said.

As he led Augustus on, Geneva appeared from the side hallway. Before she could speak, Lucas told her, "If you want him alive, turn around and go back." She stood frozen with her hands raised over her mouth, looking pitifully at her distressed husband. Lucas jerked the sleeve down from Valentine's mouth and said sharply, "Tell her to do it—-now!"

Unable to mask his distraught, in a quavering voice Augustus said, "Do what he says, Geneva."

Geneva stood there stupefied, her face going bone-gray as it drained of its blood. Then she cast Lucas a hateful scowl, and turning, slunk away.

"All right, Augustus, open that safe and start countin out what ya owe and be thankful you're alive. Try anything and you won't be."

He watched from over the rancher's shoulder as he opened the safe, making sure there were no hideouts inside. The cattleman removed a steel strongbox and sat it on his desk. When he opened it, Lucas was surprised to see the amount of cash it held. He'd expected there wouldn't be all the money he was demanding. It was the money the cattleman was to purchase the new herd of cattle with; the one being driven to him now.

"Start with the two-thousand for the homestead," Lucas instructed.

As Valentine counted the money, his hands shook uncontrollably. Lucas glanced out the window behind him and saw that Heston and the other horses were watering at the trough, and that Wooten was spreading an armload of hay on the ground about them. Turning from the window, he looked at the west wall with all of its Indian artifacts. One quiver was empty.

"Looks like you're missing some of your arrows, Augustus."

"There's two thousand," the rancher muttered.

"Now count out my proper stake from the time ya hired me in Cheyenne, up till now. And don't forget what you were holdin in the safe for me."

When Valentine finished that, Lucas instructed him to count out what was owed to Rocha, Johnny and Carl. He told him to do it right because he'd rode with each of the men long enough to know what they had coming, even though he didn't. Augustus looked at him annoyed, as though he were being cheated.

"Count, damn ya!" Lucas growled.

He hadn't thought of collecting what was owed to the three men before, but seeing that the rancher had it, decided just then to get it from him. He didn't know why, but it seemed more proper than leaving it with the man responsible for their murders. He thought how perhaps he'd run into some of the deceased men's family members somewhere along the way. *If nothing else*, he told himself, *let it serve as a further lesson to him.* He pulled an empty cloth sack from the safe and began stuffing the counted money into it.

Outside, Jodie and Tonka were returning from their ritual afternoon ride and she saw the Negro family sitting in the wagon in the yard. Then, recognizing that Heston was there, her heart caught and she flew from her saddle and dashed through the front gate to the house.

Lucas, hearing the gate outside clang shut, turned and looked through the window, but saw no one. Only Wooten, headed towards the bunkhouse.

"Put the gun down, or I will shoot," a woman's voice snarled.

Lucas reeled to see it was Katie standing just inside the open doorway, and he heard the snick as she drew back and set the hammer on the pistol she held pointed at him. Her hair was mussed and she was wearing what looked to be bed clothing. She appeared ill. Then he saw the red welt across the right side of her face. Even without the gun, she looked more unpredictable than he'd ever previously considered her.

"I will shoot you if you do not put down that gun!" she screeched.

Lucas thought now, how she even sounded as unstable as she looked.

Just then, Jodie appeared in the doorway and seeing Lucas, paused. Then she stepped forward alongside Katie. Katie's eyes darted and Lucas flinched, about to make a move, but held fast keeping his one drawn revolver trained on Augustus. He wouldn't chance Jodie being hurt. Though Katie had a gun trained on him, which he was certainly concerned about, with Jodie's being there, he felt as a different part of his heart was suddenly jolted back to life. At the same time, he was also sorry that she had to see him like this now, holding a gun to her father.

Jodie looked spellbound past Lucas' dark beard and into his eyes. It was really him and he was alive and actually there. Turning, she looked at Katie and the gun she held. Then, looking back at Lucas, she smiled.

"Stay back, Jodie," Katie warned from the corner of her mouth.

Jodie turned again to her sister, knuckled her fists, and without a second's pause, swung with her left and wheelhouse-punched Katie square in the nose. Lucas ducked and Katie staggered backwards on her heels letting go of the pistol. It hit the floor when she did and discharged across the room into the glass-faced cabinet holding the fancy bottles of whisky and glasses. Before they'd finished crashing, Jodie snatched up the smoking gun and smiled again at Lucas. He reciprocated, smiling also.

Expecting to find Augustus shot, Geneva rushed into the room. She saw Jodie holding the gun at her side and that Augustus was still sitting upright behind his desk.

Katie, on her rump on the floor near the wall behind the door, held her hands over her bloodied nose.

"You broke my nose!" she shrieked.

"What haven't you broken?" Jodie snapped back.

Katie was stunned silent. Jodie had never spoken to her like that before. Geneva, realizing Katie was there and that she was hurt, scurried past Jodie and straight to her aid.

"And you...you've ruined everything as well, Father," Jodie said. She was glaring at him as though he were a complete stranger. "How many people have to suffer and die to satisfy your—-" she left off unable to finish.

"You *ever* send anyone after me," Lucas warned, "I *will* return. Count on it and yourself fortunate to be alive, Augustus."

Augustus jerked with fright as Lucas snatched up the money he'd just counted out. He stuffed it into the sack and started away.

Jodie looked straight into his eyes as he approached her.

"I'm coming with you," she said.

"You ready?" he asked.

"I've been ready," she replied. She sounded resolute and added, "My things are already packed. I'll be right there."

She looked for the last time at her father, then mother and sister. She shook her head regrettably then rushed from the room. A few minutes later, she exited the house carrying a valise in each hand, a bag with straps over one shoulder, and folded blankets pressed beneath both her arms. As Lucas helped load her things into the wagon, he cautiously watched for Wooten. He thought about his having not seen Todd Welles and half-wondered where he was. Then he realized he hadn't introduced Jodie and the Smiths.

"Jodie, this is Grace Smith and her two sons, Nathan and Samuel. This is Jodie, folks."

Smiling richly, Grace said, "I knew it must'a been Jodie when she rode up, unh-huh."

Jodie glowed as she smiled at Grace and the boys. "Nice to meet you all," she said. "And this is my dog, Tonka." Tonka was wagging his tail, panting and watching the boys who were half-bent over the side of the wagon in awe of him.

Lucas saw as Wooten emerged from the bunkhouse. He was unarmed and carrying a valise and bedroll. He raised them away from his sides so that Lucas wouldn't read him as a threat. He set them down in front of the barn and turning, spat. As he made his way towards the Valentine house he said, "I'm done with this loco outfit and goin ta collect my stake. Ya didn't shoot him yet, did ya?"

Partially grinning, "No," Lucas said. "Katie had an accident's all."

The gate clanged shut behind Case on his way out. He was carrying a large basket made of woven cane strands and he handed it to Lucas.

"That should accommodate you folks quite satisfactorily, I should think," he said. Then turning he called, "Wait for me, Woot. I'm done with the whole bloody lot of them, as well."

Lucas looked back at Jodie. She had her left foot in the stirrup, preparing to mount.

"No offense to you intended, Jodie," Case called back.

"None taken, Mister Case," she said smiling.

Lucas and Jodie rode just ahead of Old Mare and the Smiths. Tonka, carrying a slavered stick in his mouth, ran playfully alongside the wagon entertaining Nathan and Samuel. Two tethered and saddled horses trailed the wagon.

"I'm sorry 'bout all that...back there," Lucas said looking at Jodie.

"You've got nothing whatsoever to apologize for," she said. "Let's just leave all of that back there—-back there."

"What if ya don't like where I'm headin?" he asked. He was trying to hold a fixed face while his head spun and heart pounded. He thought something inside him might explode at any moment. Jodie looked as radiant as an angel.

"It doesn't matter if it's that cabin in the mountains or not, Lucas. Just so long as I'm with you and you'll have me along."

He couldn't get over how truly beautiful she was. It had been like that each time he saw her, always more beautiful and special than the last. He shifted slightly in his saddle and Heston nudged up alongside Jodie's mount. Leaning towards her, and she, towards him, they met and kissed. As Heston tossed his head and whinnied, Grace glowed, and Nathan and Samuel snickered.

~ 37 ~

Except the nebulous glow of a slivered moon and the stars above, it was dark when Grace and Jodie started the small fire. The two of them thought it would be comforting to have one and Grace suggested making some coffee. The notion of having a cup sounded tempting and, putting aside his concern over the fires possibly drawing unwanted attention, Lucas consented.

Case had packed more than enough food so they didn't have to prepare any. After eating fried chicken and rolls that they'd warmed over the fire, Grace talked about her older brother, the boy's uncle, who lived in Denver. She tried telling Nathan and Samuel what she imagined living in a big town might be like. As Jodie unwrapped and passed around a bundle of ginger-snap cookies, she said that she'd been there once—before there was a train line—and tried to encourage Grace and the boys as she described it. Lucas stood and told Grace he would clear the bed of the wagon so that she and the boys could sleep in it. Grace, covering her mouth as she yawned, excused herself and thanked him. She, Nathan and Samuel were exhausted physically as well as emotionally beyond every measure of the word.

After he'd cleared the wagon bed, Lucas wandered away from the camp. Grace, along with Jodie's help, prepared her and the boy's bedding. As they did, Grace told Jodie how Lucas had come into their lives. When they'd finished tucking the boys in, Grace, who couldn't stop yawning, then got herself ready for bed and after telling Jodie goodnight, climbed aboard and retired.

After preparing her own bed and one for Lucas beside it, Jodie sat alone before the campfire feeling that much of her broken heart had been restored. She'd been free-falling ever since she'd learned of Lucas' death, and had all but died herself when she'd learned the heart-rending truth behind his intended murder. And though this would be her first actual night away from her family, she'd been gone ever since that day. Regardless of what lie ahead now, she looked forward to it as long as she was with him. It was all a dream come true, a prayer answered. Looking up she whispered, "Thank you, God."

Half-expecting Wooten and Mister Case to show, Lucas sat leaning against a jut of rocks facing the long, dark trail that lay behind. Though exhausted, his mind was still churning over many things. The past two days had been eventful enough to fill a whole season, and the past season, enough to fill a life. As far as the future was concerned, he wasn't sure. His original plan of going to the mountains was no longer imperative. Closing his tired eyes, he bowed his head.

"God, you know who I am and what I've been and what I haven't. I'm truly sorry 'bout all that. And I know I've got no right askin you for anything, but help me ta be the man you'd want. And please keep over Grace and the boys, and Jodie, too. Thank you, in Jesus' name. Amen."

When he opened his eyes, he was refreshed. It was good to know there was God and forgiveness, even for someone like himself. He shook his head thinking how in light of his own pardon, the way in which he judged and looked upon others should reflect the same understanding and compassion. He thought how church pastors could have preached sermons to him about it till their dying breath, but until he'd seen it actually lived out—as he had being with the Smiths—it wouldn't have done him a jot of good. Then he remembered how Joshua kept talking about getting the seeds of his garden planted, and he thought about the seeds planted by his own parents, and how they'd lain dormant for so long in the stone-hard, frozen soil of his heart, and how now, that soil had finally been thawed, turned and the seeds started.

He smiled at Jodie's long flickering shadow as she approached and he thought of the dream that had once seemed so impossible before. The one he'd entertained as he rode unaware into the blizzard of death. The one where she was with him at the cabin he'd built so many times in the mountains of his mind. And now, here she was.

Kneeling on folded legs beside him, she huddled against his shoulder and kissed his cheek.

"How are you, Mister Christian?" she asked.

She'd never called him *Christian* before. Even after learning it was his real name from the letter her father had read concerning his past. She'd always only known him as Lucas. Grace had told her earlier how she'd known that her name was Jodie before she and Joshua ever knew that Christian was his. She'd told her how he'd called her name out repeatedly when he was unconscious and battling for his life. Jodie would never let on to anyone that Grace had told her that. It was something more precious to her than riches and that she would always treasure. It was all the proof she would ever need to know that she was in his heart and that he truly cared for her.

"I'm fine," he said and chuckled.

"What?" she asked.

"Oh, I was just thinking about the wind and how its blown non-stop every day since I come out to this country." He went on to tell her about Joshua's coughing and how he'd suffered from consumption.

"Anyway, I laughed 'cause I had the notion that maybe Josh took the wind with him when he left."

"You really cared for him, didn't you?"

"Yes. He was a special, very kind and humble man."

"I wish I could have known him. I think Grace is wonderful."

"Yes she is. And she couldn't have had a more perfect name."

It wasn't long before Case and Wooten showed up. Lucas invited them to join them at their camp for the night. Jodie went to make more coffee and let them visit.

In the course of conversation with Wooten and Case, Lucas could tell that the two older men honestly hadn't been aware of what Valentine and Farliss had actually been up to. He told them the truth about the Frenchman, the JK folks, himself and Rocha, Johnny and Carl, and, finally, of how they'd ultimately tried moving against the Smiths. The two men each expressed how, outside of the initial hiring of himself and Herron and Jahns to deal with the rustlers and free grazers, they could never have imagined the actual sinister extent of it all.

"By Jove, it's what they deserve," Wooten remarked, concerning Valentine's dead crew. Turning his head, he spat with disgusted emphasis.

He and Case went on to tell Lucas what happened to Todd Welles with Herron and Katie. Lucas shook his head remorsefully thinking of the ill-fated, love-smitten cattle-hand.

Concerning Katie he said, "Some scars can take a lot of gettin used to. They can make ya feel branded."

Breaking the silence that ensued, Lucas asked Wooten, "Would ya by chance know where 'bouts Johnny and Carl are from?"

"Somewhere around Greeley," Wooten answered. "It's maybe fifty miles south'a here. How come, if ya don't mind me nosin?"

"I was just thinkin maybe their folks should know."

"Yes, as unfortunate as it is, I believe it's the proper thing as well," Case said.

"And what about Rocha?" Lucas asked.

"I ain't sure 'bout that," Wooten said. "But I heard him mention a place called Chihuahua a coupl'a times. I figured it's somewhere in Mexico."

"Would you know his whole name?" Lucas then asked.

Wooten rubbed at his bearded chin giving it some thought then said, "I think it was Santiago or somethin like that. He was sure one helluva a cowhand, though, I know that much."

Following another moment of silence, Lucas said, "Well, gentlemen, I think I'll call it a day. I'm 'bout half-asleep as it is."

Alongside the wagon in which Grace and the boys were already fast asleep, Lucas saw that Jodie was awake and lying beneath the blankets of her own bed. Beside her there was another bedroll spread and ready.

"Are you going to bed?" she asked softly.

"Yes," he said.

Smiling, she sat up and, reaching over, unfurled the top blanket of the bedding she'd prepared for him.

~ 38 ~

The sun hadn't been long in its afternoon descent when the seven of them came into Cheyenne. Though relatively busy and populated, like Lucas, it was not the same as when he was there last. If he had any concerns at all now, it was not about himself, but only seeing Grace and the boys safely and securely aboard the train for Denver.

At the depot, they learned the next train to Denver would be leaving in a few hours. Case and Wooten said their goodbyes and wished everyone, especially Jodie, good luck then rode on. Much of the morning as they were on the trail in, the two men had been discussing between themselves the notion of joining forces and opening their own eating house, and, before they left, Jodie again encouraged them to follow through with it since they were both such talented cooks.

Lucas smiled recalling how the night before, Mister Case had told him how Jodie was the only one in the Valentine household who hadn't minded assisting him in the kitchen or with other chores. He'd then added that besides her being a fine cook, *she's quite keen-minded and has a first-rate, tiptop heart.* That was when Wooten added, *I seen by the nat'ral way she took to the horses and other critters that she weren't cut from the same cloth as the others.*

Standing at the rear of the wagon, Lucas handed Grace the sack with the money he'd gotten for her and Joshua's property. She was so surprised by the amount that she wept. She wrapped her long arms around his neck and hugged him tightly. She would cry some and then sigh. Wipe at her eyes, cry again, and then sigh. Jodie was watching and being moved, found herself wiping at her own eyes as well.

When Grace had regained herself, she told Lucas she wanted him and Jodie to take Old Mare and the wagon. He offered to pay for them, but she wouldn't hear of it. She said she thought she'd be selling them, but was more pleased now to leave them with him and Jodie.

"I'd rather they stayed in the family, unh-huh," she said.

Then he went with her to purchase their boarding passes. On their way back to the wagon, Grace said she wanted to step over to one of the shops across the street for a few things. As she and the boys started over, Lucas asked Jodie if she'd go along with them in case they should run into any unfriendly types.

"Here," he said, pulling some bills from his inner coat pocket, "take her and the boys to that mercantile and try gettin her a nice dress and hat. And the boys something too, okay?"

Taking the money from him, Jodie smiled and traipsed off after them.

Lucas unhitched Old Mare and led her and Heston over to a water trough and let them drink. Then he re-hitched Old Mare and draped Heston's reins over one of the wagon wheels. After he'd led the other two horses over to drink and re-secured them to the back of the wagon, he began loading the Smith's things onto the train car. As he was just finishing, he saw there was a group of riders coming down the street. He counted seven before noticing that the man at point and some of the others were wearing lawman's badges. He turned his back to them as they neared.

"Hey, Lucas...Lucas Jackson!" one of them called.

He bristled as he turned and focused on the group of riders. One had cut from the pack and was headed towards him. He instinctively drew his right hand towards his left revolver, but was struck with the realization that he wasn't wearing them. His gun belt was in his saddlebags on Heston. For some reason that morning, likely because of Jodie, Grace and the boys, he simply hadn't thought of his needing them. He felt as though he'd been slapped across the face and his mind reeled as he tried to imagine who it was that would be calling him by name. About to bolt for Heston, he saw as the rider pushed his hat up on his forehead that it was Charlie, the kid he'd met at the shooting contest when he'd first come to town. The one who reminded him of his best friend growing up—Tyler Heston.

Greatly relieved, "Charlie, how are ya?" he greeted.

As Charlie swung himself from the saddle, he turned back to the men now milling in the street. "I'll be right along, fellas," he called.

"I'm good, Lucas. I thought I recognized ya. Are ya fixin to take the train?"

"No, just helpin some friends who are. So, what you up to?"

He saw as Charlie's expression went serious.

"You still on with…Valentine, Lucas?" he asked.

"Not since fall."

Charlie, revealing what appeared to be some measure of relief of his own now said, "That's good. I was worried 'bout that."

"What ya mean, Charlie?"

"I just been deputized, Lucas, and me and the boys there, 'long with the sheriff, are headed to the Valentine place to arrest him and his crew."

Feeling the heat of concern returning, "That so?" Lucas said.

"Yeah, we got sworn warrants on 'em for the murders of some homestead folks north of his spread. I reckon the womenfolk reported their men were all killed by 'em. They said they seen it was white men even though it was made to look like Injuns done it."

As the subject of Charlie's report registered uncomfortably with him, he was at least glad to hear those women and kids he and Rocha found hiding in that root cellar had survived.

"They figure it was Valentine's crew, huh?" he said.

"Yeah, there was an investigation and it turns out that shortly after, Mister Valentine filed claims on their parcels 'long with some others up 'round his parts. There's been a coupl'a the larger outfits' doin it of late. They even arrested the land agent here in town for bein in cahoots on it, too."

"Stenerson?" Lucas said noticing that Jodie and the Smiths were on their way back.

"Yeah, that sounds like 'em."

"Hello, Charlie," Jodie called.

"Hello, Miss Jodie," Charlie said.

As he turned back to Lucas, his eyes showing concern again, "What about Jodie, Lucas?" he asked in a hushed voice.

"She's with me now, Charlie."

"Well, congratulations," he said. "When'd ya'll get hitched?"

"Thanks, Charlie, we ain't just yet, but aim to."

"Think she'll handle it 'bout her pa okay?"

Lucas looked back over his shoulder at Jodie and the Smiths next to the wagon.

"Yeah, I think she's done with 'em too, Charlie."

"Who'd'a thought it?" Charlie said shaking his head.

Not wanting to go into it any further, "Yeah," Lucas muttered.

"Word has it too, that a couple of Valentine's hands, who was here in town over the winter, were boastin 'bout killin rustlers and sheepherders. I was kind'a worried you might be on with 'em still."

Lucas looked him squarely in the eyes and said, "Naw, I didn't fit in with 'em, Charlie."

"Well, Lucas, I best be catchin up with the others. It was good seein ya, though."

"You too, deputy."

Shaking Charlie's hand, Lucas was glad their meeting with regard to the topic of conversation was over. He didn't want to talk about the past and didn't know what to say yet about the future. He watched as Charlie mounted and thought how he'd probably never see him again. Then, completely surprising himself, he said, "By the way, Charlie, tell the sheriff he'll likely find most of their crew gathered along the northeast side, just shy of the river."

Charlie smiled, tipped the brim of his hat, swung his mount and rode off. Turning, Lucas saw Jodie had come over and he asked if they'd had any trouble shopping.

"Some unfavorable looks initially," she said. "But after seeing the money in my hand, nothing the prospect of turning a profit wouldn't remedy."

While he smiled at her assessment, he shook his head over the pitiful truth of it. As they returned to join the Smiths, he saw the boys were sitting in the back of the wagon wearing new blue denim overalls and enjoying molasses candy on sticks and watching Tonka who was busy inhaling a bowl of food which Lucas assumed Jodie had also purchased. Then, he saw that Grace was wearing a colorful new dress and matching hat. He was struck with how much younger and stately she looked.

"Do I know this woman?" he asked Jodie, smiling at Grace. She looked embarrassed, but at the same time, pleased. Then he saw she was also wearing new shoes. It made him happy in his heart and he thought if Joshua could but see her now. *Maybe he is* a silent voice inside suggested.

Probably redirecting everyone's attention from herself, Grace asked if he'd already loaded the two windows onto the train car. He said he had and she told him she'd intended for him to keep one for his and Jodie's own place when they should have one. Having spent countless hours gazing through them himself while he was on the mend, like the Smiths, he'd come to have something of a special appreciation for them as well. As he went to retrieve one, Grace told Jodie how they'd always meant so much to her and Joshua.

When Lucas returned, he thanked her for it and securely propped it upright in the bed of the wagon. Then he asked if she thought she and the boys would be okay until the train pulled out. She said *yes* and handed him a paper sack that she'd brought back with her from across the street.

Noticing that the boys and Jodie had now gathered about him and that they were all smiling he asked, "What's this?"

"Joshua would'a wanted ya to have it," Grace said. "He just told me a mite ago, unh-huh. It's a Bible, Lucas. Yours and Jodie's own. I put a marker in at the start of the New Testament where ya might wanna start readin from it. Oh, and I jotted my brother's address in the back cover, too."

Lucas and Jodie both thanked her and the boys.

"I reckon we'll be settin out then, Grace. We'll write soon as we get where we're goin."

As the two of them hugged one another tightly, Lucas couldn't help feeling as though he were hugging and saying good-bye to his own mother. Grace told him she'd keep him and Jodie in her prayers.

Then Lucas shook hands with Nathan and Samuel.

"Take care of your ma, men, and remember—-mind what side your heart's ridin."

Samuel sprang for Lucas and wrapped his arms about his waist. Nathan did, also. Grace and Jodie hugged.

"Thanks for taking good care of him, Grace," Jodie whispered in her ear.

"Unh-huh, honey," she said, adding, "He's all yours now."

After Grace and the boys boarded the train, Lucas and Jodie stood outside and waved to them through the coach window. Then an older fellow wearing a uniform arrived and boarded. He was the coachman and Lucas saw as he was greeting the Smiths in the car. Taking Jodie's hand, they returned to the wagon. After helping her up onto the bench, he told her he forgot something and that he'd be right back. He was thinking about Joshua's asking him to see Grace and the boys safely on the train, and now, wanting to further insure they had as comfortable a trip as possible, decided to impress the point upon the coachman. As he approached the train, he kept his eyes riveted on the man now standing in the open doorway of the car. He thought to himself how, for persuasive purposes, he probably should have put on his gun belt first, but, once again, hadn't thought of it.

Stepping right up before the coachman, he said, "They're my good friends and soon as she gets to Denver, she'll be writin back 'bout her trip. I trust you'll see over 'em good till then."

"I certainly will. You can count on it, sir," the coachman said.

Lucas smiled and said, "Thank you," then turned and started away. He felt satisfied that Grace and the boys would have a reasonably safe and comfortable trip. And as he was thinking how he'd accomplished it without the influence of his revolvers, the coachman called:

"Hey...I remember *you*, now."

Stopping dead in his tracks, he thought, *Here we go again.* Drawing a slow and deep breath, he turned to face the man.

"You're the fellow who bought me breakfast once. Biscuits and gravy—-remember? I'd just come into town and was outta work. I thought I recognized you by your...scar."

Slowly parting a smile, "Yeah, I remember," Lucas said.

"Well, thanks again," the coachman said.

"You're welcome."

On his way back to the wagon, he thought about the morning he'd bought the man breakfast at the diner. What he remembered the most, though, was how he'd told the man he wasn't up for company and to go sit somewhere else; that and his thinking it similar to the mistake of feeding a stray dog. Then he was struck with the *doin unto others* business and he thought how he'd unknowingly almost had it right at the time, but had been so concerned with himself that he hadn't seen it all the way through. While it was certainly nothing to be proud of, he considered how having the fellow on the train with the Smiths was good, and that he could feel reasonably confident they *would* have a comfortable journey.

Satisfied with that, he smiled and, looking up, saw that Jodie was sitting with her one arm around Tonka's neck. He was in the center, behind the bench, watching with intent eyes and alert ears as he returned. When he'd reached and climbed into the wagon, Jodie handed him his old hat. It was the one he'd worn all the way from Missouri.

"I almost forgot I had it," she said. "I asked Wooten if I could have it after—-"

He looked gratefully at her then the hat. Then he removed his red knit cap and fitted the old one onto his head.

"It got a little crumpled in my bags," Jodie said.

He thanked her with a quick kiss on the cheek, tossed the reins and they set out. As he thought about having his old hat again, it seemed as though something similar might have happened once before, but he couldn't place it.

For some time they rode silently south from Cheyenne, each deep in their own thoughts. While Lucas couldn't help wondering if Jodie knew where Charlie and the sheriff's men were headed,

Jodie thought about the promise she'd made about her leaving and never returning.

"Lucas," she said, softly at length.

"Yeah?"

"May I have a cigarette, please?"

Trying to keep a straight face and not smile, he replied, "Is that all you want me for?"

"No, it's not," she threatened followed by a snicker.

"Good, 'cause I reckon I gave 'em up."

"Me too, then," she said without hesitation. "They always made me smell like smoke anyway." As she laughed, he looked into her eyes. They were sparkling like her smile.

"You're really sure about this, huh?" he said.

She snuggled herself closer to his right side and wound her arm about his.

"Positively, absolutely, I'm sure." With that she kissed his cheek. He could feel its warmth spreading through his entire being and he had the wonderful sensation of absolute lightness; almost as though he had wings and was soaring.

"The *only* thing I'm not sure of," she said pausing, "is what I should call you. Is it Lucas Jackson, Christian Jack, Lucky, or Mister Christian like what Nathan and Samuel call you?"

Just as he was about to respond, Heston whickered a warning followed by the screaming whistle of the train passing in the distance.

"Look, Mama, its Mister Christian and Miss Jodie," Nathan exclaimed. He and Samuel were standing and watching from the coach window.

"Mama, is Mister Christian an angel?" Samuel asked.

"No, son, he ain't no angel," Grace chuckled. "He's only a man who God used to help deliver us."

"Oh," Samuel said.

"Do you remember, Nathan, how the Lord led him to us near dead in the middle of that storm?"

"Yes ma'am," Nathan said.

"Well, we saved his life and he saved ours. Always remember the Golden Rule son, and do for others as you'd want 'em to do for you, unh-huh."

Nathan smiled and placed his arm securely around Samuel's shoulders. Turning back to the window, he caught in his own reflection a glimpse of his father's encouraging smile. He knew that regardless of what may come, with God, they would always be one—-inseparable.

Across Wyoming territory, the wind regained its breath and has blown ever since.

13224131R00152

Made in the USA
Charleston, SC
24 June 2012